THE THREE STIGMATA
OF PALMER ELDRITCH

ALSO BY PHILIP K. DICK,
AVAILABLE FROM VINTAGE BOOKS

The Divine Invasion
A Scanner Darkly
The Transmigration of Timothy Archer
Ubik
VALIS

PHILIP K. DICK

THE THREE STIGMATA OF PALMER ELDRITCH

VINTAGE BOOKS

A Division of Random House, Inc.

New York

First Vintage Books Edition, December 1991

Library of Congress Cataloging-in-Publication Data
Dick, Philip K.
The three stigmata of Palmer Eldritch / Philip K. Dick.—First
Vintage Books ed.
p. cm.
ISBN 0-679-73666-2
I. Title.
PS3554.I3T46   1991
813'.54—dc20   91-50091
CIP

Book design by Debbie Glasserman

For information about the Philip K. Dick Society, write to:
PKDS, Box 611, Glen Ellen, CA 95442.

Manufactured in the United States of America
3579B864

I mean, after all; you have to consider we're only made out of dust. That's admittedly not much to go on and we shouldn't forget that. But even considering, I mean it's a sort of bad beginning, we're not doing too bad. So I personally have faith that even in this lousy situation we're faced with we can make it. You get me?

From an interoffice audio-memo circulated to Pre-Fash level consultants at Perky Pat Layouts, Inc., dictated by Leo Bulero immediately on his return from Mars.

THE THREE STIGMATA
OF PALMER ELDRITCH

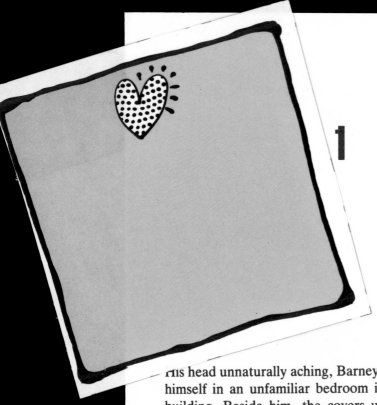

1

His head unnaturally aching, Barney Mayerson woke to find himself in an unfamiliar bedroom in an unfamiliar conapt building. Beside him, the covers up to her bare, smooth shoulders, an unfamiliar girl slept on, breathing lightly through her mouth, her hair a tumble of cottonlike white.

I'll bet I'm late for work, he said to himself, slid from the bed, and tottered to a standing position with eyes shut, keeping himself from being sick. For all he knew he was several hours' drive from his office; perhaps he was not even in the United States. However he *was* on Earth; the gravity that made him sway was familiar and normal.

And there in the next room by the sofa a familiar suitcase, that of his psychiatrist Dr. Smile.

Barefoot, he padded into the living room, and seated himself by the suitcase; he opened it, clicked switches, and turned on Dr. Smile. Meters began to register and the mechanism hummed. "Where am I?" Barney asked it. "And how far am I from New York?" That was the main point. He saw now a clock on the wall of the apt's kitchen; the time was 7:30 A.M. Not late at all.

The mechanism which was the portable extension of Dr.

Smile, connected by micro-relay to the computer itself in the basement level of Barney's own conapt building in New York, the Renown 33, tinnily declared, "Ah, Mr. Bayerson."

"Mayerson," Barney corrected, smoothing his hair with fingers that shook. "What do you remember about last night?" Now he saw, with intense physical aversion, half-empty bottles of bourbon and sparkling water, lemons, bitters, and ice cube trays on the sideboard in the kitchen. "Who is this girl?"

Dr. Smile said, "This girl in the bed is Miss Rondinella Fugate. Roni, as she asked you to call her."

It sounded vaguely familiar, and oddly, in some manner, tied up with his job. "Listen," he said to the suitcase, but then in the bedroom the girl began to stir; at once he shut off Dr. Smile and stood up, feeling humble and awkward in only his underpants.

"Are you up?" the girl asked sleepily. She thrashed about, and sat facing him; quite pretty, he decided, with lovely, large eyes. "What time is it and did you put on the coffee pot?"

He tramped into the kitchen and punched the stove into life; it began to heat water for coffee. Meanwhile he heard the shutting of a door; she had gone into the bathroom. Water ran. Roni was taking a shower.

Again in the living room he switched Dr. Smile back on. "What's she got to do with P. P. Layouts?" he asked.

"Miss Fugate is your new assistant; she arrived yesterday from People's China where she worked for P. P. Layouts as their Pre-Fash consultant for that region. However, Miss Fugate, although talented, is highly inexperienced, and Mr. Bulero decided that a short period as your assistant, I would say 'under you,' but that might be misconstrued, considering—"

"Great," Barney said. He entered the bedroom, found his clothes—they had been deposited, no doubt by him, in a heap on the floor—and began with care to dress; he still felt terrible, and it remained an effort not to give up and be violently sick. "That's right," he said to Dr. Smile as he came back to the living room buttoning his shirt. "I remember the memo from Friday about Miss Fugate. She's erratic in her talent. Picked wrong on that U. S. Civil War Picture Window item . . . if you can imagine it, she thought it'd be a smash hit in People's China." He laughed.

The bathroom door opened a crack; he caught a glimpse of Roni, pink and rubbery and clean, drying herself. "Did you call me, dear?"

"No," he said. "I was talking to my doctor."

"Everyone makes errors," Dr. Smile said, a trifle vacuously.

Barney said, "How'd she and I happen to—" He gestured toward the bedroom. "After so short a time."

"Chemistry," Dr. Smile said.

"Come on."

"Well, you're both precogs. You previewed that you'd eventually hit it off, become erotically involved. So you both decided—after a few drinks—that why should you wait? 'Life is short, art is—' " The suitcase ceased speaking, because Roni Fugate had appeared from the bathroom, naked, to pad past it and Barney back once more into the bedroom. She had a narrow, erect body, a truly superb carriage, Barney noted, and small, up-jutting breasts with nipples no larger than matched pink peas. Or rather matched pink pearls, he corrected himself.

Roni Fugate said, "I meant to ask you last night—why are you consulting a psychiatrist? And my lord, you carry it around everywhere with you; not once did you set it down— and you had it turned on right up until—" She raised an eyebrow and glanced at him searchingly.

"At least I did turn it off then," Barney pointed out.

"Do you think I'm pretty?" Rising on her toes she all at once stretched, reached above her head, then, to his amazement, began to do a brisk series of exercises, hopping and leaping, her breasts bobbing.

"I certainly do," he murmured, taken aback.

"I'd weigh a ton," Roni Fugate panted, "if I didn't do these UN Weapons Wing exercises every morning. Go pour the coffee, will you, dear?"

Barney said, "Are you really my new assistant at P. P. Layouts?"

"Yes, of course; you mean you don't remember? But I guess you're like a lot of really topnotch precogs: you see the future so well that you have only a hazy recollection of the past. Exactly what do you recall about last night?" She paused in her exercises, gasping for breath.

"Oh," he said vaguely, "I guess everything."

"Listen. The only reason why you'd be carrying a psychiatrist around with you is that you must have gotten your draft notice. Right?"

After a pause he nodded. *That* he remembered. The familiar elongated blue-green envelope had arrived one week ago; next Wednesday he would be taking his mental at the UN military hospital in the Bronx.

"Has it helped? Has he—" She gestured at the suitcase. "—Made you sick enough?"

Turning to the portable extension of Dr. Smile, Barney said, "Have you?"

The suitcase answered, "Unfortunately you're still quite viable, Mr. Mayerson; you can handle ten Freuds of stress. Sorry. But we still have several days; we've just begun."

Going into the bedroom, Roni Fugate picked up her underwear, and began to step into it. "Just think," she said reflectively. "If you're drafted, Mr. Mayerson, and you're sent to the colonies . . . maybe I'll find myself with your job." She smiled, showing superb, even teeth.

It was a gloomy possibility and his precog ability did not assist him: the outcome hung nicely, at perfect balance on the scales of cause-and-effect to be.

"You can't handle my job," he said. "You couldn't even handle it in People's China and that's a relatively simple situation in terms of factoring out pre-elements." But someday she could; without difficulty he foresaw that. She was

young and overflowing with innate talent: all she required
to equal him—and he was the best in the trade—was a few
years' experience. Now he became fully awake as awareness
of his situation filtered back to him. He stood a good chance
of being drafted, and even if he was not, Roni Fugate might
well snatch his fine, desirable job from him, a job up to which
he had worked by slow stages over a thirteen-year period.

A peculiar solution to the grimness of the situation, this
going to bed with her; he wondered how he had arrived at
it.

Bending over the suitcase, he said in a low voice to Dr.
Smile, "I wish you'd tell me why the hell with everything so
dire I decided to—"

"I can answer that," Roni Fugate called from the bedroom;
she had now put on a somewhat tight pale green sweater and
was buttoning it before the mirror of her vanity table. "You
informed me last night, after your fifth bourbon and water.
You said—" She paused, eyes sparkling. "It's inelegant.
What you said was this. 'If you can't lick 'em, join 'em.' Only
the verb you used, I regret to say, wasn't 'join.' "

"Hmm," Barney said, and went into the kitchen to pour
himself a cup of coffee. Anyhow, he was not far from New
York; obviously if Miss Fugate was a fellow employee at
P. P. Layouts he was within commute distance of his job.
They could ride in together. Charming. He wondered if their
employer Leo Bulero would approve of this if he knew. Was
there an official company policy about employees sleeping
together? There was about almost everything else . . . although how a man who spent all his time at the resort beaches
of Antarctica or in German E Therapy clinics could find time
to devise dogma on every topic eluded him.

Someday, he said to himself, I'll live like Leo Bulero;
instead of being stuck in New York City in 180 degree
heat—

Beneath him now a throbbing began; the floor shook. The
building's cooling system had come on. Day had begun.

Outside the kitchen window the hot, hostile sun took shape

beyond the other conapt buildings visible to him; he shut his eyes against it. Going to be another scorcher, all right, probably up to the twenty Wagner mark. He did not need to be a precog to foresee this.

In the miserably high-number conapt building 492 on the outskirts of Marilyn Monroe, New Jersey, Richard Hnatt ate breakfast indifferently while, with something greater than indifference, he glanced over the morning homeopape's weather-syndrome readings of the previous day.

The key glacier, Ol' Skintop, had retreated 4.62 Grables during the last twenty-four-hour period. And the temperature, at noon in New York, had exceeded the previous day's by 1.46 Wagners. In addition the humidity, as the oceans evaporated, had increased by 16 Selkirks. So things were hotter and wetter; the great procession of nature clanked on, and toward what? Hnatt pushed the 'pape away, and picked up the mail which had been delivered before dawn . . . it had been some time since mailmen had crept out in daylight hours.

The first bill which caught his eye was the apt's cooling pro-rated swindle; he owed Conapt 492 exactly ten and a half skins for the last month—a rise of three-fourths of a skin over April. Someday, he said to himself, it'll be so hot that *nothing* will keep this place from melting; he recalled the day his l-p record collection had fused together in a lump, back around '04, due to a momentary failure of the building's cooling network. Now he owned iron oxide tapes; they did not melt. And at the same moment every parakeet and Venusian ming bird in the building had dropped dead. And his neighbor's turtle had been boiled dry. Of course this had been during the day and everyone—at least the men—had been at work. The wives, however, had huddled at the lowest subsurface level, thinking (he remembered Emily telling him this) that the fatal moment had at last arrived. And not a century from now but *now*. The Caltech predictions had been wrong . . . only of course they hadn't been; it had just been a broken power-lead from the N.Y. utility people. Robot workmen had quickly shown up and repaired it.

In the living room his wife sat in her blue smock, painstakingly painting an unfired ceramic piece with glaze; her tongue protruded and her eyes glowed . . . the brush moved expertly and he could see already that this was going to be a good one. The sight of Emily at work recalled to him the task that lay before him, today: one which he did not relish.

He said, peevishly, "Maybe we ought to wait before we approach him."

Without looking up, Emily said, "We'll never have a better display to present to him than we have now."

"What if he says no?"

"We'll go on. What did you expect, that we'd give up just because my onetime husband can't foresee—or won't foresee—how successful these new pieces will eventually be in terms of the market?"

Richard Hnatt said, "You know him; I don't. He's not vengeful, is he? He wouldn't carry a grudge?" And anyhow what sort of grudge could Emily's former husband be carrying? No one had done him any harm; if anything it had gone the other way, or so he understood from what Emily had related.

It was strange, hearing about Barney Mayerson all the time and never having met him, never having direct contact with the man. Now that would end, because he had an appointment to see Mayerson at nine this morning in the man's office at P. P. Layouts. Mayerson of course would hold the whip hand; he could take one brief glance at the display of ceramics and decline ad hoc. No, he would say, P. P. Layouts is not interested in a min of this. Believe my precog ability, my Pre-Fash marketing talent and skill. And—out would go Richard Hnatt, the collection of pots under his arm, with absolutely no other place to go.

Looking out the window he saw with aversion that already it had become too hot for human endurance; the footer runnels were abruptly empty as everyone ducked for cover. The time was eight-thirty and he now had to leave; rising, he went to the hall closet to get his pith helmet and his mandatory cooling-unit; by law one had to be strapped to every commuter's back until nightfall.

"Goodbye," he said to his wife, pausing at the front door.

"Goodbye and lots of luck." She had become even more involved in her elaborate glazing and he realized all at once that this showed how vast her tension was; she could not afford to pause even a moment. He opened the door and stepped out into the hall, feeling the cool wind of the portable unit as it chugged from behind him. "Oh," Emily said, as he began to shut the door; now she raised her head, brushing her long brown hair back from her eyes. "Vid me as soon as you're out of Barney's office, as soon as you know one way or another."

"Okay," he said, and shut the door behind him.

Downramp, at the building's bank, he unlocked their safety deposit box and carried it to a privacy room; there he lifted out the display case containing the spread of ceramic ware which he was to show Mayerson.

Shortly, he was aboard a thermosealed interbuilding commute car, on his way to downtown New York City and P. P. Layouts, the great pale synthetic-cement building from which Perky Pat and all the units of her miniature world originated. The doll, he reflected, which had conquered man as man at the same time had conquered the planets of the Sol system. Perky Pat, the obsession of the colonists. What a commentary on colonial life . . . what more did one need to know about those unfortunates who, under the selective service laws of the UN, had been kicked off Earth, required to begin new, alien lives on Mars or Venus or Ganymede or wherever else the UN bureaucrats happened to imagine they could be deposited . . . and after a fashion survive.

And we think we've got it bad here, he said to himself.

The individual in the seat next to him, a middle-aged man wearing the gray pith helmet, sleeveless shirt, and shorts of bright red popular with the businessman class, remarked, "It's going to be another hot one."

"Yes."

"What you got there in that great big carton? A picnic lunch for a hovel of Martian colonists?"

"Ceramics," Hnatt said.

"I'll bet you fire them just by sticking them outdoors at high noon." The businessman chuckled, then picked up his morning 'pape, opened it to the front page. "Ship from outside the Sol system reported crash-landed on Pluto," he said. "Team being sent to find it. You suppose it's *things?* I can't stand those things from other star systems."

"It's more likely one of our own ships reporting back," Hnatt said.

"Ever seen a Proxima thing?"

"Only pics."

"Grisly," the businessman said. "If they find that wrecked ship on Pluto and it is a thing I hope they laser it out of existence; after all we do have a law against them coming into our system."

"Right."

"Can I see your ceramics? I'm in neckties, myself. The Werner simulated-handwrought living tie in a variety of Titanian colors—I have one on, see? The colors are actually a primitive life form that we import and then grow in cultures here on Terra. Just how we induce them to reproduce is our trade secret, you know, like the formula for Coca-Cola."

Hnatt said, "For a similar reason I can't show you these ceramics, much as I'd like to. They're new. I'm taking them to a Pre-Fash precog at P. P. Layouts; if he wants to miniaturize them for the Perky Pat layouts then we're in: it's just a question of flashing the info to the P. P. disc jockey—what's his name?—circling Mars. And so on."

"Werner handwrought ties are part of the Perky Pat layouts," the man informed him. "Her boyfriend Walt has a closetful of them." He beamed. "When P. P. Layouts decided to min our ties—"

"It was Barney Mayerson you talked to?"

"*I* didn't talk to him; it was our regional sales manager. They say Mayerson is difficult. Goes on what seems like impulse and once he's decided it's irreversible."

"Is he ever wrong? Declines items that become fash?"

"Sure. He may be a precog but he's only human. I'll tell you one thing that might help. He's very suspicious of women. His marriage broke up a couple of years ago and he never got over it. See, his wife became pregnant *twice,* and the board of directors of his conapt building, I think it's 33, met and voted to expel him and his wife because they had violated the building code. Well, you know 33; you know how hard it is to get into any of the buildings in that low range. So instead of giving up his apt he elected to divorce his wife and let her move, taking their child. And then later on apparently he decided he made a mistake and he got embittered; he blamed himself, naturally, for making a mistake like that. A natural mistake, though; for God's sake, what wouldn't you and I give to have an apt in 33 or 34? He never remarried; maybe he's a Neo-Christian. But anyhow when you go to try to sell him on your ceramics, be very careful about how you deal with the feminine angle; don't say 'these will appeal to the ladies' or anything like that. Most retail items are purchased—"

"Thanks for the tip," Hnatt said, rising; carrying his case of ceramics he made his way down the aisle to the exit. He sighed. It was going to be tough, possibly even hopeless; he wasn't going to be able to lick the circumstances which long predated his relationship with Emily and her pots, and that was that.

Fortunately he managed to snare a cab; as it carried him through downtown cross-traffic he read his own morning 'pape, in particular the lead story about the ship believed to have returned from Proxima only to crash on Pluto's frozen wastes—an understatement! Already it was conjectured that this might be the well-known interplan industrialist Palmer Eldritch, who had gone to the Prox system a decade ago at the invitation of the Prox Council of humanoid types; they had wanted him to modernize their autofacs along Terran lines. Nothing had been heard from Eldritch since. Now this.

It would probably be better for Terra if this wasn't Eldritch coming back, he decided. Palmer Eldritch was too wild and dazzling a solo pro; he had accomplished miracles in getting autofac production started on the colony planets, but—as always he had gone too far, schemed too much. Consumer goods had piled up in unlikely places where no colonists existed to make use of them. Mountains of debris, they had become, as the weather corroded them bit by bit, inexorably. Snowstorms, if one could believe that such still existed somewhere . . . there were places which were actually cold. Too cold, in actual fact.

"Thy destination, your eminence," the autonomic cab informed him, halting before a large but mostly subsurface structure. P. P. Layouts, with employees handily entering by its many thermal-protected ramps.

He paid the cab, hopped from it, and scuttled across a short open space for a ramp, his case held with both hands; briefly, naked sunlight touched him and he felt—or imagined—himself sizzle. Baked like a toad, dried of all life-juices, he thought as he safely reached the ramp.

Presently he was subsurface, being allowed into Mayerson's office by a receptionist. The rooms, cool and dim, invited him to relax but he did not; he gripped his display case tighter and tensed himself and, although he was not a Neo-Christian, he mumbled a prolix prayer.

"Mr. Mayerson," the receptionist, taller than Hnatt and impressive in her open-bodice dress and resort-style heels, said, speaking not to Hnatt but to the man seated at the desk. "This is Mr. Hnatt," she informed Mayerson. "This is Mr. Mayerson, Mr. Hnatt." Behind Mayerson stood a girl in a pale green sweater and with absolutely white hair. The hair was too long and the sweater too tight. "This is Miss Fugate, Mr. Hnatt. Mr. Mayerson's assistant. Miss Fugate, this is Mr. Richard Hnatt."

At the desk Barney Mayerson continued to study a document without acknowledging the entrance of anyone and Richard Hnatt waited in silence, experiencing a mixed bag of emotions; anger touched him, lodged in his windpipe and chest, and of course *Angst,* and then, above even those, a tendril of growing curiosity. So this was Emily's former husband, who, if the living necktie salesman could be believed, still chewed mournfully, bitterly, on the regret of having abolished the marriage. Mayerson was a rather heavy-set man, in his late thirties, with unusually—and not particularly fashionable—loose and wavy hair. He looked bored but there was no sign of hostility about him. But perhaps he had not as yet—

"Let's see your pots," Mayerson said suddenly.

Laying the display case on the desk Richard Hnatt opened it, got out the ceramic articles one by one, arranged them, and then stepped back.

After a pause Barney Mayerson said, "No."

" 'No'?" Hnatt said. "No what?"

Mayerson said, "They won't make it." He picked up his document and resumed reading it.

"You mean you decided just like that?" Hnatt said, unable to believe that it was already done.

"Exactly like that," Mayerson agreed. He had no further interest in the display of ceramics; as far as he was concerned Hnatt had already packed up his pots and left.

Miss Fugate said, "Excuse me, Mr. Mayerson."

Glancing at her Barney Mayerson said, "What is it?"

"I'm sorry to say this, Mr. Mayerson," Miss Fugate said; she went over to the pots, picked one up and held it in her hands, weighing it, rubbing its glazed surface. "But I get a distinctly different impression than you do. I feel these ceramic pieces will make it."

Hnatt looked from one to the other of them.

"Let me have that." Mayerson pointed to a dark gray vase; at once Hnatt handed it to him. Mayerson held it for a time. "No," he said finally. He was frowning, now. "I still get no impression of this item making it big. In my opinion you're mistaken, Miss Fugate." He set the vase back down. "However," he said to Richard Hnatt, "in view of the disagreement between myself and Miss Fugate—" He scratched his nose thoughtfully. "Leave this display with me for a few days; I'll give it further attention." Obviously, however, he would not.

Reaching, Miss Fugate picked up a small, oddly shaped piece and cradled it against her bosom almost tenderly. "This one in particular. I receive very powerful emanations from it. This one will be the most successful of all."

In a quiet voice Barney Mayerson said, "You're out of your mind, Roni." He seemed really angry, now; his face was violent and dark. "I'll vid you," he said to Richard Hnatt. "When I've made my final decision. I see no reason why I should change my mind, so don't be optimistic. In fact don't bother to leave them." He shot a hard, harsh glance toward his assistant, Miss Fugate.

2

In his office at ten that morning Leo Bulero, chairman of the board of directors of P. P. Layouts, received a vid-call—which he had been expecting—from Tri-Planetary Law Enforcement, a private police agency. He had retained it within minutes of learning of the crash on Pluto by the intersystem ship returning from Prox.

He listened idly, because despite the momentousness of the news he had other matters on his mind.

It was idiotic, in view of the fact that P. P. Layouts paid an enormous yearly tribute to the UN for immunity, but idiotic or not a UN Narcotics Control Bureau warship had seized an entire load of Can-D near the north polar cap of Mars, almost a million skins' worth, on its way from the heavily guarded plantations on Venus. Obviously the squeeze money was not reaching the right people within the complicated UN hierarchy.

But there was nothing he could do about it. The UN was a windowless monad over which he had no influence.

He could without difficulty perceive the intentions of the Narcotics Control Bureau. It wanted P. P. Layouts to initiate litigation aimed at regaining the shipload. Because this would establish that the illegal drug Can-D, chewed by so many colonists, was grown, processed, and distributed by a hidden subsidiary of P. P. Layouts. So, valuable as the shipload was, better to let it go than to make a stab at claiming it.

"The homeopape conjectures were correct," Felix Blau, boss of the police agency, was saying on the vidscreen. "It is Palmer Eldritch and he appears to be alive although badly injured. We understand that a UN ship of the line is bringing him back to a base hospital, location of course undisclosed."

"Hmm," Leo Bulero said, nodding.

"However, as to what Eldritch found in the Prox system—"

"You'll never find that out," Leo said. "Eldritch won't say and it'll end there."

"One fact has been reported," Blau said, "of interest. Aboard his ship Eldritch had—still has—a carefully maintained culture of a lichen very much resembling the Titanian lichen from which Can-D is derived. I thought in view of—" Blau broke off tactfully.

"Is there any way those lichen cultures can be destroyed?" It was an instinctive impulse.

"Unfortunately Eldritch employees have already reached the remains of the ship. They undoubtedly would resist efforts in that direction." Blau looked sympathetic. "We could of course try . . . not a forceful solution but perhaps we could buy our way in."

"Try," Leo said, although he agreed; it was undoubtedly a waste of time and effort. "Isn't there that law, that major UN ordinance, against importing life forms from other systems?" It would certainly be handy if the UN military could be induced to bomb the remains of Eldritch's ship. On his note pad he scratched a memo to himself: call lawyers, lodge complaint with UN over import of alien lichens. "I'll talk to you later," he said to Blau and rang off. Maybe I'll complain directly, he decided. Pressing the tab on his intercom he said to his secretary, "Get me UN, top, in New York. Ask for Secretary Hepburn-Gilbert personally."

Presently he found himself connected with the crafty Indian politician who last year had become UN Secretary. "Ah, Mr. Bulero." Hepburn-Gilbert smiled shyly. "You wish to complain as to the seizure of that shipment of Can-D which—"

"I know nothing about any shipment of Can-D," Leo said. "This has to do with another matter completely. Do you people realize what Palmer Eldritch is up to? He's brought non-Sol lichens into our system; it could be the beginning of another plague like we had in '98."

"We realize this. However, the Eldritch people are claiming it to be a Sol lichen which Mr. Eldritch took with him on his Prox trip and is now bringing back . . . it was a source of protein to him, they claim." The Indian's white teeth shone in gleeful superiority; the meager pretext amused him.

"You believe that?"

"Of course not." Hepburn-Gilbert's smile increased. "What interests you in this matter, Mr. Bulero? You have an, ah, special concern for lichens?"

"I'm a public-spirited citizen of the Sol system. And I insist that you act."

"We are acting," Hepburn-Gilbert said. "We have made inquiries . . . we have assigned our Mr. Lark—you know him—to this detail. You see?"

The conversation droned to a frustrating conclusion and Leo Bulero at last hung up, feeling irked at politicians; they managed to take forceful steps when it came to *him* but in connection with Palmer Eldritch . . . ah, Mr. Bulero, he mimicked to himself. That, sir, is something else again.

Yes, he knew Lark. Ned Lark was chief of the UN Narcotics Bureau and the man responsible for the seizure of this last shipment of Can-D; it had been a ploy on the part of the UN Secretary, bringing Lark into this hassle with Eldritch. What the UN was angling for here was a quid pro quo; they would drag their feet, not act against Eldritch unless and until Leo Bulero made some move to curtail his Can-D shipments; he sensed this, but could not of course prove it. After all, Hepburn-Gilbert, that dark-skinned sneaky little unevolved politician, hadn't exactly *said* that.

That's what you find yourself involved in when you talk to the UN, Leo reflected. Afro-Asian politics. A swamp. It's run, staffed, directed by foreigners. He glared at the blank vidscreen.

While he was wondering what to do his secretary Miss Gleason clicked on the intercom at her end and said, "Mr. Bulero, Mr. Mayerson is in the outer office; he'd like a few moments with you."

"Send him in." He was glad for a respite.

A moment later his expert in the field of tomorrow's fashions came in, scowling. Silently, Barney Mayerson seated himself facing Leo.

"What's eating you, Mayerson?" Leo demanded. "Speak up; that's what I'm here for, so you can cry on my shoulder. Tell me what it is and I'll hold your hand." He made his tone withering.

"My assistant. Miss Fugate."

"Yes, I hear you're sleeping with her."

"That's not the issue."

"Oh I see," Leo said. "That's just a minor aside."

"I just meant I'm here about another aspect of Miss Fugate's behavior. We had a basic disagreement a little while ago; a salesman—"

Leo said, "You turned something down and she disagreed."

"Yes."

"You precogs." Remarkable. Maybe there were alternate futures. "So you want me to order her in the future always to back you up?"

Barney Mayerson said, "She's my assistant; that means she's supposed to do as I direct."

"Well . . . isn't sleeping with you a pretty fair move in that direction?" Leo laughed. "However, she should back you up while salesmen are present, then if she has any qualms she should air them privately later on."

"I don't even go for that." Barney scowled even more.

Acutely, Leo said, "You know because I take that E Therapy I've got a huge frontal lobe; I'm practically a precog myself, I'm so advanced. Was it a pot salesman? Ceramics?"

With massive reluctance Barney nodded.

"They're your ex-wife's pots," Leo said. Her ceramics were selling well; he had seen ads in the homeopapes for them, as retained by one of New Orleans' most exclusive art-object shops, and here on the East Coast and in San Francisco. "Will they go over, Barney?" He studied his precog. *"Was Miss Fugate right?"*

"They'll never go over; that's God's truth." Barney's tone, however, was leaden. The wrong tone, Leo decided, for what he was saying; it was too lacking in vitality. "That's what I foresee," Barney said doggedly.

"Okay." Leo nodded. "I'll accept what you're saying. But if her pots become a sensation and we don't have mins of them available for the colonists' layouts—" He pondered. "You might find your bed-partner also occupying your chair," he said.

Rising, Barney said, "You'll instruct Miss Fugate, then, as to the position she should take?" He colored. "I'll rephrase that," he murmured, as Leo began to guffaw.

"Okay, Barney. I'll lower the fnard on her. She's young; she'll survive. And you're aging; you need to keep your dignity, not have anyone disagree with you." He, too, rose; walking up to Barney, he slapped him on the back. "But listen. Stop eating your heart out; forget that ex-wife of yours. Okay?"

"I've forgotten her."

"There are always more women," Leo said, thinking of Scotty Sinclair, his mistress at the moment; Scotty right now, frail and blonde but huge in the balcony, hung out at his satellite villa five hundred miles at apogee, waiting for him to knock off work for the week. "There's an infinite supply; they're not like early U. S. postage stamps or the truffle skins we use as money." It occurred to him, then, that he could smooth matters by making available to Barney one of his discarded—but still serviceable—former mistresses. "I tell you what," he began, but Barney at once cut him off with a savage swipe of his hand. "No?" Leo asked.

"No. Anyhow I'm wound up tight with Roni Fugate. One at a time is enough for any normal man." Barney eyed his employer severely.

"I agree. Lord, I only can see one at a time, myself; what do you think, I've got a harem up there at Winnie-ther-Pooh Acres?" He bristled.

"The last time I was up there," Barney said, "which was at that birthday party for you back in January—"

"Oh well. Parties. That's something else; you don't count what goes on during parties." He accompanied Barney to the door of the office. "You know, Mayerson, I heard a rumor about you, one I didn't like. Someone saw you lugging one of those suitcase-type extensions of a conapt psychiatric computer around with you . . . *did you get a draft notice?*"

There was silence. Then, at last, Barney nodded.

"And you weren't going to say anything to us," Leo said. "We were to find out when? The day you board ship for Mars?"

"I'm going to beat it."

"Sure you are. Everyone does; that's the way the UN's managed to populate four planets, six moons—"

"I'm going to fail my mental," Barney said. "My precog ability tells me I am; it's helping me. I can't endure enough Freuds of stress to satisfy them—look at me." He held up his hands; they perceptibly trembled. "Look at my reaction to Miss Fugate's harmless remark. Look at my reaction to Hnatt bringing in Emily's pots. Look at—"

"Okay," Leo said, but he still was worried. Generally the draft notices gave only a ninety-day period before induction, and Miss Fugate would hardly be ready to assume Barney's chair that soon. Of course he could transfer Mac Ronston from Paris—but even Ronston, after fifteen years, was not of the same caliber as Barney Mayerson; he had the experience, but talent could not be stored up: it had to be there as God-given.

The UN is really getting to me, Leo thought. He wondered if Barney's draft notice, coming at this particular moment, was only a coincidence or if this was another probe of his weak points. If it is, he decided, it's a bad one. And there's no pressure I can put on the UN to exempt him.

And simply because I supply those colonists with their Can-D, he said to himself. I mean, somebody has to; they've got to have it. Otherwise what good are the Perky Pat layouts to them?

And in addition it was one of the most profitable trading operations in the Sol system. Many truffle skins were involved.

The UN knew that, too.

At twelve-thirty New York time Leo Bulero had lunch with a new girl who had joined the secretary pool. Pia Jurgens, seated across from him in a secluded chamber of the Purple Fox, ate with precision, her small, neat jaw working in an orderly manner. She was a redhead and he liked redheads; they were either outrageously ugly or almost supernaturally attractive. Miss Jurgens was the latter. Now, if he could find a pretext by which to transfer her to Winnie-ther-Pooh Acres . . . assuming that Scotty didn't object, however. And such did not at the present seem very likely; Scotty had a will of her own, which was always dangerous in a woman.

Too bad I couldn't wangle Scotty off onto Barney Mayerson, he said to himself. Solve two problems at once; make Barney more psychologically secure, free myself for—

Nuts! he thought. Barney needs to be *insecure,* otherwise he's as good as on Mars; that's why he's hired that talking suitcase. I don't understand the modern world at all, obviously. I'm living back in the twentieth century when psychoanalysts made people *less* prone to stress.

"Don't you ever talk, Mr. Bulero?" Miss Jurgens asked.

"No." He thought, Could I dabble successfully in Barney's pattern of behavior? Help him to—what's the word—become less viable?

But it was not as easy as it sounded; he instinctively appreciated that, expanded frontal lobe-wise. You can't make healthy people sick just by giving an order.

Or can you?

Excusing himself, he hunted up the robot waiter and asked that a vidphone be brought to his table.

A few moments later he was in touch with Miss Gleason back at the office. "Listen, I want to see Miss Rondinella Fugate, from Mr. Mayerson's staff, as soon as I get back. And Mr. Mayerson is not to know. Understand?"

"Yes sir," Miss Gleason said, making a note.

"I heard," Pia Jurgens said, when he had hung up. "You know, I could tell Mr. Mayerson; I see him nearly every day in the—"

Leo laughed. The idea of Pia Jurgens throwing away the burgeoning future opening for her vis-à-vis himself amused him. "Listen," he said, patting her hand, "don't worry; it's not within the spectrum of human nature. Finish your Ganymedean wap-frog croquette and let's get back to the office."

"What I meant," Miss Jurgens said stiffly, "is that it seems a little odd to me that you'd be so open in front of someone else, someone you don't hardly know." She eyed him, and her bosom, already overextended and enticing, became even more so; it expanded with indignation.

"Obviously the answer is to know you better," Leo said, greedily. "Have you ever chewed Can-D?" he asked her, rhetorically. "You should. Despite the fact that it's habit-forming. It's a real experience." He of course kept a supply, grade AA, on hand at Winnie-ther-Pooh Acres; when guests assembled it often was brought out to add color to what otherwise might have passed as dull. "The reason I ask is that you look like the sort of woman who has active imagination, and the reaction you get to Can-D depends—varies with—your imaginative-type creative powers."

"I'd enjoy trying it sometime," Miss Jurgens said. She glanced about, lowered her voice, and leaned toward him. "But it's illegal."

"It is?" He stared at her.

"You know it is." The girl looked nettled.

"Listen," Leo said. "I can get you some." He would, of course, chew it with her; in concert the users' minds fused, became a new unity—or at least that was the experience. A few sessions of Can-D chewing in togetherness and he would know all there was to know about Pia Jurgens; there was something about her—beyond the obvious physical, anatomical enormity—that fascinated him; he yearned to be closer to her. "We won't use a layout." By an irony he, the creator and manufacturer of the Perky Pat micro-world, preferred to use Can-D in a vacuum; what did a Terran have to gain from a layout, inasmuch as it was a min of the conditions obtaining in the average Terran city? For settlers on a howling, gale-swept moon, huddled at the bottom of a hovel against frozen methane crystals and things, it was something else again; Perky Pat and her layout were an entree back to the world they had been born to. But he, Leo Bulero, he was damn tired of the world he had been born to and still dwelt on. And even Winnie-ther-Pooh Acres, with all its quaint and not-so-quaint diversions did not fill the void. However—

"That Can-D," he said to Miss Jurgens, "is great stuff, and no wonder it's banned. It's like religion; Can-D is the religion of the colonists." He chuckled. "One plug of it, wouzzled for fifteen minutes, and—" He made a sweeping gesture. "No more hovel. No more frozen methane. It provides a reason for living. Isn't that worth the risk and expense?"

But what is there of equal value for us? he asked himself, and felt melancholy. He had, by manufacturing the Perky Pat layouts and raising and distributing the lichen-base for the final packaged product Can-D, made life bearable for over one million unwilling expatriates from Terra. But what the hell did he get back? My life, he thought, is dedicated to others, and I'm beginning to kick; it's not enough. There was his satellite, where Scotty waited; there existed as always the tangled details of his two large business operations, the one legal, the other not . . . but wasn't there more in life than this?

He did not know. Nor did anyone else, because like Barney Mayerson they were all engaged in their various imitations of him. Barney with his Miss Rondinella Fugate, small-time replica of Leo Bulero and Miss Jurgens. Wherever he looked it was the same; probably even Ned Lark, the Narcotics Bureau chief, lived this sort of life—probably so did Hepburn-Gilbert, who probably kept a pale, tall Swedish starlet with breasts the size of bowling balls—and equally firm. Even Palmer Eldritch. No, he realized suddenly. Not Palmer Eldritch; he's found something else. For ten years he's been in the Prox system or at least coming and going. *What did he find?* Something worth the effort, worth the terminal crash on Pluto?

"You saw the homeopapes?" he asked Miss Jurgens. "About the ship on Pluto? There's a man in a billion, that Eldritch. No one else like him."

"I read," Miss Jurgens said, "that he was practically a nut."

"Sure. Ten years out of his life, all that agony, and for what?"

"You can be sure he got a good return for the ten years," Miss Jurgens said. "He's crazy but smart; he looks out for himself, like everyone else does. He's not *that* nuts."

"I'd like to meet him," Leo Bulero said. "Talk to him, even if only just a minute." He resolved, then, to do that, go to the hospital where Palmer Eldritch lay, force or buy his way into the man's room, learn what he had found.

"I used to think," Miss Jurgens said, "that when the ships first left our system for another star—remember that?—we'd hear that—" She hesitated. "It's so silly, but I was only a kid then, when Arnoldson made his first trip to Prox and back; I was a kid when he got *back*, I mean. I actually thought maybe by going that far he'd—" She ducked her head, not meeting Leo Bulero's gaze. "He'd find God."

Leo thought, I thought so, too. And I was an adult, then. In my mid-thirties. As I've mentioned to Barney on numerous occasions.

And, he thought, I still believe that, even now. About the ten-year-flight of Palmer Eldritch.

After lunch, back in his office at P. P. Layouts, he met Rondinella Fugate for the first time; she was waiting for him when he arrived.

Not bad-looking, he thought as he shut the office door. Nice figure, and what glorious, luminous eyes. She seemed nervous; she crossed her legs, smoothed her skirt, watched him furtively as he seated himself at his desk facing her. Very young, Leo realized. A child who would speak up and contradict her superior when she thought he was wrong. Touching . . .

"Do you know why you're here in my office?" he inquired.

"I guess you're angry because I contradicted Mr. Mayerson. But I really experienced the futurity in the life-line of those ceramics. So what else could I do?" She half-rose imploringly, then reseated herself.

Leo said, "I believe you. But Mr. Mayerson is sensitive. If you're living with him, you know he has a portable psychiatrist that he lugs wherever he goes." Opening his desk drawer he got out his box of Cuesta Reys, the very finest; he offered the box to Miss Fugate, who gratefully accepted one of the slender dark cigars. He, too, took a cigar; he lit hers and then his, and leaned back in his chair. "You know who Palmer Eldritch is?"

"Yes."

"Can you use your precog powers for something other than Pre-Fash foresight? In another month or so the homeopapes will be routinely mentioning Eldritch's location. I'd like you to look ahead to those 'papes and then tell me where the man is at this moment. I know you can do it." You had better be able to, he said to himself, if you want to keep your job here. He waited, smoking his cigar, watching the girl and thinking to himself, with a trace of envy, that if she was as good in bed as she looked—

Miss Fugate said in a soft, halting voice, "I get only the most vague impression, Mr. Bulero."

"Well, let's hear it anyhow." He reached for a pen.

It took her several minutes, and, as she reiterated, her impression was not distinct. Nonetheless he presently had on his note pad the words: James Riddle Veterans' Hospital, Base III, Ganymede. A UN establishment, of course. But he had anticipated that. It was not decisive; he still might be able to find a way in.

"And he's not there under that name," Miss Fugate said, pale and enervated from the effort of foreseeing; she relit her cigar, which had gone out; sitting straighter in her chair, she once more crossed her supple legs. "The homeopapes will say that Eldritch was listed in the hospital records as a Mr.—" She paused, squeezed her eyes shut, and sighed. "Oh hell," she said. "I can't make it out. One syllable. Frent. Brent. No, I think it's Trent. Yes, it's Eldon Trent." She smiled in relief; her large eyes sparkled with naïve, childlike pleasure. "They really have gone to a lot of trouble to keep him hidden. And they're interrogating him, the 'papes will say. So obviously he's conscious." She frowned then, all at once. "Wait. I'm looking at a headline; I'm in my own con-apt, by myself. It's early morning and I'm reading the front page. Oh dear."

"What's it say?" Leo demanded, bending rigidly forward; he could catch the girl's dismay.

Miss Fugate whispered, "The headlines say that Palmer Eldritch is dead." She blinked, looked around her with amazement, then slowly focused on him; she regarded him with a confused mixture of fear and uncertainty, almost palpably edging back; she retreated from him, huddled against her chair, her fingers interlocked. "And you're accused of having done it, Mr. Bulero. Honest; that's what the headline says."

"You mean I'm going to *murder* him?"

She nodded. "But—it's not a certainty; I only pick it up in some of the futures . . . do you understand? I mean, we precogs see—" She gestured.

"I know." He was familiar with precogs; Barney Mayerson had, after all, worked for P. P. Layouts thirteen years, and some of the others even longer. "It could happen," he said gratingly. Why would I do a thing like that? he asked himself. No way to tell now. Perhaps after he reached Eldritch, talked to him . . . as evidently he would.

Miss Fugate said, "I don't think you ought to try to contact Mr. Eldritch in view of this possible future; don't you agree, Mr. Bulero? I mean, the risk is there—it hangs very large. About—I'd guess—in the neighborhood of forty."

"What's 'forty'?"

"Percent. Almost half the possibilities." Now, more composed, she smoked her cigar and faced him; her eyes, dark and intense, flickered as she regarded him, undoubtedly speculating with vast curiosity why he would do such a thing.

Rising, he walked to the door of the office. "Thank you, Miss Fugate; I appreciate your assistance in this matter." He waited, indicating clearly his expectations that she would leave.

However, Miss Fugate remained seated. He was encountering the same peculiar streak of firmness that had upset Barney Mayerson. "Mr. Bulero," she said quietly, "I think I'd really have to go to the UN police about this. We precogs—"

He reshut the office door. "You precogs," he said, "are too preoccupied with other people's lives." But she had him. He wondered what she would manage to do with her knowledge.

"Mr. Mayerson may be drafted," Miss Fugate said. "You

knew that, of course. Are you going to try to influence them to let him off?''

Candidly, he said, "I had some intentions in the direction of helping him beat it, yes."

"Mr. Bulero," she said in a small, steady voice, "I'll make a deal with you. Let them draft him. And then I'll be your New York Pre-Fash consultant." She waited; Leo Bulero said nothing. "What do you say?" she asked. Obviously she was unaccustomed to such negotiations. However, she intended to make it stick if possible; after all, he reflected, everyone, even the smartest operator, had to begin somewhere. Perhaps he was seeing the initial phase of what would be a brilliant career.

And then he remembered something. Remembered why she had been transferred from the Peking office to come here to New York as Barney Mayerson's assistant. Her predictions had proved erratic. Some of them—too many of them, in fact—had proved erroneous.

Perhaps her preview of the headline relating his indictment as the alleged murderer of Palmer Eldritch—assuming that she was being truthful, that she had really experienced it— was only another of her errors. The faulty precognition which had brought her here.

Aloud he said, "Let me think it over. Give me a couple of days."

"Until tomorrow morning," Miss Fugate said firmly.

Leo laughed. "I see why Barney was so riled up." And Barney probably sensed with his own precog faculty, at least nebulously, that Miss Fugate was going to make a decisive strike at him, jeopardizing his whole position. "Listen." He walked over to her. "You're Mayerson's mistress. How'd you like to give that up? I can offer you the use of an entire satellite." Assuming, of course, that he could pry Scotty out of there.

"No thank you," Miss Fugate said.

"Why?" He was amazed. "Your career—"

"I like Mr. Mayerson," she said. "And I don't particularly care for bub—" She caught herself. "Men who've evolved in those clinics."

Again he opened the office door. "I'll let you know by tomorrow morning." As he watched her pass through the doorway and out into the receptionist's office he thought, That'll give me time to reach Ganymede and Palmer Eldritch; I'll know more, then. Know if your foresight seems spurious or not.

Shutting the door behind the girl, he turned at once to his desk, and clicked the vidphone button connecting him with the outside. To the New York City operator he said, "Get me the James Riddle Veterans' Hospital at Base III on Ganymede; I want to speak to a Mr. Eldon Trent, a patient there. Person to person." He gave his name and number, then rang off, jiggled the hook, and dialed Kennedy Spaceport.

He booked passage for the express ship leaving New York for Ganymede that evening, then paced about his office, waiting for the call-back from James Riddle Veterans' Hospital.

Bubblehead, he thought. She'd call even her employer that.

Ten minutes later the call came.

"I'm sorry, Mr. Bulero," the operator apologized. "Mr. Trent is not receiving calls, by doctors' orders."

So Rondinella Fugate was right; an Eldon Trent did exist at James Riddle and in all probability he was Palmer Eldritch. It was certainly worth making the trip; the odds looked good.

—Looked good, he thought wryly, that I'll encounter Eldritch, have some kind of altercation with him, God knows what, and eventually bring about his death. A man that at this point in time I don't even know. And I'll find myself arraigned; I won't get away with it. What a prospect.

But his curiosity was aroused. In all his manifold operations he had never found the need of killing anyone under any circumstances. Whatever it was that would occur between him and Palmer Eldritch had to be unique; definitely a trip to Ganymede was indicated.

It would be difficult to turn back now. Because he had the acute intuition that this would turn out to be what he hoped. And Rondinella Fugate had only said that he would be accused of the murder; there was no datum as to a successful conviction.

Convicting a man of his stature of a capital crime, even through the UN authorities, would take some doing.

He was willing to let them try.

3

In a bar hard by P. P. Layouts, Richard Hnatt sat sipping a Tequila Sour, his display case on the table before him. He knew goddamn well there was nothing wrong with Emily's pots; her work was saleable. The problem had to do with her ex-husband and his position of power.

And Barney Mayerson had exercised that power.

I have to call Emily and tell her, Hnatt said to himself. He started to his feet.

A man blocked his way, a peculiar round specimen mounted on spindly legs.

"Who are you?" Hnatt said.

The man bobbed toylike in front of him, meanwhile digging into his pocket as if scratching at a familiar microorganism that possessed parasitic proclivities that had survived the test of time. However, what he produced at last was a business card. "We're interested in your ceramic ware, Mr. Hatt. Natt. However you say it."

"Icholtz," Hnatt said, reading the card; it gave only the name, no further info, not even a vidnumber. "But what I have with me are just samples. I'll give you the names of retail outlets stocking our line. But these—"

"Are for minning," the toylike man, Mr. Icholtz, said, nodding. "And that's what we want. We intend to min your ceramics, Mr. Hnatt; we believe that Mayerson is wrong—they will become fash, and very soon."

Hnatt stared at him. "You want to min, and you're not from P. P. Layouts?" But no one else minned. Everyone knew P. P. Layouts had a monopoly.

Seating himself at the table beside the display case, Mr. Icholtz brought out his wallet and began counting out skins. "Very little publicity will be attached to this at first. But eventually—" He offered Hnatt the stack of brown, wrinkled, truffle-skins which served as tender in the Sol system: the only molecule, a unique protein amino acid, which could not be duplicated by the Printers, the Biltong life forms employed in place of automated assembly lines by many of Terra's industries.

"I'll have to check with my wife," Hnatt said.

"Aren't you the representative of your firm?"

"Y-yes." He accepted the pile of skins.

"The contract." Icholtz produced a document, spread it flat on the table; he extended a pen. "It gives us an exclusive."

As he bent to sign, Richard Hnatt saw the name of Icholtz' firm on the contract. Chew-Z Manufacturers of Boston. He had never heard of them. Chew-Z . . . it reminded him of another product, exactly which he could not recall. It was only after he had signed and Icholtz was tearing loose his copy that he remembered.

The illegal hallucinogenic drug Can-D, used in the colonies in conjunction with the Perky Pat layouts.

He had an intuition compounded by deep unease. But it was too late to back out. Icholtz was gathering up the display case; the contents belonged to Chew-Z Manufacturers of Boston, U.S.A., Terra, now.

"How—can I get in touch with you?" Hnatt asked, as Icholtz started away from the table.

"You won't be getting in touch with us. If we want you we'll call you." Icholtz smiled briefly.

How in hell was he going to tell Emily? Hnatt counted the skins, read the contract, realized by degrees exactly how much Icholtz had paid him; it was enough to provide him and Emily with a five-day vacation in Antarctica, at one of the great, cool resort cities frequented by the rich of Terra, where no doubt Leo Bulero and others like him spent the summer . . . and these days summer lasted all year round.

Or—he pondered. It could do even more; it could get himself and his wife into the most exclusive establishment on the planet—assuming he and Emily wanted it. They could fly to the Germanies and enter one of Dr. Willy Denkmal's E Therapy clinics. Wowie, he thought.

He shut himself up in the bar's vidphone booth and called Emily. "Pack your bag. We're going to Munich. To—" He picked the name of a clinic at random; he had seen this one advertised in exclusive Paris magazines. "To Eichenwald," he told her. "Dr. Denkmal is—"

"Barney took them," Emily said.

"No. But there's someone else in the field of minning, now, besides P. P. Layouts." He felt elated. "So Barney turned us down; so what? We did better with this new outfit; they must have plenty. I'll see you in half an hour; I'll arrange for accommodations on TWA's express flight. Think of it: E Therapy for both of us."

In a low voice Emily said, "I'm not sure I want to evolve, when it comes right down to it."

Staggered, he said, "Sure you do. I mean, it could save our lives, and if not ours then our kids'—our potential kids that we might be having, someday. And even if we're only there a short time and only evolve a little, look at the doors it'll open to us; we'll be personae gratae everywhere. Do *you* personally know anyone who's had E Therapy? You read about so-and-so in the homeopapes all the time, society people . . . but—"

"I don't want that hair all over me," Emily said. "And I don't want to have my head expand. No. I won't go to Eichenwald Clinic." She sounded completely decided; her face was placid.

He said, "Then I'll go alone." It would still be of economic value; after all, it was he who dealt with buyers. And he could stay at the clinic twice as long, evolve twice as much . . . assuming that the treatments took. Some people did not respond, but that was hardly Dr. Denkmal's fault; the capacity for evolution was not bestowed on everyone alike. About himself he felt certitude; he'd evolve remarkably, catch up with the big shots, even pass some of them, in terms of the familiar horny rind which Emily out of mistaken prejudice had called "hair."

"What am I supposed to do while you're gone? Just make pots?"

"Right," he said. Because orders would be arriving thick and fast; otherwise Chew-Z Manufacturers of Boston would have no interest in the min. Obviously they employed their own Pre-Fash precogs as P. P. Layouts did. But then he remembered; Icholtz had said *very little publicity at first.* That meant, he realized, that the new firm had no network of disc jockeys circling the colony moons and planets; unlike P. P. Layouts, they had no Allen and Charlotte Faine to flash the news to.

But it took time to set up disc jockey satellites. This was natural.

And yet it made him uneasy. He thought all at once in panic, Could they be an illegal firm? Maybe Chew-Z, like Can-D, is banned; maybe I've got us into something dangerous.

"Chew-Z," he said aloud to Emily. "Ever heard of it?"

"No."

He got the contract out and once more examined it. What

a mess, he thought. How'd I get into it? If only that damn
Mayerson had said yes on the pots . . .

At ten in the morning a terrific horn, familiar to him, hooted
Sam Regan out of his sleep, and he cursed the UN ship
upstairs; he knew the racket was deliberate. The ship, circling
above the hovel Chicken Pox Prospects, wanted to be certain
that colonists—and not merely indigenous animals—got the
parcels that were to be dropped.

We'll get them, Sam Regan muttered to himself as he
zipped his insulated overalls, put his feet into high boots,
and then grumpily sauntered as slowly as possible toward the
ramp.

"He's early today," Tod Morris complained. "And I'll bet
it's all staples, sugar and food-basics like lard—nothing interesting such as, say, candy."

Putting his shoulders against the lid at the top of the ramp,
Norman Schein pushed; bright cold sunlight spilled down on
them and they blinked.

The UN ship sparkled overhead, set against the black sky
as if hanging from an uneasy thread. Good pilot, this drop,
Tod decided. Knows the Fineburg Crescent area. He waved
at the UN ship and once more the huge horn burst out its
din, making him clap his hands to his ears.

A projectile slid from the under part of the ship, extended
stabilizers, and spiraled toward the ground.

"Sheoot," Sam Regan said with disgust. "It is staples; they
don't have the parachute." He turned away, not interested.

How miserable the upstairs looked today, he thought as
he surveyed the landscape of Mars. Dreary. Why did we
come here? Had to, were forced to.

Already the UN projectile had landed; its hull cracked
open, torn by the impact, and the three colonists could see
cannisters. It looked to be five hundred pounds of salt. Sam
Regan felt even more despondent.

"Hey," Schein said, walking toward the projectile and peering. "I believe I see something we can use."

"Looks like radios in those boxes," Tod said. "Transistor radios." Thoughtfully he followed after Schein. "Maybe we can use them for something new in our layouts."

"Mine's already got a radio," Schein said.

"Well, build an electronic self-directing lawn mower with the parts," Tod said. "You don't have that, do you?" He knew the Scheins' Perky Pat layout fairly well; the two couples, he and his wife with Schein and his, had fused together a good deal, being compatible.

Sam Regan said, "Dibs on the radios, because I can use them." His layout lacked the automatic garage-door opener that both Schein and Tod had; he was considerably behind them. Of course all those items could be purchased. But he was out of skins. He had used his complete supply in the service of a need which he considered more pressing. He had, from a pusher, bought a fairly large quantity of Can-D; it was buried, hidden out of sight, in the earth under his sleep-compartment at the bottom level of their collective hovel.

He himself was a believer; he affirmed the miracle of translation—the near-sacred moment in which the miniature artifacts of the layout no longer merely represented Earth but *became* Earth. And he and the others, joined together in the fusion of doll-inhabitation by means of the Can-D, were transported outside of time and local space. Many of the colonists were as yet unbelievers; to them the layouts were merely symbols of a world which none of them could any longer experience. But, one by one, the unbelievers came around.

Even now, so early in the morning, he yearned to go back down below, chew a slice of Can-D from his hoard, and join with his fellows in the most solemn moment of which they were capable.

To Tod and Norm Schein he said, "Either of you care to

seek transit?" That was the technical term they used for participation. "I'm going back below," he said. "We can use my Can-D; I'll share it with you."

An inducement like that could not be ignored; both Tod and Norm looked tempted. "So early?" Norm Schein said. "We just got out of bed. But I guess there's nothing to do anyhow." He kicked glumly at a huge semi-autonomous sand dredge; it had remained parked near the entrance of the hovel for days now. No one had the energy to come up to the surface and resume the clearing operations inaugurated earlier in the month. "It seems wrong, though," he muttered. "We ought to be up here working in our gardens."

"And that's some garden you've got," Sam Regan said, with a grin. "What is that stuff you've got growing there? Got a name for it?"

Norm Schein, hands in the pockets of his coveralls, walked over the sandy, loose soil with its sparse vegetation to his once carefully maintained vegetable garden; he paused to look up and down the rows, hopeful that more of the specially prepared seeds had sprouted. None had.

"Swiss chard," Tod said encouragingly. "Right? Mutated as it is, I can still recognize the leaves."

Breaking off a leaf Norm chewed it, then spat it out; the leaf was bitter and coated with sand.

Now Helen Morris emerged from the hovel, shivering in the cold Martian sunlight. "We have a question," she said to the three men. "I say that psychoanalysts back on Earth were charging fifty dollars an hour and Fran says it was for only forty-five minutes." She explained, "We want to add an analyst to our layout and we want to get it right, because it's an authentic item, made on Earth and shipped here, if you remember that Bulero ship that came by last week—"

"We remember," Norm Schein said sourly. The prices that the Bulero salesman had wanted. And all the time in their satellite Allen and Charlotte Faine talked up the different items so, whetting everyone's appetite.

"Ask the Faines," Helen's husband Tod said. "Radio them the next time the satellite passes over." He glanced at his wristwatch. "In another hour. They have all the data on authentic items; in fact that particular datum should have been included with the item itself, right in the carton." It perturbed him because it had of course been his skins—his and Helen's together—that had gone to pay for the tiny figure of the human-type psychoanalyst, including the couch, desk, carpet, and bookcase of incredibly well-minned impressive books.

"You went to the analyst when you were still on Earth," Helen said to Norm Schein. "What was the charge?"

"Well, I mostly went to group therapy," Norm said. "At the Berkeley State Mental Hygiene Clinic, and they charged according to your ability to pay. And of course Perky Pat and her boyfriend go to a private analyst." He walked down the length of the garden solemnly deeded to him, between the rows of jagged leaves, all of which were to some extent shredded and devoured by microscopic native pests. If he could find one healthy plant, one untouched—it would be enough to restore his spirits. Insecticides from Earth simply had not done the job, here; the native pests thrived. They had been waiting ten thousand years, biding their time, for someone to appear and make an attempt to raise crops.

Tod said, "You better do some watering."

"Yeah," Norm Schein agreed. He meandered gloomily in the direction of Chicken Pox Prospects' hydro-pumping system; it was attached to their now partially sand-filled irrigation network which served all the gardens of their hovel. Before watering came sand-removal, he realized. If they didn't get the big Class-A dredge started up soon they wouldn't be able to water even if they wanted to. But he did not particularly want to.

And yet he could not, like Sam Regan, simply turn his back on the scene up there, return below to fiddle with his layout, build or insert new items, make improvements . . .

or, as Sam proposed, actually get out a quantity of the carefully hidden Can-D and begin the communication. We have
responsibilities, he realized.

To Helen he said, "Ask my wife to come up here." She
could direct him as he operated the dredge; Fran had a good
eye.

"I'll get her," Sam Regan agreed, starting back down
below. "No one wants to come along?"

No one followed him; Tod and Helen Morris had gone
over to inspect their own garden, now, and Norm Schein was
busy pulling the protective wrapper from the dredge, pre-
paratory to starting it up.

Back below, Sam Regan hunted up Fran Schein; he found
her crouched at the Perky Pat layout which the Morrises and
the Scheins maintained together, intent on what she was
doing.

Without looking up, Fran said, "We've got Perky Pat all
the way downtown in her new Ford hardtop convert and
parked and a dime in the meter and she's shopped and now
she's in the analyst's office reading *Fortune*. But what does
she pay?" She glanced up, smoothed back her long dark hair,
and smiled at him. Beyond a doubt Fran was the handsomest
and most dramatic person in their collective hovel; he observed this now, and not for anything like the first time.

He said, "How can you fuss with that layout and not
chew—" He glanced around; the two of them appeared to
be alone. Bending down he said softly to her, "Come on and
we'll chew some first-rate Can-D. Like you and I did before.
Okay?" His heart labored as he waited for her to answer;
recollections of the last time the two of them had been translated in unison made him feel weak.

"Helen Morris will be—"

"No, they're cranking up the dredge, above. They won't
be back down for an hour." He took hold of Fran by the
hand, led her to her feet. "What arrives in a plain brown
wrapper," he said as he steered her from the compartment
out into the corridor, "should be used, not just buried. It

gets old and stale. Loses its potency." And we pay a lot for that potency, he thought morbidly. Too much to let it go to waste. Although some—not in this hovel—claimed that the power to insure translation did not come from the Can-D but from the accuracy of the layout. To him this was a nonsensical view, and yet it had its adherents.

As they hurriedly entered Sam Regan's compartment Fran said, "I'll chew in unison with you, Sam, but let's not do anything while we're there on Terra that—you know. We wouldn't do here. I mean, just because we're Pat and Walt and not ourselves that doesn't give us license." She gave him a warning frown, reproving him for his former conduct and for leading her to that yet unasked.

"Then you admit we really go to Earth." They had argued this point—and it was cardinal—many times in the past. Fran tended to take the position that the translation was one of appearance only, of what the colonists called *accidents*—the mere outward manifestations of the places and objects involved, not the essences.

"I believe," Fran said slowly, as she disengaged her fingers from his and stood by the hall door of the compartment, "that whether it's a play of imagination, of drug-induced hallucination, or an actual translation from Mars to Earth-as-it-was by an agency we know nothing of—" Again she eyed him sternly. "I think we should abstain. In order not to contaminate the experience of communication." As she watched him carefully remove the metal bed from the wall and reach, with an elongated hook, into the cavity revealed, she said, "It should be a purifying experience. We lose our fleshly bodies, our corporeality, as they say. And put on imperishable bodies instead, for a time anyhow. Or forever, if you believe as some do that it's outside of time and space, that it's eternal. Don't you agree, Sam?" She sighed. "I know you don't."

"Spirituality," he said with disgust as he fished up the packet of Can-D from its cavity beneath the compartment. "A denial of reality, and what do you get instead? Nothing."

"I admit," Fran said as she came closer to watch him open the packet, "that I can't *prove* you get anything better back, due to abstention. But I do know this. What you and other sensualists among us don't realize is that when we chew Can-D and leave our bodies *we die*. And by dying we lose the weight of—" She hesitated.

"Say it," Sam said as he opened the packet; with a knife he cut a strip from the mass of brown, tough, plant-like fibers.

Fran said, "Sin."

Sam Regan howled with laughter. "Okay—at least you're orthodox." Because most colonists would agree with Fran. "But," he said, redepositing the packet back in its safe place, "that's not why I chew it; I don't want to lose anything . . . I want to gain something." He shut the door of the compartment, then swiftly got out his own Perky Pat layout, spread it on the floor, and put each object in place, working at eager speed. "Something to which we're not normally entitled," he added, as if Fran didn't know.

Her husband—or his wife or both of them or everyone in the entire hovel—could show up while he and Fran were in the state of translation. And their two bodies would be seated at proper distance one from the other; no wrong-doing could be observed, however prurient the observers were. Legally this had been ruled on; no cohabitation could be proved, and legal experts among the ruling UN authorities on Mars and the other colonies had tried—and failed. While translated one could commit incest, murder, anything, and it remained from a juridical standpoint a mere fantasy, an impotent wish only.

This highly interesting fact had long inured him to the use of Can-D; for him life on Mars had few blessings.

"I think," Fran said, "you're tempting me to do wrong." As she seated herself she looked sad; her eyes, large and dark, fixed futilely on a spot at the center of the layout, near Perky Pat's enormous wardrobe. Absently, Fran began to fool with a mink sable coat, not speaking.

He handed her half of a strip of Can-D, then popped his own portion into his mouth and chewed greedily.

Still looking mournful, Fran also chewed.

He was Walt. He owned a Jaguar XXB sports ship with a flatout velocity of fifteen thousand miles an hour. His shirts came from Italy and his shoes were made in England. As he opened his eyes he looked for the little G.E. clock TV set by his bed; it would be on automatically, tuned to the morning show of the great newsclown Jim Briskin. In his flaming red wig Briskin was already forming on the screen. Walt sat up, touched a button which swung his bed, altered to support him in a sitting position, and lay back to watch for a moment the program in progress.

"I'm standing here at the corner of Van Ness and Market in downtown San Francisco," Briskin said pleasantly, "and we're just about to view the opening of the exciting new subsurface conapt building Sir Francis Drake, the first to be *entirely underground*. With us, to dedicate the building, standing right by me is that enchanting female of ballad and—"

Walt shut off the TV, rose, and walked barefoot to the window; he drew the shades, saw out then onto the warm sparkling early-morning San Francisco street, the hills and white houses. This was Saturday morning and he did not have to go to his job down in Palo Alto at Ampex Corporation; instead—and this rang nicely in his mind—he had a date with his girl, Pat Christensen, who had a modern little apt over on Potrero Hill.

It was always Saturday.

In the bathroom he splashed his face with water, then squirted on shave cream, and began to shave. And, while he shaved, staring into the mirror at his familiar features, he saw a note tacked up, in his own hand.

THIS IS AN ILLUSION. YOU ARE SAM REGAN, A COLONIST ON MARS. MAKE USE OF YOUR TIME OF

TRANSLATION, BUDDY BOY. CALL UP PAT
PRONTO!

And the note was signed Sam Regan.

An illusion, he thought, pausing in his shaving. In what
way? He tried to think back; Sam Regan and Mars, a dreary
colonists' hovel . . . yes, he could dimly make the image out,
but it seemed remote and vitiated and not convincing. Shrugging, he resumed shaving, puzzled, now, and a little depressed. All right, suppose the note was correct; maybe he
did remember that other world, that gloomy quasi-life of
involuntary expatriation in an unnatural environment. So
what? Why did he have to wreck this? Reaching, he yanked
down the note, crumpled it and dropped it into the bathroom
disposal chute.

As soon as he had finished shaving he vidphoned Pat.

"Listen," she said at once, cool and crisp; on the screen
her blonde hair shimmered: she had been drying it. "I don't
want to see you, Walt. Please. Because I know what you
have in mind and I'm just not interested; do you understand?" Her blue-gray eyes were cold.

"Hmm," he said, shaken, trying to think of an answer.
"But it's a terrific day—we ought to get outdoors. Visit
Golden Gate Park, maybe."

"It's going to be too hot to go outdoors."

"No," he disagreed, nettled. "That's later. Hey, we could
walk along the beach, splash around in the waves. Okay?"

She wavered, visibly. "But that conversation we had just
before—"

"There was no conversation. I haven't seen you in a week,
not since last Saturday." He made his tone as firm and full
of conviction as possible. "I'll drop by your place in half an
hour and pick you up. Wear your swimsuit, you know, the
yellow one. The Spanish one that has a halter."

"Oh," she said disdainfully, "that's completely out of fash
now. I have a new one from Sweden; you haven't seen it.

I'll wear that, if it's permitted. The girl at A & F wasn't sure."

"It's a deal," he said, and rang off.

A half hour later in his Jaguar he landed on the elevated field of her conapt building.

Pat wore a sweater and slacks; the swimsuit, she explained, was on underneath. Carrying a picnic basket, she followed him up the ramp to his parked ship. Eager and pretty, she hurried ahead of him, pattering along in her sandals. It was all working out as he had hoped; this was going to be a swell day after all, after his initial trepidations had evaporated . . . as thank God they had.

"Wait until you see this swimsuit," she said as she slid into the parked ship, the basket on her lap. "It's really daring; it hardly exists: actually you sort of have to have faith to believe in it." As he got in beside her she leaned against him. "I've been thinking over that conversation we had—let me finish." She put her fingers against his lips, silencing him. "I *know* it took place, Walt. But in a way you're right; in fact basically you have the proper attitude. We should try to obtain as much from this as possible. Our time is short enough as it is . . . at least so it seems to me." She smiled wanly. "So drive as fast as you can; I want to get to the ocean."

Almost at once they were setting down in the parking lot at the edge of the beach.

"It's going to be hotter," Pat said soberly. "Every day. Isn't it? Until finally it's unbearable." She tugged off her sweater, then, shifting about on the seat of the ship, managed to struggle out of her slacks. "But we won't live that long . . . it'll be another fifty years before no one can go outside at noon. Like they say, become mad dogs and Englishmen; we're not that yet." She opened the door and stepped out in her swimsuit. And she had been correct; it took faith in things unseen to make the suit out at all. It was perfectly satisfactory, to both of them.

Together, he and she plodded along the wet, hard-packed

sand, examining jelly fish, shells, and pebbles, the debris tossed up by the waves.

"What year is this?" Pat asked him suddenly, halting. The wind blew her untied hair back; it lifted in a mass of cloudlike yellow, clear and bright and utterly clean, each strand separate.

He said, "Well, I guess it's—" And then he could not recall; it eluded him. "Damn," he said crossly.

"Well, it doesn't matter." Linking arms with him she trudged on. "Look, there's that little secluded spot ahead, past those rocks." She increased her tempo of motion; her body rippled as her strong, taut muscles strained against the wind and the sand and the old, familiar gravity of a world lost long ago. "Am I what's-her-name—Fran?" she asked suddenly. She stepped past the rocks, foam and water rolled over her feet, her ankles; laughing, she leaped, shivered from the sudden chill. "Or am I Patricia Christensen?" With both hands she smoothed her hair. "This is blonde, so I must be Pat. Perky Pat." She disappeared beyond the rocks; he quickly followed, scrambling after her. "I used to be Fran," she said over her shoulder, "but that doesn't matter now. I could have been anyone before, Fran or Helen or Mary, and it wouldn't matter now. Right?"

"No," he disagreed, catching up with her. Panting, he said, "It's important that you're Fran. In essence."

" 'In essence.' " She threw herself down on the sand, lay resting on her elbow, drawing by means of a sharp black rock in savage swipes which left deeply gouged lines; almost at once she tossed the rock away, and sat around to face the ocean. "But the accidents . . . they're Pat." She put her hands beneath her breasts, then, languidly lifting them, a puzzled expression on her face. "These," she said, "are Pat's. Not mine. Mine are smaller; I remember."

He seated himself beside her, saying nothing.

"We're here," she said presently, "to do what we can't do back at the hovel. Back where we've left our corruptible bodies. As long as we keep our layouts in repair this—" She gestured at the ocean, then once more touched herself, unbelievingly. "It can't decay, can it? We've put on immortality." All at once she lay back, flat against the sand, and shut her eyes, one arm over her face. "And since we're here, and we can do things denied us at the hovel, then your theory is we *ought* to do those things. We ought to take advantage of the opportunity."

He leaned over her, bent and kissed her on the mouth.

Inside his mind a voice thought, "But I can do this any time." And, in the limbs of his body, an alien mastery asserted itself; he sat back, away from the girl. "After all," Norm Schein thought, "I'm married to her." He laughed, then.

"Who said you could use my layout?" Sam Regan thought angrily. "Get out of my compartment. And I bet it's my Can-D, too."

"You offered it to us," the co-inhabitant of his mind-body answered. "So I decided to take you up on it."

"I'm here, too," Tod Morris thought. "And if you want my opinion—"

"Nobody asked you for yours," Norm Schein thought angrily. "In fact nobody asked you to come along; why don't you go back up and mess with that rundown no-good garden of yours, where you ought to be?"

Tod Morris thought calmly, "I'm with Sam. I don't get a chance to do this, except here." The power of his will combined with Sam's; once more Walt bent over the reclining girl; once again he kissed her on the mouth, and this time heavily, with increased agitation.

Without opening her eyes Pat said in a low voice, "I'm here, too. This is Helen." She added, "And also Mary. But we're not using your supply of Can-D, Sam; we brought some we had already." She put her arms around him as the three inhabitants of Perky Pat joined in unison in one endeavor. Taken by surprise, Sam Regan broke contact with Tod Morris; he joined the effort of Norm Schein, and Walt sat back away from Perky Pat.

The waves of the ocean lapped at the two of them as they silently reclined together on the beach, two figures comprising the essences of six persons. Two in six, Sam Regan thought. The mystery repeated; how is it accomplished? The old question again. But all I care about, he thought, is whether they're using up my Can-D. And I bet they are; I don't care what they say: I don't believe them.

Rising to her feet Perky Pat said, "Well, I can see I might just as well go for a swim; nothing's doing here." She padded into the water, splashed away from them as they sat in their body, watching her go.

"We missed our chance," Tod Morris thought wryly.

"My fault," Sam admitted. By joining, he and Tod managed to stand; they walked a few steps after the girl and then, ankle-deep in the water, halted.

Already Sam Regan could feel the power of the drug wearing off; he felt weak and afraid and bitterly sickened at the realization. So goddam soon, he said to himself. All over; back to the hovel, to the pit in which we twist and cringe like worms in a paper bag, huddled away from the daylight. Pale and white and awful. He shuddered.

—Shuddered, and saw, once more, his compartment with its tinny bed, washstand, desk, kitchen stove . . . and, in slumped, inert heaps, the empty husks of Tod and Helen Morris, Fran and Norm Schein, his own wife Mary; their eyes stared emptily and he looked away, appalled.

On the floor between them was his layout; he looked down and saw the dolls, Walt and Pat, placed at the edge of the ocean, near the parked Jaguar. Sure enough, Perky Pat had on the near-invisible Swedish swimsuit, and next to them reposed a tiny picnic basket.

And, by the layout, a plain brown wrapper that had contained Can-D; the five of them had chewed it out of existence, and even now as he looked—against his will—he saw a thin trickle of shiny brown syrup emerge from each of their slack, will-less mouths.

Across from him Fran Schein stirred, opened her eyes, moaned; she focused on him, then wearily sighed.

"They got to us," he said.

"We took too long." She rose unsteadily, stumbled, and almost fell; at once he was up, too, catching hold of her. "You were right; we should have done it right away if we intended to. But—" She let him hold her, briefly. "I like the preliminaries. Walking along the beach, showing you the swimsuit that is no swimsuit." She smiled a little.

Sam said, "They'll be out for a few more minutes, I bet."

Wide-eyed, Fran said, "Yes, you're right." She skipped away from him, to the door; tugging it open, she disappeared out into the hall. "In our compartment," she called back. "Hurry!"

Pleased, he followed. It was too amusing; he was convulsed with laughter. Ahead of him the girl scampered up the ramp to her level of the hovel; he gained on her, caught hold of her as they reached her compartment. Together they tumbled in, rolled giggling and struggling across the hard metal floor to bump against the far wall.

We won after all, he thought as he deftly unhooked her bra, began to unbutton her shirt, unzipped her skirt, and removed her laceless slipperlike shoes in one swift operation; he was busy everywhere and Fran sighed, this time not wearily.

"I better lock the door." He rose, hurried to the door and shut it, fastening it securely. Fran, meanwhile, struggled out of her undone clothes.

"Come back," she urged. "Don't just watch." She piled them in a hasty heap, shoes on top like two paperweights.

He descended back to her side and her swift, clever fingers began on him; dark eyes alit she worked away, to his delight.

And right here in their dreary abode on Mars. And yet—they had still managed it in the old way, the sole way: through the drug brought in by the furtive pushers. Can-D had made this possible; they continued to require it. In no way were they free.

As Fran's knees clasped his bare sides he thought, And in no way do we want to be. In fact just the opposite. As his hand traveled down her flat, quaking stomach he thought, We could even use a little more.

4

At the reception desk at James Riddle Veterans' Hospital at Base III on Ganymede, Leo Bulero tipped his expensive hand-fashioned wubfur derby to the girl in her starched white uniform and said, "I'm here to see a patient, a Mr. Eldon Trent."

"I'm sorry, sir," the girl began, but he cut her off.

"Tell him Leo Bulero is here. Got it? Leo Bulero." And he saw past her hand, to the register; he saw the number of Eldritch's room. As the girl turned to the switchboard he strode in the direction of that number. The hell with waiting, he said to himself; I came millions of miles and I expect to see the man or the thing, whichever it is.

An armed UN soldier with a rifle halted him at the door, a very young man with clear, cold eyes like a girl's; eyes that emphatically said no, even to him.

"Okay," Leo grumbled. "I get the picture. But if he knew who it was out here he'd say let me in."

Beside him, at his ear, startling him, a sharp female voice said, "How did you find out my father was here, Mr. Bulero?"

He turned and saw a rather heavy-set woman in her mid-thirties; she regarded him intently and he thought, This is Zoe Eldritch. I ought to know; she's on the society pages of the homeopapes enough.

A UN official approached. "Miss Eldritch, if you'd like we can evict Mr. Bulero from this building; it's up to you." He smiled pleasantly at Leo and all at once Leo identified him. This was the chief of the UN's legal division, Ned Lark's superior, Frank Santina. Dark-eyed, alert, somatically vibrant, Santina looked quickly from Leo to Zoe Eldritch, waiting for a response.

"No," Zoe Eldritch said at last. "At least not right now. Not until I find out how he found out dad is here; he can't know. Can you, Mr. Bulero?"

Santina murmured, "Through one of his Pre-Fash precogs, probably. Isn't that so, Bulero?"

Presently Leo, reluctantly, nodded.

"You see, Miss Eldritch," Santina explained, "a man like Bulero can hire anything he wants, any form of talent. So we expected him." He indicated the two uniformed armed guards at Palmer Eldritch's door. "That's why we require both of them at all times. As I tried to explain."

"Isn't there any way I can do business with Eldritch?" Leo demanded. "That's what I came here for; I've got nothing illegal in mind. I think all of you are nuts, or else you're trying to hide something; maybe you've got guilty consciences." He eyed them, but saw nothing. "Is it really Palmer Eldritch in there?" he asked. "I bet it isn't." Again he got no response; neither of them rose to the jibe. "I'm tired," he said. "It was a long-type trip here. The hell with it; I'm going to go get something to eat and then I'm going to find a hotel room and sleep for ten hours and forget this." Turning, he stalked off.

Neither Santina nor Miss Eldritch tried to stop him. Disappointed, he continued on, feeling oppressive disgust.

Obviously he would have to reach Palmer Eldritch through some medium agency. Perhaps, he reflected, Felix Blau and his private police could gain entry here. It was worth a try.

But once he became this depressed, nothing seemed to matter. Why not do as he had said, eat and then get some needed rest, forget about reaching Eldritch for the time being? The hell with all of them, he said to himself as he left the hospital building and marched out onto the sidewalk to search for a cab. That daughter, he thought. Tough-looking, like a lesbian, with her hair cut short and no makeup. Ugh.

He found a cab and rode airborne for a time while he pondered.

Using the cab's vidsystem he contacted Felix back on Earth.

"I'm glad you called," Felix Blau said, as soon as he made out who it was. "There's an organization that's come into existence in Boston under strange circumstances; it *seems* to have sprung up overnight completely intact, including—"

"What's it doing?"

"They're preparing to market something; the machinery is there, including three ad satellites, similar to your own, one on Mars, one on Io, one on Titan. The rumor we hear is that they're preparing to approach the market with a commodity directly competing with your own Perky Pat layouts. It'll be called Connie Companion Doll." He smiled briefly. "Isn't that cute?"

Leo said, "What about—you know. The additive."

"No information on that. Assuming there is one, it would be beyond the legal scope of merchandising operations, presumably. Is a min layout any use minus the—'additive'?"

"No."

"Then that would seem to answer that."

Leo said, "I called you to find out if you can get me in to see Palmer Eldritch. I've located him here at Base III on Ganymede."

"You recall my report on Eldritch's importation of a lichen similar to that used in the manufacture of Can-D. Has it occurred to you that this new Boston outfit may have been set up by Eldritch? Although it would seem rather soon for that; however, he could have radioed ahead years ago to his daughter."

"I've got to see him," Leo said.

"It's James Riddle Hospital, I assume. We thought he might be there. By the way; you ever heard of a man named Richard Hnatt?"

"Never."

"A rep from this new Boston outfit met with him and transacted some kind of business deal. This rep, Icholtz—"

"What a mess," Leo said. "And I can't even get to Eldritch; Santina is hanging around at the door, along with that dike daughter of Palmer's." No one would get past the two of them, he decided.

He gave Felix Blau the address of a hotel at Base III, the one at which he had left his baggage, and then rang off.

I bet he's right, he said to himself. Palmer Eldritch is this competitor. Just my luck: I have to be in the particular line that Eldritch, on his way back from Prox, decides to enter. Why couldn't I be making rocket guidance systems and be only competing with G.E. and General Dynamics?

Now he really wondered about the lichen which Eldritch had brought with him. An improvement on Can-D, perhaps. Cheaper to produce, capable of creating translation of longer duration and intensity. Jeez!

Mulling, here and now a bizarre recollection came to him. An organization, emanating from the United Arab Republic; trained assassins for hire. Fat chance they would have against Palmer Eldritch . . . a man like that, once he had made his mind up—

And yet Rondinella Fugate's precognition remained; in the future he would be arraigned for the murder of Palmer Eldritch.

Evidently he would find a way despite the obstacles.

He had with him a weapon so small, so intangible, that even the most thorough search couldn't disclose it. Some time ago a surgeon at Washington, D.C. had sewn it into his tongue: a self-guiding, high-velocity poison dart, modeled on Soviet Russian lines . . . but vastly improved, in that once it had reached its victim it obliterated itself, leaving no remains. The poison, too, was original; it did not curtail heart or respiratory action; in fact it was not a poison but a filterable virus which multiplied in the victim's blood stream, causing death within forty-eight hours. It was carcinomatous, an importation from one of Uranus's moons, and still generally unknown; it had cost him a great deal. All he needed to do was stand within arm's length of his intended victim and manually squeeze the base of his tongue, protruding the same simultaneously in the victim's direction. So if he could see Eldritch—

And I had better arrange it, he realized, before this new Boston corporation is in production. Before it can function without Eldritch. Like any weed it had to be caught early or not at all.

When he reached his hotel room he placed a call to P. P. Layouts to see if any vital-type messages or events were awaiting his attention.

"Yes," Miss Gleason said, as soon as she recognized him. "There's an urgent call from a Miss Impatience White—if that's her name, if I did get it right. Here's the number. It's on Mars." She held the slip to the vidscreen.

At first Leo could not place any woman named White. And then he identified her—and felt fright. Why had *she* called?

"Thanks," he mumbled, and at once rang off. God, if the UN legal division had monitored the call . . . because Impy White, operating out of Mars, was a top pusher of Can-D.

With great reluctance he called the number.

Small-faced and sharp-eyed, pretty in a short sort of way, Impy White obtained on the vidscreen. He had imagined her as much more brawny; she looked quite bantamlike, but fierce, though. "Mr. Bulero, as soon as I say it—"

"There's no other way? No channels?" A method existed by which Conner Freeman, chief of the Venusian operation, could contact him. Miss White could have worked through Freeman, her superior.

"I visited a hovel, Mr. Bulero, at the south of Mars this morning with a shipment. The hovelists declined. On the grounds they had spent all their skins for a new product. In the same class as—what we sell. Chew-Z." She went on, "And—"

Leo Bulero rang off. And sat shakily in silence, thinking.

I've got to not get rattled, he told himself. After all, I'm an evolved human variety. So this is it; this is that Boston firm's new product. Derived from Eldritch's lichen; I have to assume that. He's lying there on his hospital bed not a mile from me, giving the orders no doubt through Zoe, and there's not a fligging thing I can do. The operation is all set up and functioning. I'm already too late. Even this thing in my tongue, he realized. It's futile, now.

But I'll think of something, he knew. I always do.

This was not the end of P. P. Layouts, exactly.

The only thing was, what *could* he do? It eluded him, and this did not decrease his sweaty, nervous alarm.

Come to me, artificially accelerated cortical-development idea, he said in prayer. God help me to overcome my enemies, the bastards. Maybe if I make use of my Pre-Fash precogs, Roni Fugate and Barney . . . maybe they can come up with something. Especially that old pro Barney; he hasn't been brought in on this at all, as yet.

Once more he placed a vidcall to P. P. Layouts back on Terra. This time he requested Barney Mayerson's department.

And then he remembered Barney's problem with the draft, his need of developing an inability to endure stress, in order not to wind up in a hovel on Mars.

Grimly, Leo Bulero thought, I'll provide that proof; for him the danger of being drafted is already over.

When the call came from Leo Bulero on Ganymede, Barney Mayerson was alone in his office.

The conversation did not last long; when he had hung up

he glanced at his watch, and marveled. Five minutes. It had seemed a major interval in his life.

Rising, he touched the button of his intercom and said, "Don't let anyone in for a while. Not even—especially not even—Miss Fugate." He walked to the window and stood gazing out at the hot, bright, empty street.

Leo was dumping the entire problem in his lap. It was the first time he had seen his employer collapse; imagine, he thought, Leo Bulero baffled—by the first competition that he had ever experienced. He very simply was not used to it. The new Boston company's existence had totally, for the time being, disoriented him; the man became the child.

Eventually Leo would snap out of it, but meanwhile— *what can I get from this?* Barney Mayerson asked himself, and did not immediately see any answer. I can help Leo . . . but exactly what can Leo do for me? That was a question more to his liking. In fact, he had to think of it that way; Leo himself had taught him to, over the years. His employer would not have wanted it any other way.

For a time he sat meditating and then, as Leo had directed, he turned his attention to the future. And while he was at it he poked once more into his own draft situation; he tried to see precisely how that would finally resolve itself.

But the topic of his being drafted was too small, too much an iota, to be recorded in the public annals of the great; he could scan no homeopape headlines, hear no newscasts . . . in Leo's case, however, it was something else again. Because he previewed a number of 'pape lead articles pertaining to Leo and Palmer Eldritch. Everything of course was blurred, and alternates presented themselves in a chaos of profusion. Leo would meet Eldritch; Leo would not. And—at this he focused intently—Leo arraigned for the murder of Palmer Eldritch; good lord, what did *that* mean?

It meant, he discovered from closer scrutiny, just what it said. And if Leo were arrested, tried, and sentenced, it might mean the termination of P. P. Layouts as a salary-paying enterprise. Hence the end of a career to which he had already sacrificed everything else in his life, his marriage and the woman he—even now!—loved.

Obviously it was to his advantage, a necessity in fact, to warn Leo. And yet even this datum could be turned to advantage.

He phoned Leo back. "I have your news."

"Good." Leo beamed, his florid, elongated, rind-topped face suffused with relief. "Go ahead, Barney."

Barney said, "There will soon be a situation which you can exploit. You can get in to see Palmer Eldritch—not there at the hospital but elsewhere. He'll be removed from Ganymede by his own order." He added with caution, not wanting to give away too much of the data he had collected, "There'll be a falling-out between him and the UN; he's using them now, while he's incapacitated, to protect him. But when he's well—"

"Details," Leo said at once, cocking his big head alertly.

"There is something I'd like in exchange."

"For what?" Leo's palpably evolved face clouded.

Barney said, "In exchange for my telling you the exact date and locus at which you can successfully reach Palmer Eldritch."

Grumbling, Leo said, "And what d'ya want, for chrissakes?" He eyed Barney apprehensively; E Therapy had not brought tranquillity.

"One quarter of one percent of your gross. Of P. P. Layouts' . . . not including revenue from any other source." Meaning the plantation network on Venus where Can-D was obtained.

"Good food in heaven," Leo said, and breathed raggedly.

"There's more."

"What more? I mean, you'll be rich!"

"And I want a restructuring of your use of Pre-Fash consultants. Each will stay at his post, nominally handle the job he has now, but with this alteration. All their decisions will be referred to me for final review; I'll have the ultimate sayso on their determinations. So I no longer will represent any one region; you can turn New York over to Roni as soon as—"

"Power hungry," Leo said in a grating voice.

Barney shrugged. Who cared what it was called? It represented the culmination of his career; this was what counted. And they were all in it for this, Leo included. In fact Leo first of all.

"Okay," Leo said, nodding. "You can ride herd on all the other Pre-Fash consultants; it doesn't mean anything to me. Now tell me how and when and where—"

"You can meet Palmer Eldritch in three days. One of his own ships, unmarked, will take him off Ganymede the day after tomorrow, to his demesne on Luna; there he'll continue to recuperate, but no longer in UN territory. Frank Santina won't have any more authority in this matter so you can forget about him. On the twenty-third at his demesne Eldritch will meet 'pape reporters, and give them his version of what took place on his trip; he'll be in a good mood— at least so they'll report. Apparently healthy, glad to be back, recovering satisfactorily . . . he'll give a long story about—"

"Just tell me how to get in. There'll still be a security system by his own boys."

Barney said, "P. P. Layouts—get this—puts out a trade journal four times a year. *The Mind of Minning.* It's such a small-scale operation you probably don't even know it exists."

"You mean I should go as a reporter from our house organ?" Leo stared at him. "I can get entry to his demesne on *that* basis?" He looked disgusted. "Hell. I didn't have to pay you for such garbagey information; it would have been announced in the next day or so—I mean, if 'pape reporters are going to be there it must be made public."

Barney shrugged. He did not bother to answer.

"I guess you got me," Leo said. "I was too eager. Well," he added philosophically, "maybe you can tell me what he's going to give the 'pape reporters by way of an explanation.

What *did* he find in the Prox system? Does he mention the lichens he brought back?"

"He does. He claims they're a benign form, approved by the UN's Narcotics Control Bureau, which will replace—" He hesitated. "Certain dangerous, habit-forming derivatives now in wide use. And—"

"And," Leo finished stonily, "he's going to announce the formation of a company to peddle his narcotic-exempt commodity."

"Yes." Barney said. "Called Chew-Z, with the slogan: *be choosy. Chew Chew-Z.*"

"Aw frgawdsake!"

"It was all set up by intersystem radio-laser long ago, through his daughter with the approval of Santina and Lark at the UN, in fact with Hepburn-Gilbert's own approval. They see this as a way of putting a finish to the Can-D trade."

There was silence.

"Okay," Leo said hoarsely, after a time. "It seems a shame you couldn't have previewed this a couple of years ago, but hell—you're an employee and no one told you to."

Barney shrugged.

Grim-faced, Leo Bulero rang off.

So that's that, Barney said to himself. I violated Rule One of career-oriented functioning: never tell your superior something he doesn't want to hear. I wonder what the consequences of that will be.

The vidphone all at once came back on; once again Leo Bulero's clouded features formed. "Listen, Barney. I just had a thought. This is going to make you sore, so get set."

"I'm set." He prepared himself.

"I forgot, and I shouldn't have, that I previously talked to Miss Fugate and she knows about—certain events in the future pertaining to myself and Palmer Eldritch. Events which in any case, if she were to get disturbed—and having you ride herd on her would make her disturbed—she might fly into a fit and do us harm. In fact I got to thinking that potentially all my Pre-Fash consultants could come across this information, so the idea of you supervising all of them—"

"The 'events,' " Barney interrupted, "have to do with your arraignment for the first-degree murder of Palmer Eldritch; correct?"

Leo grunted, wheezed, and stared morosely at him. At last, reluctantly, he nodded.

"I'm not going to let you pull out of the agreement you just now made with me," Barney said. "You made me certain promises and I expect you to—"

"But," Leo bleated, "that fool girl—she's erratic, she'll run to the UN cops; Barney, she's got me!"

"So have I," he pointed out quietly.

"Yeah, but I've known you for years." Leo appeared to be thinking rapidly, appraising the situation with what he enjoyed calling his next-stage-in-the-Homo-sapiens-type-evolved-knowledge powers, or some such thing. "You're a pal. You wouldn't do that, what she'd do. And anyhow I can still offer you the percentage of the gross you asked for. Okay?" He eyed Barney anxiously, but with formidable determination; he had made up his mind. "Can we finalize on that, then?"

"We already finalized."

"But dammit, like I said, I forgot about—"

"If you don't come through," Barney said, "I'll quit. And go somewhere else with my ability." He had worked too many years to turn back at this point.

"You?" Leo said unbelievingly. "I mean, you're not just talking about going to the UN police; you're talking about—switching sides and going over to Palmer Eldritch!"

Barney said nothing.

"You darn snink," Leo said. "So this is what trying to stay afloat in times like this has done to us. Listen; I'm not so sure Palmer would accept you. Probably he's got his Pre-Fash people already set up. And if he does he knows the news already, about my—" He broke off. "Yeah, I'll take the chance; I think you have that Greek sin—what did they call it? Hubris? Pride, like Satan had, reaching too far. Go ahead and reach, Barney. In fact do anything you want; it doesn't matter to me. And lots of luck, fella. Keep me posted on how you make out, and the next time you feel inclined to blackmail somebody—"

Barney cut the connection. The screen became a formless gray. Gray, he thought, like the world inside me and around me, like reality. He rose and walked stiffly back and forth, hands in his trouser pockets.

My best bet, he decided, at this point—God forbid—is to join with Roni Fugate. Because she's the one Leo is scared of, and for good reason. There must be a whole galaxy of things she'd do that I wouldn't. And Leo knows it.

Reseating himself he had Roni paged, brought at last into his office.

"Hi," she said brightly, colorful in her Peking-style silk dress, sans bra. "What's up? I tried to reach you a minute ago, but—"

"You just never," he said, "never have on all your clothes. Shut the door."

She shut the door.

"However," he said, "to give you your due, you were very good in bed last night."

"Thank you." Her youthful, clear face glowed.

Barney said, "Do you foresee *clearly* that our employer will murder Palmer Eldritch? Or is there doubt?"

Swallowing, she ducked her head and murmured, "You just reek with talent." She seated herself and crossed her legs, which were, he noticed, bare. "Of course there's doubt. First of all I think it's moronic of Mr. Bulero, because of course it means the end of his career. The 'papes don't—will not—know his motives for it, so I can't guess; it must be something enormous and dreadful, don't you think?"

"The end of his career," Barney said, "and also yours and mine."

"No," Roni said, "I don't think so, dear. Let's consider a moment. Mr. Palmer Eldritch is going to replace him in the min field; isn't that Mr. Bulero's probable motive? And doesn't that tell us something about the economic reality to come? Even with Mr. Eldritch dead it would appear that his organization will—"

"So we go over to Eldritch? Just like that?"

Screwing up her face in concentration, Roni said laboredly, "No, I don't *quite* mean that. But we must be wary of losing with Mr. Bulero; we don't want to find ourselves dragged down with him . . . I have years ahead of me and to some lesser extent so do you."

"Thanks," he said acidly.

"What we must do now is to plan carefully. And if precogs can't plan for the future—"

"I've provided Leo with info that'll lead to a meeting between him and Eldritch. Had it occurred to you that the two of them might form a syndicate together?" He eyed her intently.

"I—see nothing like that ahead. No 'pape article to that effect."

"God," he said with scorn, "it's not going to get into the 'papes."

"Oh." Chastened, she nodded. "That's so, I guess."

"And if that happened," he said, "we'd be nowhere, once we left Leo and marched over to Eldritch. He'd have us back and on his own terms; we'd be better off getting out of the Pre-Fash business entirely." That was obvious to him and he saw by the expression on Roni Fugate's face that it was obvious to her, too. "If we approach Palmer Eldritch—"

" 'If.' We've got to."

Barney said, "No we don't. We can stumble along like we are." As employees of Leo Bulero, whether he sinks or rises or even completely disappears, he thought to himself. "I'll tell you what else we can do; we can approach all the other Pre-Fash consultants that work for P. P. Layouts and form a syndicate of our own." It was an idea he had toyed with for years. "A guild, so to speak, with a monopoly. Then we can dictate terms to both Leo and Eldritch."

"Except," Roni said, "that Eldritch has Pre-Fash consultants of his own, evidently." She smiled at him. "You have no clear conception of what to do, have you, Barney? I can see that. What a shame. And you've worked so many years." She shook her head sadly.

"I can see," he said, "why Leo was hesitant at the idea of crossing you."

"Because I tell the truth?" She raised her eyebrows. "Yes, perhaps so; everybody's afraid of the truth. You, for instance—you don't like to face the fact that you said no to that poor pot salesman just to get back at the woman who—"

"Shut up," he said savagely.

"You know where that pot salesman probably is right now? Signed up by Palmer Eldritch. You did him—and your ex-wife—a favor. Whereas if you'd said yes you'd have chained him to a declining company, cut both of them out of their chance to—" She broke off. "I'm making you feel bad."

Gesturing, he said, "This is just not relevant to what I called you in here for."

"That's right." She nodded. "You called me in here so we could work out a way of betraying Leo Bulero together."

Baffled, he said, "Listen—"

"But it's so. You can't handle it alone; you need me. I haven't said no. Keep calm. However, I don't think this is the place or the time to discuss it; let's wait until we're home at the conapt. Okay?" She gave him, then, a brilliant smile, one of absolute warmth.

"Okay," he agreed. She was right.

"Wouldn't it be sad," Roni said, "if this office of yours were bugged? Perhaps Mr. Bulero is going to get a tape of everything we've said just now." Her smile continued, even grew; it dazzled him. The girl was afraid of no one and nothing on Earth or in the whole Sol system, he realized.

He wished he felt the same way. Because there was one problem that haunted him, one he had not discussed with either Leo or her, although it was certainly bothering Leo, too . . . and should, if she were as rational as she seemed, be bothering her.

It had yet to be established that what had come back from Prox, the person or thing that had crashed on Pluto, was really Palmer Eldritch.

5

Set up financially by the contract with the Chew-Z people, Richard Hnatt placed a call to one of Dr. Willy Denkmal's E Therapy clinics in the Germanies; he picked the central one, in Munich, and began making arrangements for both himself and Emily.

I'm up with the greats, he said to himself as he waited, with Emily, in the swanky gnoff-hide decorated lounge of the clinic; Dr. Denkmal, as was his custom, proposed to interview them initially personally, although of course the therapy itself would be carried out by members of his staff.

"It makes me nervous," Emily whispered; she held a magazine on her lap but was unable to read. "It's so—unnatural."

"Hell," Hnatt said vigorously, "that's what it's not; it's an acceleration of the *natural* evolutionary process that's going on all the time anyway, only usually it's so slow we don't perceive it. I mean, look at our ancestors in caves; they were covered with body-hair and they had no chins and a very limited frontal-area brain-wise. And they had huge fused molars in order to chew uncooked seeds."

"Okay," Emily said, nodding.

"The farther away we can get from them the better. Anyhow, they evolved to meet the Ice Age; we have to evolve to meet the Fire Age, just the opposite. So we need that chitinous-type skin, that rind and the altered metabolism that lets us sleep in midday and also the improved ventilation and the—"

From the inner office Dr. Denkmal, a small, round style of middle-class German with white hair and an Albert Schweitzer mustache, emerged. With him came another man, and Richard Hnatt saw for the first time close-up the effects of E Therapy. And it was not like seeing pics on the society pages of the homeopape. Not at all.

The man's head reminded Hnatt of a photograph he had once seen in a textbook; the photo had been labeled *hydrocephalic*. The same enlargement above the browline; it was clearly domelike and oddly fragile-looking and he saw at once why these well-to-do persons who had evolved were popularly called *bubbleheads*. Looks about to burst, he thought, impressed. And—the massive rind. Hair had given way to the darker, more uniform pattern of chitinous shell. Bubblehead? More like a coconut.

"Mr. Hnatt," Dr. Denkmal said to Richard Hnatt, pausing. "And Frau Hnatt, too. I'll be with you in a moment." He turned back to the man beside him. "It's just chance that we were able to squeeze you in today, Mr. Bulero, on such short notice. Anyhow you haven't lost a bit of ground; in fact you've gained."

However, Mr. Bulero was gazing at Richard Hnatt. "I've heard your name before. Oh, yes. Felix Blau mentioned you." His supremely intelligent eyes became dark and he said, "Did you recently sign a contract with a Boston firm called—" The elongated face, distorted as if by a permanent optically impaired mirror, twisted. "Chew-Z Manufacturers?"

"N-nuts to you," Hnatt stammered. "Your Pre-Fash consultant turned us down."

Leo Bulero eyed him, then with a shrug turned back to Dr. Denkmal. "I'll see you in two weeks."

"Two! But—" Denkmal gestured protestingly.

"I can't make it next week; I'll be off Terra again." Again Bulero eyed Richard and Emily Hnatt, lingeringly, then strode off.

Watching him go, Dr. Denkmal said, "Very evolved, that man. Both physically and spiritually." He turned to the Hnatts. "Welcome to Eichenwald Clinic." He beamed.

"Thank you," Emily said nervously. "Does—it hurt?"

"Our therapy?" Dr. Denkmal tittered with amusement. "Not in the slightest, although it may shock—in the figurative sense—at first. As you experience a growth of your cortex area. You'll have many new and exciting concepts occur to you, especially of a religious nature. Oh, if only Luther and Erasmus were alive today; their controversies could be solved so easily now, by means of E Therapy. Both would see the truth, as *zum Beiszspiel* regard transubstantiation—you know, the *Blut und*—" He interrupted himself with a cough. "In English, blood and wafer; you know, in the Mass. Is very much like the takers of Can-D; have you noticed that affinity? But come on; we begin." He slapped Richard Hnatt on the back and led the two of them into his inner office, eyeing Emily with what seemed to Richard to be a rather unspiritual, covetous look.

They faced a gigantic chamber of scientific gadgets and two Dr. Frankenstein tables, complete with arm and leg brackets. At the sight Emily moaned and shrank back.

"Nothing to fear, Frau Hnatt. Like electro-convulsive shock, causes certain musculature reactions; reflex, you know?" Denkmal giggled. "Now you must, ah, you know: take off your clothes. Each of you in private, of course; then don smocks and *auskommen*—understand? A nurse will assist you. We have your medical charts from Nord Amerika already; we know your histories. Both quite healthy, virile; good Nord Amerikanische people." He led Richard Hnatt to a side room, secluded by a curtain; there he left him off and returned to Emily. As he entered the side room Richard heard Dr. Denkmal talking to Emily in a soothing but commanding tone; the combination was a neat bit of business and Hnatt felt both envious and suspicious and then, at last, glum. It was not quite as he had pictured it, not quite big-time enough to suit him.

However, Leo Bulero had emerged from this room so that proved it was authentic big-time; Bulero would never have settled for less.

Heartened, he began to undress.

Somewhere out of sight Emily squeaked.

He redressed and left the side room, boiling with concern. However, he found Denkmal at a desk, reading Emily's medical chart; she was off, he realized, with a female nurse, so everything was all right.

Criminy, he thought, I certainly am edgy. Once more entering the side room he resumed undressing; his hands, he found, were shaking.

Presently he lay strapped to one of the twin tables, Emily in a similar state beside him. She, too, seemed frightened; she was very pale and quiet.

"Your glands," Dr. Denkmal explained, jovially rubbing his hands together and wantonly eyeing Emily, "will be stimulated by this, especially Kresy's Gland, which controls rate of evolution, *nicht Wahr?* Yes, you know that; every schoolchild knows that, is taught now what we've discovered here. Today what you will notice is no growth of chitinous shell or brainshield or loss of fingernails and toenails—you didn't know that, I bet!—but only a slight but very, very important change in the frontal lobe . . . it will smart; that is a pun, you know? It smarts and you become, ah, smart." Again he giggled. Richard Hnatt felt miserable; he waited like some hog-tied animal for whatever they had in store for him. What a way to make business contacts, he said ruefully to himself, and shut his eyes.

A male attendant materialized and stood by him, looking blond, Nordic, and without intelligence.

"We play soothing *Musik*," Dr. Denkmal said, pressing a button. Multiphonic sound, from every corner of the room, filtered out, an insipid orchestral version of some popular Italian opera, Puccini or Verdi; Hnatt did not know. "Now *höre*, Herr Hnatt." Denkmal bent down beside him, suddenly serious. "I want you to understand; every now and then this therapy—what do you say?—*blasts back*."

"Backfires," Hnatt said gratingly. He had been expecting this.

"But mostly we have successes. Here, Herr Hnatt, is what the backfires consist of, I am afraid; instead of evoluting the Kresy Gland is very stimulated to—regress. Is that correct in English?"

"Yes," Hnatt muttered. "Regress how far?"

"Just a trifle. But it could be unpleasant. We would catch it quickly, of course, and cease therapy. And generally that stops the regression. But—not always. Sometimes once the Kresy Gland has been stimulated to—" He gestured. "It keeps on. I should tell you this in case you might have scruples. Right?"

"I'll take the chance," Richard Hnatt said. "I guess. Everyone else does, don't they? Okay, go ahead." He squirmed, saw Emily, even paler now, almost imperceptibly nodding; her eyes were glassy.

What'll probably happen, he thought fatalistically, is that one of us will evolve—probably Emily—and the other, me, will devolve back to Sinanthropus. Back to fused molars, tiny brain, bent legs, and cannibalistic tendencies. I'll have a hell of a time closing sales that way.

Dr. Denkmal clamped a switch shut, whistling along with the opera happily to himself.

The Hnatts' E Therapy had begun.

He seemed to feel a loss of weight, nothing more, at least not at first. And then his head ached as if rapped by a hammer. With the ache came almost instantly a new and acute comprehension; it was a dreadful risk he and Emily were taking, and it wasn't fair to her to subject her to this, just to further sales. Obviously she didn't want this; suppose she evolved back just enough to lose her ceramic talent? And they both would be ruined; his career hung on seeing Emily remain one of the planet's top ceramists.

"Stop," he said aloud, but the sound did not seem to emerge; he did not hear it, although his vocal apparatus seemed to function—he felt the words in his throat. And then it came to him. He was evolving; it was functioning. His insight was due to the change in his brain metabolism. Assuming Emily was all right then everything was all right.

He perceived, too, that Dr. Willy Denkmal was a cheap little pseudo-quack, that this whole business preyed off the vanity of mortals striving to become more than they were entitled to be, and in a purely earthly, transitory way. The hell with his sales, his contacts; what did that matter in comparison to the possibility of evolving the human brain to entire new orders of conception? For instance—

Below lay the tomb world, the immutable cause-and-effect world of the demonic. At median extended the layer of the human, but at any instant a man could plunge—descend as if sinking—into the hell-layer beneath. Or: he could ascend to the ethereal world above, which constituted the third of the trinary layers. Always, in his middle level of the human, a man risked the sinking. And yet the possibility of ascent lay before him; any aspect or sequence of reality *could become either,* at any instant. Hell and heaven, not after death but now! Depression, all mental illness, was the sinking. And the other . . . how was it achieved?

Through empathy. Grasping another, not from outside but from the inner. For example, had he ever really looked at Emily's pots as anything more than merchandise for which a market existed? No. What I ought to have seen in them, he realized, is the artistic intention, the spirit she's revealing intrinsically.

And that contract with Chew-Z Manufacturers, he realized; I signed without consulting her—how unethical can one become? I chained her to a firm which she may not want as a minner of her products . . . we have no knowledge of the worth of their layouts. They may be shoddy. Substandard. But too late, now; the road to the hell-layer is paved with second-guessing. And they may be involved in the illegal manufacture of a translation drug; that would explain the name Chew-Z . . . it would correspond with Can-D. But— the fact that they've selected that name openly suggests they have nothing illegal in mind.

With a lightning leap of intuition it came to him: someone had found a translation drug which satisfied the UN's nar- cotics agency. The agency had already passed on Chew-Z, would allow it on the open market. So, for the first time, a translation drug would be available on thoroughly policed Terra, not in the remote, unpoliced colonies only.

And this meant that Chew-Z's layouts—unlike Perky Pat—would be marketable on Terra, along with the drug. And as the weather worsened over the years, as the home planet became more of an alien environment, the layouts would sell faster. The market which Leo Bulero controlled was pitifully meager compared to what lay eventually—but not now—before Chew-Z Manufacturers.

So he had signed a good contract after all. And—no won- der Chew-Z had paid him so much. They were a big outfit, with big plans; they had, obviously, unlimited capital backing them.

And where would they obtain unlimited capital? Nowhere on Terra; he intuited that, too. Probably from Palmer El- dritch, who had returned to the Sol system after having joined economically with the Proxers; it was they who were behind Chew-Z. So, for the chance to ruin Leo Bulero, the UN was allowing a non-Sol race to begin operations in the system.

It was a bad, perhaps even terminal, exchange.

The next he knew, Dr. Denkmal was slapping him into wake- fulness. "How goes it?" Denkmal demanded, peering at him. "Broad, all-inclusive preoccupations?"

"Y-yes," he said, and managed to sit up; he was un-strapped.

"Then we have nothing to fear," Dr. Denkmal said, and beamed, his white mustache twitching like antennae. "Now we will consult with Frau Hnatt." A female attendant was already unstrapping her; Emily sat up groggily and yawned. Dr. Denkmal looked nervous. "How do you feel, Frau?" he inquired.

"Fine," Emily murmured. "I had all sorts of pot ideas. One after another." She glanced timidly at first him and then at Richard. "Does that mean anything?"

"Paper," Dr. Denkmal said, producing a tablet. "Pen." He extended them to Emily. "Put down your ideas, Frau."

Tremblingly, Emily sketched her pot ideas. She seemed to have difficulty controlling the pen, Hnatt noticed. But presumably that would pass.

"Fine," Dr. Denkmal said, when she had finished. He showed the sketches to Richard Hnatt. "Highly organized cephalic activity. Superior inventiveness, right?"

The pot sketches were certainly good, even brilliant. And yet Hnatt felt there was something wrong. Something about the sketches. But it was not until they had left the clinic, were standing together under the antithermal curtain outside the building, waiting for their jet-express cab to land, that he realized what it was.

The ideas were good—but Emily had done them al-ready. Years ago, when she had designed her first pro-fessionally adequate pots: she had shown him sketches of them and then the pots themselves, even before the two of them were married. Didn't she remember this? Obviously not.

He wondered why she didn't remember and what it meant; it made him deeply uneasy.

However, he had been continually uneasy since receiving the first E Therapy treatment, first about the state of mankind and the Sol system in general and now about his wife. Maybe it's merely a sign of what Denkmal calls "highly organized cephalic activity," he thought to himself. Brain metabolism stimulation.

Or—maybe not.

Arriving on Luna, with his official press card from P. P. Layouts' house journal clutched, Leo Bulero found himself squeezed in with a gaggle of homeopape reporters on their way by surface tractor across the ashy face of the moon to Palmer Eldritch's demesne.

"Your ident-pape, sir," an armed guard, but not wearing the colors of the UN, yapped at him as he prepared to exit into the parking area of the demesne. Leo Bulero was there-upon wedged in the doorway of the tractor, while behind him the legitimate homeopape reporters surged and clam-ored restively, wanting to get out. "Mr. Bulero," the guard said leisurely, and returned the press card. "Mr. Eldritch is expecting you. Come this way." He was immediately re-placed by another guard, who began checking the i.d. of the reporters one by one.

Nervous, Leo Bulero accompanied the first guard through an air-filled pressurized and comfortably heated tube to the demesne proper.

Ahead of him, blocking the tube, appeared another uni-formed guard from Palmer Eldritch's staff; he raised his arm and pointed something small and shiny at Leo Bulero.

"Hey," Leo protested feebly, freezing in his tracks; he spun, ducked his head, and then stumbled a few steps back the way he had come.

The beam—of a variety he knew nothing about—touched him and he pitched forward, trying to break his fall by throw-ing his arms out.

The next he knew he was once more conscious and swad-dled—absurdly—to a chair in a barren room. His head rang and he looked blearily around, but saw only a small table in the center of the room on which an electronic contraption rested.

"Let me out of here," he said.

At once the electronic contraption said, "Good morning, Mr. Bulero. I am Palmer Eldritch. You wanted to see me, I understand."

"This is cruel conduct," Bulero said. "Having me put to sleep and then tying me up like this."

"Have a cigar." The electronic contraption sprouted an extension which carried in its grasp a long green cigar; the end of the cigar puffed into flame and then the elongated pseudopodium presented it to Leo Bulero. "I brought ten boxes of these back from Prox, but only one box survived the crash. It's not tobacco; it's superior to tobacco. What is it, Leo? What did you want?"

Leo Bulero said, "Are you in that thing there, Eldritch? Or are you somewhere else, speaking through it?"

"Be content," the voice from the metal construct resting on the table said. It continued to extend the lighted cigar, then withdrew it, stubbed it out, and dropped the remains from sight within itself. "Do you care to see color slides of my visit to the Prox system?"

"You're kidding."

"No," Palmer Eldritch said. "They'll give you some idea of what I was up against there. They're 3-D time-lapse slides, very good."

"No thanks."

Eldritch said, "We found that dart embedded in your tongue; it's been removed. But you may have something more, or so we suspect."

"You're giving me a lot of credit," Leo said. "More than I ought to get."

"In four years on Prox I learned a lot. Six years in transit, four in residence. The Proxers are going to invade Earth."

"You're putting me on," Leo said.

Eldritch said, "I can understand your reaction. The UN, in particular Hepburn-Gilbert, reacted the same way. But it's true—not in the conventional sense, of course, but in a deeper, coarser manner that I don't quite get, even though

I was among them for so long. It may be involved with Earth's heating up, for all I know. Or there may be worse to come."

"Let's talk about that lichen you brought back."

"I obtained that illegally; the Proxers didn't know I took any of it. They use it themselves, in religious orgies. As our Indians made use of mescal and peyotl. Is that what you wanted to see me about?"

"Sure. You're getting into my business. I know you've already set up a corporation; haven't you? Nuts to this business about Proxers invading our system; it's you I'm sore about, what you're doing. Can't you find some other field to go into besides min layouts?"

The room blew up in his face. White light descended, blanketing him, and he shut his eyes. Jeez, he thought. Anyhow I don't believe that about the Proxers; he's just trying to turn our attention away from what he's up to. I mean, it's strategy.

He opened his eyes, and found himself sitting on a grassy bank. Beside him a small girl played with a yo-yo.

"That toy," Leo Bulero said, "is popular in the Prox system." His arms and legs, he discovered, were untied; he stood up stiffly and moved his limbs. "What's your name?" he asked.

The little girl said, "Monica."

"The Proxers," Leo said, "the humanoid types anyhow, wear wigs and have false teeth." He took hold of the bulk of the child's luminous blonde hair and pulled.

"Ouch," the girl said. "You're a bad man." He let go and she retreated, still playing with her yo-yo and glaring at him defiantly.

"Sorry," he murmured. Her hair was real; perhaps he was not in the Prox system. Anyhow, wherever he was Palmer Eldritch was trying to tell him something. "Are you planning to invade Earth?" he asked the child. "I mean, you don't look as if you are." Could Eldritch have gotten it wrong? he wondered. Misunderstood the Proxers? After all, to his knowledge Palmer hadn't evolved, didn't possess the powerful, expanded comprehension which came with E Therapy.

"My yo-yo," the child said, "is magic. I can do anything I want with it. What'll I do? You tell me; you look like a kindly man."

"Take me to your leader," Leo said. "An old joke; you wouldn't understand it. Went out a century ago." He looked around him and saw no signs of habitation, only the grassy plain. Too cool for Earth, he realized. Above, the blue sky. Good air, he thought. Dense. "Do you feel sorry for me," he asked, "because Palmer Eldritch is horning into my business and if he does I'll probably be ruined? I'm going to have to make some kind of a deal with him." It now looks like killing him is out, he said to himself morosely. "But," he said, "I can't figure out any deal he'll take; he seems to hold all the cards. Look for instance how he's got me here, and I don't even know where this is." Not that it matters, he realized. Because wherever it is it's a place Eldritch controls.

"Cards," the child said. "I have a deck of cards, in my suitcase."

He saw no suitcase. "Where?"

Kneeling, the girl touched the grass here and there. All at once a section slid smoothly back; the girl reached into the cavity and brought out a suitcase. "I keep it hidden," she explained. "From the sponsors."

"What's that mean, that 'sponsors'?"

"Well, to be here you need a sponsor. All of us have them; I guess they pay for everything, pay until we're well and then we can go home, if we have homes." She seated herself by the suitcase, and opened it—or at least tried to. The lock did not respond. "Darn," she said. "This is the wrong one. This is Dr. Smile."

"A psychiatrist?" Leo asked, alertly. "From one of those big conapts? Is it working? Turn it on."

Obligingly the girl turned the psychiatrist on. "Hello, Monica," the suitcase said tinnily. "Hello to you, too, Mr. Bulero." It pronounced his name wrong, getting the stress on the final syllable. "What are you doing here, sir? You're much too old to be here. Tee-hee. Or are you regressed, due to malappropriate so-called E Therapy rggggg *click!*" It whirred in agitation. "Therapy in Munich?" it finished.

"I feel fine," Leo assured it. "Look, Smile; who do you know that I know that could get me out of here? Name someone, anyone. I can't stay here any more, get it?"

"I know a Mr. Bayerson," Dr. Smile said. "In fact I'm with him right now, via portable extension, of course, right in his office."

"There's noboby I know named Bayerson," Leo said. "What is this place? Obviously it's a rest camp of some sort for sick kids or kids with no money or some damn thing. I thought this was maybe in the Prox system but if you're here obviously it isn't. Bayerson." It came to him, then. "Hell, you mean Mayerson. Barney. Back at P. P. Layouts."

"Yes, that's so," Dr. Smile said.

"Contact him," Leo said. "Tell him to get in touch with Felix Blau right away, that Tri-Planet Police Agency or whatever they call themselves. Have him have Blau do research, find out where exactly I am and then send a ship here. Got it?"

"All right," Dr. Smile said. "I'll address Mr. Mayerson right away. He's conferring with Miss Fugate, his assistant, who is also his mistress and who today is wearing—hmm. They're talking about you this very minute. But of course I can't report what they're saying; seal of the medical profession, you realize. She is wearing—"

"Okay, who cares?" Leo said irritably.

"You'll excuse me a moment," the suitcase said. "While I sign off." It sounded huffy. And then there was silence.

"I have bad news for you," the child said.

"What is it?"

"I was kidding. That's not really Dr. Smile; it's just pretend, to keep us from loneliness. It's alive but it's not connected with anything outside itself; it's what they call being on intrinsic."

He knew what that meant; the unit was self-contained. But

then how could it have known about Barney and Miss Fugate, even down to details about their personal life? Even as to what she had on? The child was not telling the truth, obviously. "Who are you?" he demanded, "Monica what? I want to know your full name." Something about her was familiar.

"I'm back," the suitcase announced suddenly. "Well, Mr. Bulero—" Again the faulty pronunciation. "I've discussed your dilemma with Mr. Mayerson and he will contact Felix Blau as you requested. Mr. Mayerson thinks he recalls reading in a homeopape once about a UN camp much as you are experiencing, somewhere in the Saturn region, for retarded children. Perhaps—"

"Hell," Leo said, "this girl isn't retarded." If anything she was precocious. It did not make sense. But what did make sense was the realization that Palmer Eldritch wanted something out of him; this was not merely a matter of edifying him: it was a question of intimidation.

On the horizon a shape appeared, immense and gray, bloating as it rushed at terrific speed toward them. It had ugly spiked whiskers.

"That's a rat," Monica said calmly.

Leo said, "That big?" No place in the Sol system, on none of the moons or planets, did such an enormous, feral creature exist. "What will it do to us?" he asked, wondering why she wasn't afraid.

"Oh," Monica said, "I suppose it'll kill us."

"And that doesn't frighten you?" He heard his own voice rise in a shriek. "I mean, you want to die like that, and right now? Eaten by a rat the size of—" He grabbed the girl with one hand, picked up Dr. Smile the suitcase in the other, and began lumbering away from the rat.

The rat reached them, passed on by, and was gone; its shape dwindled until at last it disappeared.

The girl snickered. "It scared you. I knew it wouldn't see us. They can't; they're blind to us, here."

"They are?" He knew, then, where he was. Felix Blau

wouldn't find him. Nobody would, even if they looked forever.

Eldritch had given him an intravenous injection of a translating drug, no doubt Chew-Z. This place was a nonexistent world, analogous to the irreal "Earth" to which the translated colonists went when they chewed his own product, Can-D.

And the rat, unlike everything else, was genuine. Unlike themselves; he and this girl—they were not real, either. At least not here. Somewhere their empty, silent bodies lay like sacks, discarded by the cerebral contents for the time being. No doubt their bodies were at Palmer Eldritch's Lunar demesne.

"You're Zoe," he said. "Aren't you? This is the way you want to be, a little girl-child again, about eight. Right? With long blonde hair." And even, he realized, with a different name.

Stiffly, the child said, "There is no one named Zoe."

"No one but you. Your father is Palmer Eldritch, right?" With great reluctance the child nodded.

"Is this a special place for you?" he asked. "To which you come often?"

"This is *my* place," the girl said. "No one comes here without my permission."

"Why did you let me come here, then?" He knew that she did not like him. Had not from the very start.

"Because," the child said, "we think perhaps you can stop the Proxers from whatever it is they're doing."

"That again," he said, simply not believing her. "Your father—"

"My father," the child said, "is trying to save us. He didn't want to bring back Chew-Z; they made him. Chew-Z is the agent by which we're going to be delivered over to them. You see?"

"How?"

"Because they control these areas. Like this, where you go when you're given Chew-Z."

"You don't seem under any sort of alien control; look what you're telling me."

"But I will be," the girl said, nodding soberly. "Soon. Just like my father is now. He was given it on Prox; he's been taking it for years. It's too late for him and he knows it."

"Prove all this to me," Leo said. "In fact prove any of it, even one part; give me something actual to go on."

The suitcase, which he still held, now said, "What Monica says is true, Mr. Bulero."

"How do you know?" he demanded, annoyed with it.

"Because," the suitcase replied, "I'm under Prox influence, too; that's why I—"

"You did nothing," Leo said. He set the suitcase down. "Damn that Chew-Z," he said, to both of them, the suitcase and the girl. "It's made everything confused; I don't know what the hell's going on. You're not Zoe—you don't even know who she is. And you—you're not Dr. Smile, and you didn't call Barney, and he wasn't talking to Roni Fugate; it's all just a drug-induced hallucination. It's my own fears about Palmer Eldritch being read back to me, this trash about him being under Prox influence, and you, too. Who ever heard of a suitcase being dominated by minds from an alien star-system?" Highly indignant, he walked away from them.

I know what's going on, he realized. This is Palmer's way of gaining domination over my mind; this is a form of what they used to call brainwashing. He's got me running scared. Carefully measuring his steps, he continued on without looking back.

It was a near-fatal mistake. Something—he caught sight of it out of the corner of his eye—launched itself at his legs; he leaped aside and it passed him, circling back at once as it reoriented itself, and picked him up again as its prey.

"The rats can't see you," the girl called, "but the glucks can! You better run!"

Without clearly seeing it—he had seen enough—he ran.

And what he had seen he could not blame on Chew-Z.

Because it was not an illusion, not a device of Palmer Eldritch's to terrorize him. The gluck, whatever it was, did not originate on Terra nor from a Terran mind.

Behind him, leaving the suitcase, the girl ran, too.

"What about me?" Dr. Smile called anxiously.

No one came back for him.

On the vidscreen the image of Felix Blau said, "I've processed the material you gave me, Mr. Mayerson. It adds up to a convincing case that your employer Mr. Bulero—who is also a client of mine—is at present on a small artificial satellite orbiting Earth, legally titled Sigma 14-B. I have consulted the records of ownership and it appears to belong to a rocket-fuel manufacturer in St. George, Utah." He inspected the papers before him. "Robard Lethane Sales. Lethane is their trade-name for their brand of—"

"Okay," Barney Mayerson said. "I'll contact them." How in God's name had Leo Bulero gotten *there*?

"There is one further item of possible interest. Robard Lethane Sales incorporated the same day, four years ago, as Chew-Z Manufacturers of Boston. It seems more than a coincidence to me."

"What about getting Leo off the satellite?"

"You could file a write of mandamus with the courts demanding—"

"Too much time," Barney said. He had a deep, ill sense of personal responsibility for what had happened. Evidently Palmer Eldritch had set up the news conference with the 'pape reporters as a pretext by which to lure Leo to the Lunar demesne—and he, precog Barney Mayerson, the man who could perceive the future, had been taken in, had expertly done his part to get Leo there.

Felix Blau said, "I can supply you with about a hundred men, from various offices of my organization. And you ought to be able to raise fifty more from P. P. Layouts. You could try to invest the satellite."

"And find him dead."

"True." Blau appeared to pout. "Well, you could go to Hepburn-Gilbert and plead for UN assistance. Or try to contact—and this sticks in the craw even worse—contact Palmer or whatever's taking Palmer's place, and deal directly with *it*. See if you can buy Leo back."

Barney cut the circuit. He at once dialed for an outplan line, saying, "Get me Mr. Palmer Eldritch on Luna. It's an emergency; I'd like you to hurry it up, miss."

As he waited for the call to be put through, Roni Fugate said from the far end of the office, "Apparently we're not going to have time to sell out to Eldritch."

"It does look that way." How smoothly it had all been handled; Eldritch had let his adversary do the work. And us, too, he realized, Roni and I; he'll probably get us the same way. In fact Eldritch could indeed be waiting for our flight to the satellite; that would explain his supplying Leo with Dr. Smile.

"I wonder," Roni said, fooling with the clasp of her blouse, "if we want to work for a man that clever. If it is a man. It looks more and more to me as if it's not actually Palmer who came back but one of them; I think we're going to have to accept that. The next thing we can look forward to is Chew-Z flooding the market. With UN sanction." Her tone was bitter. "And Leo, who at least is one of us and who just wants to make a few skins, will be dead or driven out—" She stared straight ahead in fury.

"Patriotism," Barney said.

"Self-preservation. I don't want to find myself, some morning, chewing away on the stuff, doing whatever you do when you chew it instead of Can-D. Going—not to Perky Pat land; that's for sure."

The vidphone operator said, "I have a Miss Zoe Eldritch on the line, sir. Will you speak to her?"

"Okay," Barney said, resigned.

A smartly dressed woman, sharp-eyed, with heavy hair pulled back in a bun, gazed at him in miniature. "Yes?"

"This is Mayerson at P. P. Layouts. What do we have to do to get Leo Bulero back?" He waited. No response. "You do know what I'm talking about, don't you?" he said.

Presently she said, "Mr. Bulero arrived here at the demesne and was taken sick. He's resting in our infirmary. When he's better—"

"May I dispatch an official company physician to examine him?"

"Of course." Zoe Eldritch did not bat an eye.

"Why didn't you notify us?"

"It just now occurred. My father was about to call. It seems to be nothing more than a reaction to the change of gravity; actually it's very common with older persons who arrive here. We haven't tried to approximate Earth gravity as Mr. Bulero has at his satellite, Winnie-ther-Pooh Acres. So you see it's really quite simple." She smiled slightly. "You'll have him back sometime later today at the very latest. Did you suspect something else?"

"I suspect," Barney said, "that Leo is not on Luna any longer. That he's on an Earth-satellite called Sigma 14-B which belongs to a St. George firm that you own. Isn't that the case? And what we'll find in your infirmary at the demesne will not be Leo Bulero."

Roni stared at him.

"You're welcome to see for yourself," Zoe said stonily. "It *is* Leo Bulero, at least as far as we know. It's what arrived here with the homeopape reporters."

"I'll come to the demesne," Barney said. And knew he was making a mistake. His precog ability told him that. And, at the far end of the office, Roni Fugate hopped to her feet and stood rigid; her ability had picked it up, too. Shutting off the vidphone he turned to her and said, "P. P. Layouts employee commits suicide. Correct? Or some such wording. The 'papes tomorrow morning."

"The exact wording—" Roni began.

"I don't care to hear the exact wording." But it would be by exposure, he knew. Man's body found on pedestrian ramp at noon; dead from excessive solar radiation. Downtown New York somewhere. At whatever spot the Eldritch organization had dropped him off. Would drop him off.

He could have done without his precog faculty, in this. Since he did not intend to act on its foresight.

What disturbed him the most was the pic on the 'pape page, a close-up view of his sun-shriveled body.

At the office door he stopped and simply stood.

"You can't go," Roni said.

"No." Not after previewing the pic. Leo, he realized, will have to take care of himself. Returning to his desk he re-seated himself.

"The only problem," Roni said, "is that if he does get back he's going to be hard to explain the situation to. That you didn't do anything."

"I know." But that was not the only problem; in fact that was barely an issue at all.

Because Leo would probably not be getting back.

6

The gluck had him by the ankle and it was trying to drink him; it had penetrated his flesh with tiny tubes like cilia. Leo Bulero cried out—and then, abruptly, there stood Palmer Eldritch.

"You were wrong," Eldritch said. "I did *not* find God in the Prox system. But I found something better." With a stick he poked at the gluck; it reluctantly withdrew its cilia, and contracted into itself until at last it was no longer clinging to Leo; it dropped to the ground and traveled away, as Eldritch continued to prod it. "God," Eldritch said, "promises eternal life. I can do better; *I can deliver it.*"

"Deliver it how?" Trembling and weak with relief, Leo dropped to the grassy soil, seated himself, and gasped for breath.

"Through the lichen which we're marketing under the name Chew-Z," Eldritch said. "It bears very little resemblance to your own product, Leo. Can-D is obsolete, because what does it do? Provides a few moments of escape, nothing but fantasy. Who wants it? Who needs that when they can get the genuine thing from me?" He added, "We're there, now."

"So I assumed. And if you imagine people are going to pay out skins for an experience like this—" Leo gestured at the gluck, which still lurked nearby keeping an eye on both himself and Eldritch. "You're not just out of your body; you're out of your mind, too."

"This is a special situation. To prove to you that this is authentic. Nothing excels physical pain and terror in that respect; the glucks showed you with absolute clarity that this is *not* a fantasy. They could actually have killed you. And if you died here that would be it. Not like Can-D, is it?" Eldritch was probably enjoying the situation. "When I discovered the lichen in the Prox system I couldn't believe it. I've lived a hundred years, Leo, already, using it in the Prox system under the direction of their medical people; I've taken it orally, intravenously, in suppository form—I've burned it and inhaled the fumes, made it into a water-soluble solution and boiled it, sniffed the vapors: I've experienced it every way possible and it hasn't hurt me. The effect on Proxers is minor, nothing like what it does to us; to them it's less of a stimulant than their very best grade tobacco. Want to hear more?"

"Not particularly."

Eldritch seated himself nearby, rested his artificial arm on his bent knees, and idly swung his stick from side to side, scrutinizing the gluck, which had still not departed. "When we return to our former bodies—you notice the use of the word 'former,' a term you wouldn't apply with Can-D, and for good reason—*you'll find that no time has passed.* We could stay here fifty years and it'd be the same; we'd emerge back at the demense on Luna and find everything unchanged, and anyone watching us would see no lapse of consciousness, as you have with Can-D, no trance, no stupor. Oh, maybe a flicker of the eyelids. A split second; I'm willing to concede that."

"What determines our length of time here?" Leo asked.

"Our attitude. Not the quantity taken. We can return whenever we want to. So the amount of the drug need not be—"

"That's not true. Because I've wanted out of here for some time, now."

"But," Eldritch said, "you didn't construct this—establishment, here; I did and it's mine. I created the glucks, this landscape—" He gestured with his stick. "Every damn thing you see, including your body."

"My body?" Leo examined himself. It was his regular, familiar body, known to him intimately; it was his, not Eldritch's.

"I willed you to emerge here exactly as you are in our universe," Eldritch said. "You see, that's the point that appealed to Hepburn-Gilbert, who of course is a Buddhist. You can reincarnate in any form you wish, or that's wished for you, as in this situation."

"So that's why the UN bit," Leo said. It explained a great deal.

"With Chew-Z one can pass from life to life, be a bug, a physics teacher, a hawk, a protozoon, a slime mold, a streetwalker in Paris in 1904, a—"

"Even," Leo said, "a gluck. Which one of us is the gluck, there?"

"I told you; I made it out of a portion of myself. You could shape something. Go ahead—project a fraction of your essence; it'll take material form on its own. What you supply is the logos. Remember that?"

"I remember," Leo said. He concentrated, and presently there formed not far off an unwieldy mass of wires and bars and gridlike extensions.

"What the hell is that?" Eldritch demanded.

"A gluck trap."

Eldritch put his head back and laughed. "Very good. But please don't build a Palmer Eldritch trap; I still have things I want to say." He and Leo watched the gluck suspiciously approach the trap, sniffing. It entered and the trap banged shut. The gluck was caught, and now the trap dispatched it; one quick sizzle, a small plume of smoke, and the gluck had vanished.

In the air before Leo a small section shimmered; out of it emerged a black book, which he accepted, thumbed through, then, satisfied, put down on his lap.

"What's that?" Eldritch asked.

"A King James Bible. I thought it might help protect me."

"Not here," Eldritch said. "This is my domain." He gestured at the bible and it vanished. "You could have your own, though, and fill it with bibles. As can everyone. As soon as our operations are underway. We're going to have layouts, of course, but that comes later with our Terran activities. And anyhow that's a formality, a ritual to ease the transition. Can-D and Chew-Z will be marketed on the same basis, in open competition; we'll claim nothing for Chew-Z that you don't claim for your product. We don't want to scare people away; religion has become a touchy subject. It will only be after a few tries that they realize the two different aspects: the lack of a time lapse and the other, perhaps the more vital. That it isn't fantasy, that they enter a genuine new universe."

"Many persons feel that about Can-D," Leo pointed out. "They hold it as an article of faith that they're actually on Earth."

"Fanatics," Eldritch said with disgust. "Obviously it's illusion because there is no Perky Pat and no Walt Essex and anyhow the structure of their fantasy environment is limited to the artifacts actually installed in their layout; they can't operate the automatic dishwasher in the kitchen unless a min of one was installed in advance. And a person who doesn't participate can watch and see that the two dolls don't go anywhere; no one is in them. It can be demonstrated—"

"But you're going to have trouble convincing those people," Leo said. "They'll stay loyal to Can-D. There's no real dissatisfaction with Perky Pat; why should they give up—"

"I'll tell you," Eldritch said. "Because however wonderful being Perky Pat and Walt is for a while, eventually they're forced to return to their hovels. Do you know how that feels,

Leo? Try it sometime; wake up in a hovel on Ganymede after you've been freed for twenty, thirty minutes. It's an experience you'll never forget."

"Hmm."

"And there's something else—and you know what it is, too. When the little period of escape is over and the colonist returns . . . he's not fit to resume a normal, daily life. He's demoralized. But if instead of Can-D he's chewed—"

He broke off. Leo was not listening; he was involved in constructing another artifact in the air before him.

A short flight of stairs appeared, leading into a luminous hoop. The far end of the flight of stairs could not be seen.

"Where does that go?" Eldritch demanded, an irritated expression on his face.

"New York City," Leo said. "It'll take me back to P. P. Layouts." He rose and walked to the flight of stairs. "I have a feeling, Eldritch, *that something's wrong,* some aspect of this Chew-Z product. And we won't discover what it is until too late." He began climbing the stairs and then he remembered the girl, Monica; he wondered if she was all right, here in Palmer Eldritch's world. "What about the child?" He stopped his climb. Below him, but seemingly far off, he could make out Eldritch, still seated with his stick on the grass. "The glucks didn't get her, did they?"

Eldritch said, "I was the little girl. That's what I'm trying to explain to you; that's why I say it means genuine reincarnation, triumph over death."

Blinking, Leo said, "Then the reason she was familiar—" He ceased, and looked again.

On the grass Eldritch was gone. The child Monica, with her suitcase full of Dr. Smile, sat there instead. So it was evident, now.

He was telling—she, they were telling—the truth.

Slowly, Leo walked back down the stairs and out onto the grass once more.

• • •

The child, Monica, said, "I'm glad you're not leaving, Mr. Bulero. It's nice to have someone smart and evolved like you to talk to." She patted the suitcase resting on the grass beside her. "I went back and got him; he was terrified of the glucks. I see you found something that would handle them." She nodded toward his gluck trap, which now, empty, awaited another victim. "Very ingenious of you. I hadn't thought of it; I just got the hell out of there. A diencephalic panic-reaction."

To her Leo said hesitantly, "You're Palmer, are you? I mean, down underneath? Actually?"

"Take the medieval doctrine of substance versus accidents," the child said pleasantly. "My accidents are those of this child, but my substance, as with the wine and the wafer in transubstantiation—"

"Okay," Leo said. "You're Eldritch; I believe you. But I still don't like this place. Those glucks—"

"Don't blame them on Chew-Z," the child said. "Blame them on me; they're a product of my mind, not of the lichen. Does every new universe constructed have to be *nice?* I like glucks in mine; they appeal to something in me."

"Suppose I want to construct my own universe," Leo said. "Maybe there's something evil in me, too, some aspect of my personality I don't know about. That would cause me to produce a thing even more ugly than what you've brought into being." At least with the Perky Pat layouts one was limited to what one had provided in advance, as Eldritch himself had pointed out. And—there was a certain safety in this.

"Whatever it was could be abolished," the child said indifferently. "If you found you didn't like it. And if you did like it—" She shrugged. "Keep it, then. Why not? Who's hurt? You're alone in your—" Instantly she broke off, clapping her hand to her mouth.

"Alone," Leo said. "You mean each person goes to a different subjective world? It's not like the layouts, then, because everyone in the group who takes Can-D goes to the layout, the men to Walt, the women into Perky Pat. But that means you're not here." Or, he thought, I'm not here. But in that case—

The child watched him intently, trying to gauge his reaction.

"We haven't taken Chew-Z," Leo said quietly. "This is all a hypnogogic, absolutely artificially induced pseudo-environment. We're not anywhere except where we started from; we're still at your demesne on Luna. Chew-Z doesn't create any new universe and you know it. There's no bona fide reincarnation with it. This is all just one big snow-job."

The child was silent. But she had not taken her eyes from him; her eyes burned, cold and bright, unwinking.

Leo said, "Come on, Palmer; what does Chew-Z *really* do?"

"I told you." The child's voice was harsh.

"This is not even as real as Perky Pat, as the use of our own drug. And even *that* is open to the question as regards the validity of the experience, its authenticity versus it as purely hypnogogic or hallucinatory. So obviously there won't be any discussion about this; it's patently the latter."

"No," the child said. "And you better believe me, because if you don't you won't get out of this world alive."

"You can't die in a hallucination," Leo said. "Any more than you can be born again. I'm going back to P. P. Layouts." Once more he started toward the stairs.

"Go ahead and climb," the child said from behind him. "See if I care. Wait and see where it gets you."

Leo climbed the stairs, and passed through the luminous hoop.

Blinding, ferociously hot sunlight descended on him; he scuttled from the open street to a nearby doorway for shelter.

A jet cab, from the towering high buildings, swooped

down, spying him. "A ride, sir? Better get indoors; it's almost noon."

Gasping, almost unable to breathe, Leo said, "Yes, thanks. Take me to P. P. Layouts." He unsteadily got into the cab, and fell back at once against the seat, panting in the coolness provided by its antithermal shield.

The cab took off. Presently it was descending at the enclosed field of his company's central building.

As soon as he reached his outer office he said to Miss Gleason, "Get hold of Mayerson. Find out why he didn't do anything to rescue me."

"Rescue you?" Miss Gleason said, in consternation. "What was the matter, Mr. Bulero?" She followed him to the inner office. "Where were you and in what way—"

"Just get Mayerson." He seated himself at his familiar desk, relieved to be back here. The hell with Palmer Eldritch, he said to himself, and reached into the desk drawer for his favorite English briar pipe and half-pound can of Sail tobacco, a Dutch cavendish mix.

He was busy lighting his pipe when the door opened and Barney Mayerson appeared, looking sheepish and worn.

"Well?" Leo said. He puffed energetically on his pipe.

Barney said, "I—" He turned to Miss Fugate, who had come in after him; gesturing, he turned again to Leo and said, "Anyhow you're back."

"Of course I'm back. I built myself a stairway to here. Aren't you going to answer as to why you didn't do anything? I guess not. But as you say, you weren't needed. I've now got an idea of what this new Chew-Z substance is like. It's definitely inferior to Can-D. I have no qualms in saying that emphatically. You can tell without doubt that it's merely a hallucinogenic experience you're undergoing. Now let's get down to business. Eldritch has sold Chew-Z to the UN by claiming that it induces genuine reincarnation, which ratifies the religious convictions of more than half the governing members of the General Assembly, plus that Indian skunk

Hepburn-Gilbert himself. It's a fraud, because Chew-Z doesn't do that. But the worst aspect of Chew-Z is the solipsistic quality. With Can-D you undergo a valid interpersonal experience, in that the others in your hovel are—" He paused irritably. "What is it, Miss Fugate? What are you staring at?"

Roni Fugate murmured, "I'm sorry, Mr. Bulero, but there's a creature under your desk."

Bending, Leo peered under the desk.

A thing had squeezed itself between the base of the desk and the floor; its eyes regarded him greenly, unwinking.

"Get out of there," Leo said. To Barney he said, "Get a yardstick or a broom, something to prod it with."

Barney left the office.

"Damn it, Miss Fugate," Leo said, smoking rapidly on his pipe, "I hate to think what that is under there. And what it signifies." Because it might signify that Eldritch—within the little girl Monica—had been right when she said *See if I care. Wait and see where it gets you.*

The thing from beneath the desk scuttled out, and made for the door. It squeezed under the door and was gone.

It was even worse than the glucks. He got one good look at it.

Leo said, "Well, that's that. I'm sorry, Miss Fugate, but you might as well return to your office; there's no point in our discussing what actions to take toward the imminent appearance of Chew-Z on the market. Because I'm not talking to anyone; I'm sitting here babbling away to myself." He felt depressed. Eldritch had him and also the validity, or at least the seeming validity, of the Chew-Z experience had been demonstrated; he himself had confused it with the real. Only the malign bug created by Palmer Eldritch—deliberately—had given it away.

Otherwise, he realized, I might have gone on forever.

Spent a century, as Eldritch said, in this ersatz universe.

Jeez, he thought. I'm licked. "Miss Fugate," he said, "please don't just stand there; go back to your office." He got up, went to the water cooler, and poured himself a paper cup of mineral water. Drinking unreal water for an unreal body, he said to himself. In front of an unreal employee. "Miss Fugate," he said, "are you really Mr. Mayerson's mistress?"

"Yes, Mr. Bulero," Miss Fugate said, nodding. "As I told you."

"And you won't be mine." He shook his head. "Because I'm too old and too evolved. You know—or rather you don't know—that I have at least a limited power in this universe. I could make over my body, make myself young." Or, he thought, make you old. How would you like that? he wondered. He drank the water, and tossed the cup in the waste chute; not looking at Miss Fugate he said to himself, You're my age, Miss Fugate. In fact older. Let's see; you're about ninety-two, now. In this world, anyhow; you've aged, here . . . time has rolled forward for you because you turned me down and I don't like being turned down. In fact, he said to himself, you're over one hundred years old, withered, juiceless, without teeth and eyes. A thing.

Behind him he heard a dry, rasping sound, an intake of breath. And a wavering, shrill voice, like the cry of a frightened bird. "Oh, Mr. Bulero—"

I've changed my mind, Leo thought. You're the way you were; I take it back, okay? He turned, and saw Roni Fugate or at least something standing there where she had last stood. A spider web, gray fungoid strands wrapped one around another to form a brittle column that swayed . . . he saw the head, sunken at the cheeks, with eyes like dead spots of soft, inert white slime that leaked out gummy, slow-moving tears, eyes that tried to appeal but could not because they could not make out where he was.

"You're back the way you were," Leo said harshly, and shut his own eyes. "Tell me when it's over."

Footsteps. A man's. Barney, re-entering the office. "Jesus," Barney said, and halted.

Eyes shut, Leo said, "Isn't she back the way she was yet?"

"*She*? Where's Roni? What's this?"

Leo opened his eyes.

It was not Roni Fugate who stood there, not even an ancient manifestation of her; it was a puddle, but not of water. The puddle was alive and in it bits of sharp, jagged gray splinters swam.

The thick, oozing material of the puddle flowed gradually outward, then shuddered, and retracted into itself; in the center the fragments of hard gray matter swam together, and cohered into a roughly shaped ball with tangled, matted strands of hair floating at its crown. Vague eyesockets, empty, formed; it was becoming a skull, but of some life-formation to come: his unconscious desire for her to experience evolution in its horrific aspect had conjured this monstrosity into being.

The jaw clacked, opening and shutting as if jerked by wicked, deeply imbedded wires; drifting here and there in the fluid of the puddle it croaked, "But you see, Mr. Bulero, she didn't live that long. You forgot that." It was, remotely but absolutely, the voice—not of Roni Fugate—but Monica, as if drumming at the far-distant end of a waxed string. "You made her past one hundred but she only is going to live to be seventy. So she's been dead thirty years, except you made her alive; that was what you intended. And even worse—" The toothless jaw waggled and the uninhabited pockets for eyes gaped. "She evolved not while alive but there in the ground." The skull ceased piping, then by stages disintegrated; its parts once more floated away and the semblance of organization again dissipated.

After a time Barney said, "Get us out of here, Leo."

Leo said, "Hey, Palmer." His voice was uncontrolled, babylike with fear. "Hey, you know what? I give up; I really do."

The carpet of the office beneath his feet rotted, became mushy, and then sprouted, grew, alive, into green fibers; he saw that it was becoming grass. And then the walls and the ceiling caved in, collapsed into fine dust; the particles rained noiselessly down like ashes. And the blue, cool sky appeared, untouched, above.

Seated on the grass, with the stick in her lap and the suitcase containing Dr. Smile beside her, Monica said, "Did you want Mr. Mayerson to remain? I didn't think so. I let him go with the rest that you made. Okay?" She smiled up at Leo.

"Okay," he agreed chokingly. Looking around him he saw now only the plain of green; even the dust which had composed P. P. Layouts, the building and its core of people, had vanished, except for a dim layer that remained on his hands, on his coat; he brushed it off, reflexively.

Monica said, " 'From dust thou art come, o man; to dust shalt—' "

"Okay!" he said loudly. "I get it; you don't have to hammer me over the noggin with it. So it was irreal; so what? I mean, you made your goddam point, Eldritch; you can do anything here you want, and I'm nothing, I'm just a phantom." He felt hatred toward Palmer Eldritch and he thought, If I ever get out of here, if I can escape from you, you bastard . . .

"Now, now," the girl said, her eyes dancing. "You are not going to use language like that; you really aren't, because I won't let you. I won't even say what I'll do if you continue, but you know me, Mr. Bulero. Right?"

Leo said, "Right." He walked off a few steps, got out his handkerchief, and mopped the perspiration from his upper lip and neck, the hollow beneath his adam's apple where it was so hard, in the mornings, to shave. God, he thought, help me. Will You? And if You do, if You can reach into this world, I'll do anything, whatever You want; I'm not afraid now, I'm sick. This is going to kill my body, even if it's just an ectoplasmic, phantom-type body.

Hunched over, he was sick; he vomited onto the grass. For a long time—it seemed a long time—that kept up and then he was better; he was able to turn, and walk slowly back toward the seated child with her suitcase.

"Terms," the child said flatly. "We're going to work out an exact business relationship between my company and yours. We need your superb network of ad satellites and your transportation system of late-model interplan ships and your God-knows-how-extensive plantations on Venus; we want everything, Bulero. We're going to grow the lichen where you now grow Can-D, ship it in the same ships, reach the colonists with the same well-trained, experienced pushers you use, advertise through pros like Allen and Charlotte Faine. Can-D and Chew-Z won't be competing because there'll just be the one product, Chew-Z; you're about to announce your retirement. Understand me, Leo?"

"Sure," Leo said, "I hear."

"Will you do it?"

"Okay," Leo said. And pounced on the child.

His hands closed about her windpipe; he squeezed. She stared into his face, rigidly, her mouth pursed, saying nothing, not even trying to struggle, to claw him or get away. He continued squeezing, for a time so long that it seemed as if his hands had grown fast to her, become fixed in place forever, like gnarled roots of some ancient, diseased, but still-living plant.

When he let go she was dead. Her body settled forward, then twisted and fell to one side, to come to rest supine on the grass. No blood. No sign even of a struggle, except that her throat was a dark, mottled, blackish red.

He stood up, thinking, Well, did I do it? If he—she or it, whatever it is—dies here, does that take care of it?

But the simulated world remained. He had expected it to dwindle away as her—Eldritch's—life dwindled away.

Puzzled, he stood without moving an inch, smelling the air, listening to a far-off wind. *Nothing* had changed except that the girl had died. Why? What ailed the basis on which he had acted? Incredibly, it was wrong.

Bending, he snapped on Dr. Smile. "Explain it to me," he said.

Obligingly, Dr. Smile tinnily declared, "He is dead here, Mr. Bulero. But at the demesne on Luna—"

"Okay," Leo said roughly. "Well, tell me how to get out of this place. How do I get back to Luna, to—" He gestured. "You know what I mean. Actuality."

"At this moment," Dr. Smile explained, "Palmer Eldritch, although considerably upset and angered, is intravenously providing you with a substance which counters the injectable Chew-Z previously administered; you will return shortly." It added, "That is, shortly, even instantly, in terms of the time-flow in that world. As to this—" It chuckled. "It could seem longer."

"*How* longer?"

"Oh, years," Dr. Smile said. "But quite possibly less. Days? Months? Time sense is subjective, so let's see how it feels to you; do you not agree?"

Seating himself wearily by the body of the child, Leo sighed, put his head down, chin against his chest, and prepared to wait.

"I'll keep you company," Dr. Smile said, "if I can. But I'm afraid without Mr. Eldritch's animating presence—" Its voice, Leo realized, had become feeble, as well as slowed down. "Nothing can sustain this world," it intoned weakly, "but Mr. Eldritch. So I am afraid . . ."

Its voice faded out entirely.

There was only silence. Even the distant wind had ceased.

How long? Leo asked himself. And then he wondered if he could, as before, make something.

Gesturing in the manner of an inspired symphony conductor, his hands writhing, he tried to create before him in the air a jet cab.

At last a meager outline appeared. Insubstantial, it remained without color, almost transparent; he rose, walked closer to it, and tried with all his strength once more. For a moment it seemed to gain color and reality and then suddenly it became fixed; like a hard, discarded chitinous shell it sagged, and burst. Its sections, only two-dimensional at best, blew and fluttered, tearing into ragged pieces—he turned his back on it and walked away in disgust. What a mess, he said to himself dismally.

He continued, without purpose, to walk. Until he came, all at once, to something in the grass, something dead; he saw it lying there and warily he approached it. This, he thought. The final indication of what I've done.

He kicked the dead gluck with the toe of his shoe; his toe passed entirely through it and he drew back, repelled.

Going on, hands deep in his pockets, he shut his eyes and once more prayed but this time vaguely; it was only a wish, inchoate, and then it became clear. I'm going to get him in the real world, he said to himself. Not just here, as I've done, but as the 'papes are going to report. Not for myself; not to save P. P. Layouts and the Can-D trade. But for—he knew what he meant. Everyone in the system. Because Palmer Eldritch is an invader and this is how we'll all wind up, here like this, on a plain of dead things that have become nothing more than random fragments; this is the "reincarnation" that he promised Hepburn-Gilbert.

For a time he wandered on and then, by degrees, he made his way back to the suitcase which had been Dr. Smile.

Something bent over the suitcase. A human or quasi-human figure.

Seeing him it at once straightened; its bald head glistened as it gaped at him, taken by surprise. And then it leaped and rushed off.

A Proxer.

It seemed to him as he watched it go that this put everything in perspective. Palmer Eldritch had peopled his landscape with things such as this; he was still highly involved with them, even now that he had returned to his home system. This, which had appeared just now, gave an insight into the man's mind at the deepest level; and Palmer Eldritch himself might not have known that he had so populated his hallucinatory establishment—the Proxer might have been just as much a surprise to him.

Unless of course this was the Prox system.

Perhaps it would be a good idea to follow the Proxer.

He set off in that direction and trudged for what seemed to be hours; he saw nothing, only the grass underfoot, the level horizon. And then at last a shape formed ahead; he made for it and found himself all at once confronting a parked ship. Halting, he regarded it in amazement. For one thing it was not a Terran ship and yet it was not a Prox ship either.

Simply, it was not from either system.

Nor were the two creatures lounging nearby it Proxers or Terrans; he had never seen such life forms before. Tall, slender, with reedlike limbs and grotesque, egg-shaped heads which, even at this distance, seemed oddly delicate, a highly evolved race, he decided, and yet related to Terrans; the resemblance was closer than to the Proxers.

He walked toward them, hand raised in greeting.

One of the two creatures turned toward him, saw him, gaped, and nudged its companion; both stared and then the first one said. "My God, Alec; it's one of the old forms. You know, the near-men."

"Yeah," the other creature agreed.

"Wait," Leo Bulero said. "You're speaking the language of Terra, twenty-first-century English—so you must have seen a Terran before."

"Terran?" the one named Alec said. "We're Terrans. What the hell are you? A freak that died out centuries ago, that's what. Well, maybe not centuries but anyhow a long time ago."

"An enclave of them must still exist on this moon," the first said. To Leo he said, "How many dawn men are there besides you? Come on, fella; we won't treat you bad. Any women? Can you reproduce?" To his companion he said, "It just seems like centuries. I mean, you've got to remember we been evolving in terms of a hundred thousand years at a crack. If it wasn't for Denkmal these dawn men would still be—"

"Denkmal," Leo said. Then this was the end-result of Denkmal's E Therapy; this was only a little ahead in time, perhaps merely decades. Like them he felt a gulf of a million years, and yet it was in fact an illusion; he himself, when he finished with his therapy, might resemble these. Except that the chitinous hide was gone, and that had been one of the prime aspects of the evolving types. "I go to his clinic," he said to the two of them. "Once a week. At Munich. I'm evolving; it's working on me." He came up close to them, and studied them intently. "Where's the hide?" he asked. "To shield you from the sun?"

"Aw, that phony hot period's over," the one named Alec said, with a gesture of derision. "That was those Proxers, working with the Renegade. You know. Or maybe you don't."

"Palmer Eldritch," Leo said.

"Yeah," Alec said, nodding. "But we got him. Right here on this moon, in fact. Now it's a shrine—not to us but to the Proxers; they sneak in here to worship. Seen any? We're supposed to arrest any we find; this is Sol system territory, belongs to the UN."

"What planet's this a moon of?" Leo asked.

The two evolved Terrans both grinned. "Terra," Alec said. "It's artificial. Called Sigma 14-B, built years ago. Didn't it exist in your time? It must have; it's a real old one."

"I think so," Leo said. "Then you can get me to Earth."

"Sure." Both of the evolved Terrans nodded in agreement. "As a matter of fact we're taking off in half an hour; we'll take you along—you and the rest of your tribe. Just tell us the location."

"I'm the only one," Leo said testily, "and we would hardly be a tribe anyhow; we're not out of prehistoric times." He wondered how he had gotten here to this future epoch. Or was this an illusion, too, constructed by the master hallucinator, Palmer Eldritch? Why should he assume this was any more real than the child Monica or the glucks or the synthetic P. P. Layouts which he had visited—visited and seen collapse? This was Palmer Eldritch imagining the future; these were meanderings of his brilliant, creative mind as he waited at his demesne on Luna for the effects of the intravenous injection of Chew-Z to wear off. Nothing more.

In fact, even as he stood here, he could see, faintly, the horizon-line through the parked ship; the ship was slightly transparent, not quite substantial enough. And the two evolved Terrans; they wavered in a mild but pervasive distortion which reminded him of the days when he had had astigmatic vision, before he had received, by surgical transplant, totally healthy eyes. The two of them had not exactly locked in place.

He reached his hand out to the first Terran. "I'd like to shake hands with you," he said. Alec, the Terran, extended his hand, too, with a smile.

Leo's hand passed through Alec's and emerged on the far side.

"Hey," Alec said, frowning; he at once, pistonlike, withdrew his hand. "What's going on?" To his companion he said, "This guy isn't real; we should have suspected it. He's a—what did they used to call them? From chewing that diabolical drug that Eldritch picked up in the Prox system. A *chooser;* that's what. He's a phantasm." He glared at Leo.

"I am?" Leo said feebly, and then realized that Alec was right. His actual body was on Luna; he was not really here.

But what did that make the two evolved Terrans? Perhaps they were not constructs of Eldritch's busy mind; perhaps they, alone, were genuinely here. Meanwhile, the one named Alec was now staring at him.

"You know," Alec said to his companion, "this *chooser* looks familiar to me. I've seen a pic in the 'papes of him; I'm sure of it." To Leo he said, "What's your name, *chooser?*" His stare became harsher, more intense.

"I'm Leo Bulero," Leo said.

Both the evolved Terrans jumped with shock. "Hey," Alec

exclaimed, "no wonder I thought I recognized him. He's the guy who killed Palmer Eldritch!" To Leo he said, "You're a hero, fella. I bet you don't know that, because you're just a mere *chooser;* right? And you've come back here to haunt this place because this is historically the—"

"He didn't come back," his companion broke in. "He's from the past."

"He can still come back," Alec said. "This is a second coming for him, after his own time; he's returned—okay, can I say that?" To Leo he said, "You've returned to this spot because of its association with Palmer Eldritch's death." He turned, and started on a run toward the parked ship. "I'm going to tell the 'papes," he called. "Maybe they can get a pic of you—the ghost of Sigma 14-B." He gestured excitedly. "Now the tourists really will want to visit here. But look out: maybe Eldritch's ghost, his *chooser,* will show up here, too. To pay you back." At that thought he did not look too pleased.

Leo said, "Eldritch already has."

Alec halted, then came slowly back. "He has?" He looked around nervously. "Where is he? Near here?"

"He's dead," Leo said. "I killed him. Strangled him." He felt no emotion about it, just weariness. How could one become elated over the killing of any living person, especially a child?

"They've got to re-enact it through eternity," Alec said, impressed and wide-eyed. He shook his great egglike head.

Leo said, "I wasn't re-enacting anything. This was the first time." Then he thought, And not the real one. That's still to come.

"You mean," Alec said slowly, "it—"

"I've still got to do it," Leo grated. "But one of my Pre-Fash consultants tells me it won't be long. Probably." It was not inevitable and he could never forget that fact. And Eldritch knew it, too; this would go a long way in explaining Eldritch's efforts here and now; he was staving off—or so he hoped—his own death.

"Come on," Alec said to Leo, "and take a look at the marker commemorating the event." He and his companion led the way; Leo, reluctantly, followed. "The Proxers," Alec said over his shoulder, "always seek to—you know. Desiccate this."

"Desecrate," his companion corrected.

"Yeah," Alec said, nodding. "Anyhow, here it is." He stopped.

Ahead of them jutted an imitation—but impressive— granite pillar; on it a brass plaque had been bolted securely at eye-level. Leo, against his better judgment, read the plaque.

IN MEMORIAM. 2016 A.D. NEAR THIS SPOT THE ENEMY OF THE SOL SYSTEM PALMER ELDRITCH WAS SLAIN IN FAIR COMBAT WITH THE CHAMPION OF OUR NINE PLANETS, LEO BULERO OF TERRA.

"Hoopla," Leo ejaculated, impressed despite himself. He read it again. And again. "I wonder," he said, half to himself, "if Palmer's seen this."

"If he's a *chooser*," Alec said, "he probably has. The original form of Chew-Z produced what the manufacturer— Eldritch himself—called 'time-overtones.' That's you right now; you occupy a locus years after you're dead. I guess you're dead by now, anyhow." To his companion he said, "Leo Bulero's dead by now, isn't he?"

"Oh hell, sure," his companion said. "By several decades."

"In fact I think I read—" Alec began, then ceased, looking past Leo; he nudged his companion. Leo turned to see what it was.

A scraggly, narrow, ungainly white dog was approaching.

"Yours?" Alec asked.

"No," Leo said.

"It looks like a *chooser* dog," Alec said. "See, you can look through it a little." The three of them watched the dog as it marched up to them, then past them to the monument itself.

Picking up a pebble, Alec chucked it at the dog; the pebble passed through the dog and landed in the grass beyond. It was a *chooser* dog.

As the three of them watched, the dog halted at the monument, seemed to gaze up at the plaque for a brief interval, and then it—

"Defecation!" Alec shouted, his face turning bright red with rage. He ran toward the dog, waving his arms and trying to kick it, then reaching for the laser pistol at his belt but missing its handle in his excitement.

"Desecration," his companion corrected.

Leo said, "It's Palmer Eldritch." Eldritch was showing his contempt for the monument, his lack of fear toward the future. There would never be such a monument. The dog leisurely strolled off, the two evolved Terrans cursing futilely at it as it departed.

"You're sure that's not your dog?" Alec demanded suspiciously. "As far as I can make out you're the only *chooser* around." He eyed Leo.

Leo started to answer, to explain to them what had happened; it was important that they understand. And then without harbinger of any kind the two evolved Terrans disappeared; the grassy plain, the monument, the departing dog—the entire panorama evaporated, as if the method by which it had been projected, stabilized, and maintained had clicked to the off position. He saw only an empty white expanse, a focused glare, as if there were now no 3-D slide in the projector at all. The light, he thought, that underlies the play of phenomena which we call "reality."

And then he was sitting in the barren room in Palmer Eldritch's demesne on Luna, facing the table with its electronic gadget.

The gadget or contraption or whatever it was said, "Yes, I've seen the monument. About 45 percent of the futures have it. Slightly less than equal chances obtain so I'm not terribly concerned. Have a cigar." Once again the machine extended a lighted cigar to Leo.

"No," Leo said.

"I'm going to let you go," the gadget said, "for a short time, for about twenty-four hours. You can return to your little office at your minuscule company on Terra; while you're there I want you to ponder the situation. Now you've seen Chew-Z in force; you comprehend the fact that your antediluvian product Can-D can't even remotely compare to it. And furthermore—"

"Bull," Leo said. "Can-D is far superior."

"Well, you think it over," the electronic contraption said, with confidence.

"All right," Leo said. He stood stiffly. Had he actually been on the artificial Earth-satellite Sigma 14-B? It was a job for Felix Blau; experts could trace it down. No use worrying about that now. The immediate problem was serious enough; he still had not gotten out from under Palmer Eldritch's control.

He could escape only when—and if—Eldritch decided to release him. That was an undisguised piece of factual reality, hard as it was to face.

"I'd like to point out," the gadget said, "that I've shown mercy to you, Leo. I could have put an—well, let's say a period to the sentence that constitutes your rather short life. And at any time. Because of this I expect—I insist—that you consider very seriously doing the same."

"As I said, I'll think it over," Leo answered. He felt irritable, as if he had drunk too many cups of coffee, and he wanted to leave as soon as possible; he opened the door of the room, and made his way out into the corridor.

As he started to shut the door after him the electronic gadget said, "If you don't decide to join me, Leo, *I'm not going to wait*. I'm going to kill you. I must, to save my own self. Do you understand?"

"I understand," Leo said, and shut the door after him. And I have to, too, he thought. Must kill you . . . or couldn't we both put it in a less direct way, something like they say about animals: put you to sleep.

And I have to do it not just to save myself but everyone in the system, and that's my staff on which I'm leaning. For example, those two evolved Terran soldiers I ran into at the monument. For them so they'll have something to guard.

Slowly he walked up the corridor. At the far end stood the group of 'pape reporters; they had not left yet, had not even obtained their interview—almost no time had passed. So on that point Palmer was right.

Joining the reporters Leo relaxed, and felt considerably better. Maybe he would get away, now; maybe Palmer Eldritch was actually going to let him go. He would live to smell, see, drink in the world once more.

But underneath he knew better. Eldritch would never let him go; one of them would have to be destroyed, first.

He hoped it would not be himself. But he had a terrible intuition, despite the monument, that it could well be.

7

The door to Barney Mayerson's inner office, flung open, revealed Leo Bulero, hunched with weariness, travel-stained. "You didn't try to help me."

After an interval Barney answered, "That's correct." There was no use trying to explain why, not because Leo would fail to understand or believe but because of the reason itself. It was simply not adequate.

Leo said, "You are fired, Mayerson."

"Okay." And he thought, Anyhow I'm alive. And if I'd gone after Leo I wouldn't be, now. He began with numbed fingers gathering up his personal articles from his desk, dropping them into an empty sample case.

"Where's Miss Fugate?" Leo demanded. "She'll be taking your place." He came close to Barney, and scrutinized him. "*Why* didn't you come and get me? Name me the goddam reason, Barney."

"I looked ahead. It would have cost me too much. My life."

"But you didn't have to come personally. This is a big company—you could have arranged for a party from here, and stayed behind. Right?"

It was true. And he hadn't even considered it.

"So," Leo said, "you must have wanted something fatal to happen to me. No other interpretation is possible. Maybe it was unconscious. Yes?"

"I guess so," Barney admitted. Because certainly he hadn't been aware of it. Anyhow Leo was right; why else would he not have taken the responsibility, seen to it that an armed party, as Felix Blau had suggested, emerged from P. P. Layouts and headed for Luna? It was so obvious, now. So simple to see.

"I've had a terrible experience," Leo said, "in Palmer Eldritch's domain. He's a damned magician, Barney. He did all kinds of things with me, things you and I never dreamed of. Turned himself for instance into a little girl, showed me the future, only maybe that was unintentional, made a complete universe up anyhow including a horrible animal called a gluck along with an illusional New York City with you and Roni. What a mess." He shook his head blearily. "Where you going to go?"

"There's only one place I can go."

"Where's that?" Leo eyed him apprehensively.

"Only one other person would have use for my Pre-Fash talent."

"Then you're my enemy!"

"I am already. As far as you're concerned." And he was willing to accept Leo's judgment as fair, Leo's interpretation of his failure to act.

"I'll get you, too, then," Leo said. "Along with that nutty magician, that so-called Palmer Eldritch."

"Why so-called?" Barney glanced up quickly, and ceased his packing.

"Because I'm even more convinced he's not human. I never did lay eyes on him except during the period under the effect of Chew-Z; otherwise he addressed me through an electronic extension."

"Interesting," Barney said.

"Yes, isn't it? And you're so corrupt you'd go ahead and

apply to his outfit for a job. Even though he may be a wig-headed Proxer or something worse, some damn thing that got into his ship while it was coming or going, out in deep space, ate him, and took his place. If you had seen the glucks—"

"Then for chrissakes," Barney said, *"don't make me do this.* Keep me on here."

"I can't. Not after what you failed to do loyalty-wise." Leo glanced away, swallowing rapidly. "I wish I wasn't so sore in this cold, reasonable way at you, but—" He clenched his fists, futilely. "It was hideous; he virtually did it, broke me. And then I ran into those two evolved Terrans and that helped. Up until Eldritch appeared in the form of a dog that peed on the monument." He grimaced starkly. "I have to admit he demonstrated his attitude graphically; there was no mistaking his contempt." He added, half to himself, "His belief that he's going to win, that he has nothing to fear even after seeing the plaque."

"Wish me luck," Barney said. He held out his hand; they briefly, ritualistically shook and then Barney walked from his office, past his secretary's desk, out into the central corridor. He felt hollow, stuffed with some unoccupied, tasteless waste-material, like straw. Nothing more.

As he stood waiting for the elevator Roni Fugate hurried up, breathless, her clear face animated with concern. "Barney—he fired you?"

He nodded.

"Oh dear," she said. "Now what?"

"Now," he said, "over to the other side. For better or worse."

"But how can you and I go on living together, with me working here for Leo and you—"

"I don't have the foggiest notion," Barney said. The elevator had arrived, self-regulated; he stepped into it. "I'll see you," he said, and touched the button; the doors shut, cutting off his view of Roni. I'll see you in what the Neo-Christians call hell, he thought to himself. Probably not before. Not unless this already is, and it may be, hell right now.

At street level he emerged from P. P. Layouts, and stood under the antithermal protective shield searching for signs of a cab.

As a cab halted and he started toward it a voice called to him urgently from the entrance of the building, "Barney, wait."

"You're out of your mind," he said to her. "Go back on in. Don't abandon your budding, bright career along with what was left of mine."

Roni said, "We were about to work together, remember? To as I put it betray Leo; why can't we go on cooperating now?"

"It's all changed. By my sick and depraved unwillingness or inability or whatever you care to call it to go to Luna and help Leo." He felt differently about himself, now, and no longer viewed himself in the same ultra-sympathetic light. "God, you don't want to stay with me," he said to the girl. "Someday you'd be in difficulty and need my help and I'd do to you exactly what I did to Leo; I'd let you sink without moving my right arm."

"But your own life was at—"

"It always is," he pointed out. "When you do anything. That's the name of the comedy we're stuck in." It didn't excuse him, at least not in his own eyes. He entered the cab, automatically gave his conapt address, and lay back against the seat as the cab rose into the fire-drenched midday sky. Far below, under the antithermal curtain, Roni Fugate stood shielding her eyes, watching him go. No doubt hoping he would change his mind and turn back.

However, he did not.

It takes a certain amount of courage, he thought, to face yourself and say with candor, I'm rotten. I've done evil and I will again. It was no accident; it emanated from the true, authentic me.

Presently the cab began to descend; he reached into his pocket for his wallet and then discovered with shock that this was not his conapt building; in panic he tried to figure out where he was. Then it came to him. This was conapt 492. He had given Emily's address to the cab.

Whisk! Back to the past. Where things made sense. He thought, When I had my career, knew what I wanted from the future, knew even in my heart what I was willing to abandon, turn again, sacrifice—and what for. But now . . .

Now he had sacrificed his career, in order as it seemed at the time to save his life. So by logic he had at that former time sacrificed Emily to save his life; it was as simple as that. Nothing could be clearer. It was not an idealistic goal, not the old Puritan, Calvin-style high duty to vocation; it was nothing more than the instinct that inhabited and compelled every flatworm that crept. Christ! he thought. I've done this: I've put myself ahead first of Emily and now of Leo. What kind of human am I? And, as I was honest enough to tell her, next it would be Roni. Inevitably.

Maybe Emily can help me, he said to himself. Maybe that's why I'm here. She was always smart about things like this; she saw through the self-justifying delusions that I erected to obscure the reality inside. And of course that just made me more eager to get rid of her. In fact that alone was reason enough, given a person like me. But—maybe I'm better able to endure it now.

A few moments later he was at Emily's door, ringing the bell.

If she thinks I should join Palmer Eldritch's staff I will, he said to himself. And if not then not. But she and her husband are working for Eldritch; how can they, with morality, tell me not to? So it was decided in advance. And maybe I knew that, too.

The door opened. Wearing a blue smock stained with both wet and dried clay, Emily stared at him large-eyed, astonished.

"Hi," he said. "Leo fired me." He waited but she said nothing. "Can I come in?" he asked.

"Yes." She led him into the apt; in the center of the living

room her familiar potter's wheel took up, as always, enormous space. "I was potting. It's nice to see you, Barney. If
you want a cup of coffee you'll have to—"

"I came here to ask your advice," he said. "But now I've
decided it's unnecessary." He wandered to the window, set
his bulging sample case down, and gazed out.

"Do you mind if I go on working? I had a good idea, or
at least it seemed good at the time." She rubbed her forehead, then massaged her eyes. "Now I don't know . . . and
I feel so tired. I wonder if it has to do with E Therapy."

"Evolution therapy? You're taking that?" He spun at once
to scrutinize her; had she changed physically?

It seemed to him—but this was perhaps because he had
not seen her for so long—that her features had coarsened.

Age, he thought. But—

"How's it working?" he asked.

"Well, I've just had one session. But you know, my mind
feels so muddy. I can't seem to think properly; all my ideas
get scrambled up together."

"I think you had better knock off on that therapy. Even
if it is the rage; even if it is what everybody who is anybody
does."

"Maybe so. But they seem so satisfied. Richard and Dr.
Denkmal." She hung her head, an old familiar response.
"They'd know, wouldn't they?"

"Nobody knows; it's uncharted. Knock it off. And you
always let people walk all over you." He made his tone
commanding; he had used that tone with her countless times
during their years together, and generally it had worked. Not
always.

And this time, he saw, was one of them; she got that
stubborn look in her eyes, the refusal to be normally passive.
"I think it's up to me," she said with dignity. "And I intend
to continue."

Shrugging, he roamed about the conapt. He had no power
over her; nor did he care. But was that true? Did he really

not care? An image appeared in his mind, of Emily devolving . . . and at the same time trying to work on her pots, trying to be creative. It was funny—and dreadful.

"Listen," he said roughly. "If that guy actually loves you—"

"But I told you," Emily said. "It's my decision." She returned to her wheel; a great tall pot was being thrown, and he walked over to get a good look at it. A nice one, he decided. And yet—familiar. Hadn't she done such a pot already? He said nothing, however; he merely studied it. "What do you suppose you're going to do?" Emily asked. "Who could you work for?" She seemed sympathetic and it made him remember how, recently, he had blocked the sale of her pots to P. P. Layouts. Easily, she could have held a great animosity toward him, but it was typical of her not to. And of course she knew that it was he who had turned Hnatt down.

He said, "My future may be decided. I got a draft notice."

"Good grief. You on Mars; I can't picture it."

"I can chew Can-D," he said. "Only—" Instead of having a Perky Pat layout, he thought, maybe I'll have an Emily layout. And spend time, in fantasy, back with you, back to the life I deliberately, moronically, turned my back on. The only really good period of my life, when I was genuinely happy. But of course I didn't know it, because I had nothing to compare it to . . . as I have now. "Is there any chance," he said, "that you'd like to come?"

She stared at him and he stared back, both of them dumbfounded by what he had proposed.

"I mean it," he said.

"When did you decide that?"

"It doesn't matter when I decided it," he said. "All that matters is that that's how I feel."

"It also matters how *I* feel," Emily said quietly; she then resumed potting. "And I'm perfectly happy married to Richard. We get along just swell." Her face was placid; beyond doubt she meant every word of it. He was damned, doomed, consigned to the void which he had hollowed out for himself. And he deserved it. They both knew that, without either saying it.

"I guess I'll go," he said.

Emily didn't protest that, either. She merely nodded.

"I hope in the name of God," he said, "that you're not devolving. I think you are, personally. I can see it, in your face for instance. Look in the mirror." With that he departed; the door shut after him. Instantly he regretted what he had said, and yet it might be a good thing . . . it might help her, he thought. Because I could see it. And I don't want that; nobody does. Not even that jackass of a husband of hers that she prefers over me . . . for reasons I'll never know, except perhaps that marriage to him has the aspect of destiny. She's fated to live with Richard Hnatt, fated never to be my wife again; you can't reverse the flow of time.

You can when you chew Can-D, he thought. Or the new product, Chew-Z. All the colonists do. It's not available on Earth but it is on Mars or Venus or Ganymede, any of the frontier colonies.

If everything else fails, there's that.

And perhaps it already had failed. Because—

In the last analysis he could not go to Palmer Eldritch. Not after what the man had done—or tried to do—to Leo. He realized this as he stood outdoors waiting for a cab. Beyond him the midday street shimmered and he thought, Maybe I'll step out there. Would anyone find me before I died? Probably not. It would be as good a way as any . . .

So there goes my last hope of employment. It would amuse Leo that I'd balk here. He'd be surprised and probably pleased.

Just for the hell of it, he decided, I'll call Eldritch, ask him, see if he would give me a job.

He found a vidphone booth and put through a call to Eldritch's demesne on Luna.

"This is Barney Mayerson," he explained. "Previously top Pre-Fash consultant to Leo Bulero; as a matter of fact I was second in command at P. P. Layouts."

Eldritch's personnel manager frowned and said, "Well? What do you want?"

"I'd like to see about a job with you."

"We're not hiring any Pre-Fash consultants. Sorry."

"Would you ask Mr. Eldritch, please?"

"Mr. Eldritch has already expressed himself on the matter."

Barney hung up. He left the vidphone booth.

He was not really surprised.

If they had said, Come to Luna for an interview, would I have gone? Yes, he realized. I'd have gone but at some point I'd have pulled out. Once I had firmly established that they'd give me the job.

Returning to the vidphone booth he called his UN selective service board. "This is Mr. Barney Mayerson." He gave them his official code-ident number. "I received my notice the other day. I'd like to waive the formalities and go right in. I'm anxious to emigrate."

"The physical can't be bypassed," the UN bureaucrat informed him. "Nor can the mental. But if you choose you may come by any time, right now if you wish, and take both."

"Okay," he said. "I will."

"And since you are volunteering, Mr. Mayerson, you get to pick—"

"Any planet or moon is fine with me," he said. He rang off, left the booth, found a cab, and gave it the address of the selective service board near his conapt building.

As the cab hummed above downtown New York another cab rose and zipped ahead of it, wig-wagging its side fins in a rocking motion.

"They are trying to contact us," the autonomic circuit of his own cab informed him. "Do you wish to respond?"

"No," Barney said. "Speed up." And then he changed his mind. "Can you ask them who they are?"

"By radio, perhaps." The cab was silent a moment and then it stated, "They claim to have a message for you from Palmer Eldritch; he wants to tell you that he will accept you as an employee and for you not to—"

"Let's have that again," Barney said.

"Mr. Palmer Eldritch, whom they represent, will employ you as you recently requested. Although they have a general rule—"

"Let me talk to them," Barney said.

A mike was presented to him.

"Who is this?" Barney said into it.

An unfamiliar man's voice said, "This is Icholtz. From Chew-Z Manufacturers of Boston. May we land and discuss the matter of your employment with our firm?"

"I'm on my way to the draft board. To give myself up."

"There's nothing in writing, is there? You haven't signed."

"No."

"Good. Then it's not too late."

Barney said, "But on Mars I can chew Can-D."

"Why do you want to do that, for godssake?"

"Then I can be back with Emily."

"Who's Emily?"

"My previous wife. Who I kicked out because she became pregnant. Now I realize it was the only happy time of my life. In fact I love her more now than I ever did; it's grown instead of faded."

"Look," Icholtz said. "We can supply you with all the Chew-Z you want and it's superior; you can live forever in an eternal unchanging perfect now with your ex-wife. So there's no problem."

"But maybe I don't want to work for Palmer Eldritch."

"You applied!"

"I've got doubts," Barney said. "Grave ones. I tell you; don't call me, I'll call you. If I don't go into the service." He handed the mike back to the cab. "Here. Thanks."

"It's patriotic to go into the service," the cab said.

"Mind your own business," Barney said.

"I think you're doing the right thing," the cab said, anyhow.

"If only I had gone to Sigma 14-B to save Leo," he said. "Or was it Luna? Wherever he was; I can't even remember now. It all seems like a disfigured dream. Anyhow if I had I'd still be working for him and everything would be all right."

"We all make mistakes," the cab said piously.

"But some of us," Barney said, "make fatal ones." First about our loved ones, our wife and children, and then about our employer, he said to himself.

The cab hummed on.

And then, he said to himself, we make one last one. About our whole life, summing it all up. Whether to take a job with Eldritch or go into the service. And whichever we choose we can know this:

It was the wrong alternative.

An hour later he had taken his physical; he had passed and thereupon the mental was administered by something not unlike Dr. Smile.

He passed that, too.

In a daze he took the oath ("I swear to look upon Earth as the mother and leader," etc.) and then, with a folio of greetings!-type information, was ejected to go back to his conapt and pack. He had twenty-four hours before his ship left for—wherever they were sending him. They had not as yet uttered this. The notification of destination, he conjectured, probably began, " *'Mene, mene, tekel.'* " At least it should, considering the possible choices to which it was limited.

I'm in, he said to himself with every sort of reaction: gladness, relief, terror, and then the melancholy that came with an overwhelming sense of defeat. Anyhow, he thought as he rode back to his conapt, this beats stepping out into the midday sun, becoming, as they say, a mad dog or an Englishman.

Or did it?

Anyhow, *this was slower*. It took longer to die this way, possibly fifty years, and that appealed to him more. But why, he did not know.

However, he reflected, I can always decide to speed it up. On the colony world there are undoubtedly as many opportunities for that as there are here, perhaps even more.

While he was packing his possessions, ensconced for the last time in his beloved, worked-for conapt, the vidphone rang.

"Mr. Bayerson—" A girl, some minor official of some sub-front-office department of the UN's colonizing apparatus. *Smiling*.

"Mayerson."

"Yes. What I called for, you see, is to tell you your destination, and—lucky you, Mr. Mayerson!—it will be the fertile area of Mars known as Fineburg Crescent. I *know* you'll enjoy it there. Well, so goodbye, sir, and good luck." She kept right on smiling, even up until he had cut off the image. It was the smile of someone who was not going.

"Good luck to you, too," he said.

Fineburg Crescent. He had heard of it; relatively, it actually was fertile. Anyhow the colonists there had gardens: it was not, like some areas, a waste of frozen methane crystals and gas descending in violent, ceaseless storms year in, year out. Believe it or not he could go up to the surface from time to time, step out of his hovel.

In the corner of the living room of his conapt rested the suitcase containing Dr. Smile; he switched it on and said, "Doctor, you'll have a bit of trouble believing this, but I have no further need of your services. Goodbye and good luck, as the girl who isn't going said." He added by way of explanation, "I volunteered."

"Cdryxxxxx," Dr. Smile blared, slipping a cog down below in the conapt building's basement. "But for your type—that's virtually impossible. What was the reason, Mr. Mayerson?"

"The death wish," he said, and shut the psychiatrist off; he resumed his packing in silence. God, he thought. And a little while ago Roni and I had such big plans; we were going to sell out Leo on a grand scale, go over to Eldritch with an enormous splash. What happened to all that? I'll tell you what happened, he said to himself; Leo acted first.

And now Roni has my job. Exactly what she wanted.

The more he thought of it the angrier it made him, in a baffled sort of way. But there was nothing he could do about it, at least not in this world. Maybe when he chewed Can-D or Chew-Z he could inhabit a universe where—

There was a knock at the door.

"Hi," Leo said. "Can I come in?" He entered the apt, wiping his immense forehead with a folded handkerchief. "Hot day. I looked in the 'pape and it's gone up six-tenths of—"

"If you came to offer me my job back," Barney said, pausing in his packing, "it's too late because I've entered the service. I'm leaving tomorrow for the Fineburg Crescent." It would be a final irony if Leo wanted to make peace; the ultimate turn of the blind wheels of creation.

"I'm not offering you your job back. And I know you've been inducted; I've got informants in the selective service and anyhow Dr. Smile notified me. I was paying him—you didn't know this, of course—to report to me on your progress in declining under stress."

"What do you want, then?"

Leo said, "I want you to accept a job with Felix Blau. It's all worked out."

"The rest of my life," Barney said quietly, "will be spent at Fineburg Crescent. Don't you understand?"

"Take it easy. I'm trying to make the best of a bad situation and you'd better, too. Both of us acted too hastily, me in firing you, you in giving yourself up to your Dracula-type selective service board. Barney, I think I know a way to ensnare Palmer Eldritch. I've hashed it out with Blau and he likes the idea. You're to pose as a colonist—" Leo corrected himself. "Or rather go ahead, live your actual colonist-type life, become one of the group. Now, one of these days, probably in the next week, Eldritch is going to start peddling Chew-Z in your area. They may right away approach you; anyhow we hope so. We're counting on it."

Barney rose to his feet. "And I'm supposed to jump to and buy."

"Right."

"Why?"

"You file a complaint—our legal boys will draw it up for you—with the UN. Declaring that the goddam miserable unholy crap produced highly toxic side effects in you; never mind what, now. We'll escalate you into a test case, compel the UN to ban Chew-Z as harmful, dangerous—we'll keep it off Terra completely. Actually it's ideal, you quitting your job with P. P. and going into the service; it couldn't have happened at a better time."

Barney shook his head.

"What's that mean?" Leo said.

"I'm out of it."

"Why?"

Barney shrugged. Actually he did not know. "After the way I let you down—"

"You panicked. You didn't know what to do; it's not your job. I should have had Smile contact the head of our company police, John Seltzer. All right, so you made a mistake. It's over."

"No," Barney said. Because, he thought, of what I learned from it about myself; I can't forget that. Those insights, they only go one way, and that's straight at your heart. And they're poison-filled.

"Don't brood, for chrissakes. I mean, it's morbid; you still have a whole lifetime ahead, even if it is at Fineburg Crescent; I mean, you'd probably have been drafted anyhow. Right? You agree?" Agitated, Leo paced about the living room. "What a mess. All right, don't help us out; let Eldritch and those Proxers do whatever it is they're up to, taking over the Sol system or even worse, the entire universe, starting with us." He halted, glared at Barney.

"Let me—think it over."

"Wait'll you take Chew-Z. You'll find out. It's going to contaminate us all, starting inside and working to the surface—it's utter derangement." Wheezing with exertion, Leo paused to cough violently. "Too many cigars," he said, weakly. "Jeez." He eyed Barney. "The guy's given me a day, you know that? I'm supposed to capitulate and if not—" He snapped his fingers.

"I can't be on Mars that soon," Barney said. "Let alone be set up to buy a bindle of Chew-Z from a pusher."

"I know that." Leo's voice was hard. "But he can't destroy me that soon; it'll take him weeks, maybe even months. And by then we'll have someone in the courts who can show damages. I recognize this doesn't sound to you like much, but—"

Barney said, "Contact me when I'm on Mars. At my hovel."

"I'll do that! I'll do that!" And then, half to himself, Leo said, "And it'll give you a reason."

"Pardon?"

"Nothing, Barney."

"Explain."

Leo shrugged. "Hell, I know the spot you're in. Roni's got your job; you were right. And I had you traced; I know you went beeline-wise to your ex. You still love her and she won't come with you, will she? I know you better than you know yourself. I know exactly why you didn't show up to bail me out when Palmer had me; your whole life has led up to your replacing me and now that's collapsed, you have to start over with something new. Too bad, but you did it to yourself, by overreaching. See, I don't plan to step aside, never did. You're good, but not as an executive, only as Pre-

Fash boy; you're too petty. Look at how you turned down those pots of Richard Hnatt's. That was a dead giveaway, Barney. I'm sorry."

"Okay." Barney said finally. "Possibly you're right."

"Well, so you learned a lot about yourself. And you *can* start again, Fineburg Crescent-wise." Leo slapped him on the back. "Become a leader in your hovel; make it creative and productive or whatever hovels do. And you'll be a spy for Felix Blau; that's big-time."

Barney said, "I could have gone over to Eldritch."

"Yeah, but you didn't. Who cares what you *might* have done?"

"You think I did the right thing to volunteer for the service?"

Leo said quietly, "Fella, what the hell else could you do?"

There was no answer to that. And they both knew it.

"When the urge strikes you," Leo said, "to feel sorry for yourself, remember this. *Palmer Eldritch wants to kill me* . . . I'm a lot worse off than you."

"I guess so." It rang true, and he had one more intuition to accompany that.

His situation would become the same as Leo's the moment he initiated litigation against Palmer Eldritch.

He did not look forward to it.

That night he found himself on a UN transport sighted on the planet Mars as its destination. In the seat next to him sat a pretty, frightened but desperately calm dark-haired girl with features as sharply etched as those of a magazine model. Her name, she told him almost as soon as the ship had attained escape velocity—she was patently eager to break her tension by conversation with anyone, on any topic—was Anne Hawthorne. She could have avoided the draft, she declared a trifle wistfully, but she hadn't; she believed it to be her patriotic duty to accept the chilling UN greetings! summons.

"How would you have avoided it?" he asked, curious.

"A heart murmur," Anne said. "And an arrhythmia, paroxysmal tachycardia."

"How about premature contractions such as auricular, nodal, and ventricular, auricular tachycardia, auricular flutter, auricular fibrillation, not to mention night cramps?" Barney asked, having himself looked—without result—into the topic.

"I could have produced documents from hospitals and doctors and insurance companies testifying for me." She glanced him over, up and down, then, very interestedly, "It sounds as if you could have gotten out, Mr. Payerson."

"Mayerson. I volunteered, Miss Hawthorne." But I couldn't have gotten out, not for long, he said to himself.

"They're very religious in the colonies. So I hear, anyhow. What denomination are you, Mr. Mayerson?"

"Um," he said, stuck.

"I think you'd better find out before we get there. They'll ask you and expect you to attend services." She added, "It's primarily the use of that drug—you know. Can-D. It's brought about a lot of conversions to the established churches . . . although many of the colonists find in the drug itself a religious experience that's adequate for them. I have relatives on Mars; they write me so I know. I'm going to the Fineburg Crescent; where are you going?"

Up the creek, he thought. "The same," he said, aloud.

"Possibly you and I'll be in the same hovel," Anne Hawthorne said, with a thoughtful expression on her precisely cut face. "I belong to the Reformed Branch of the Neo-American Church, the New Christian Church of the United States and Canada. Actually our roots are very old: in A.D. 300 our forefathers had bishops that attended a conference in France; we didn't split off from the other churches as late as everyone thinks. So you can see we have Apostolic Succession." She smiled at him in a solemn, friendly fashion.

"Honest," Barney said. "I believe it. Whatever that is."

"There's a Neo-American mission church in the Fineburg Crescent and therefore a vicar, a priest; I expect to be able to take Holy Communion at least once a month. And confess twice a year, as we're supposed to, as I've been doing on Terra. Our church has many sacraments . . . have you taken either of the two Greater Sacraments, Mr. Mayerson?"

"Uh—" he hesitated.

"Christ specified that we observe two sacraments," Anne Hawthorne explained patiently. "Baptism—by water—and Holy Communion. The latter in memory of Him . . . it was inaugurated at the Last Supper."

"Oh. You mean the bread and the wine."

"You know how the eating of Can-D translates—as they call it—the partaker to another world. It's secular, however, in that it's temporary and only a physical world. The bread and the wine—"

"I'm sorry, Miss Hawthorne," Barney said, "but I'm afraid I can't believe in that, the body and blood business. It's too mystical for me." Too much based upon unproved premises, he said to himself. But she was right; sacral religion had, because of Can-D, become common in the colony moons and planets, and he would be encountering it, as Anne said.

"Are you going to try Can-D?" Anne asked.

"Sure."

Anne said, "You have faith in that. And yet you know that the Earth it takes you to isn't the real one."

"I don't want to argue it," he said. "It's experienced as real; that's all I know."

"So are dreams."

"But this is stronger," he pointed out. "Clearer. And it's done in—" He had started to say *communion.* "In company with others who really go along. So it can't be entirely an illusion. Dreams are private; that's the reason we identify them as illusion. But Perky Pat—"

"It would be interesting to know what the people who

make the Perky Pat layouts think about it all," Anne said reflectively.

"I can tell you. To them it's just a business. As probably the manufacture of sacramental wine and wafers is to those who—"

"If you're going to try Can-D," Anne said, "and put your faith for a new life into it, can I induce you to try baptism and confirmation into the Neo-American Christian Church? So you could see if your faith deserves to be put into that, too? Or the First Revised Christian Church of Europe which of course also observes the two Greater Sacraments. Once you've participated in Holy Communion—"

"I can't," he said. I believe in Can-D, he said to himself, and, if necessary, Chew-Z. You can put your faith in something twenty-one centuries old; I'll stick with something new. And that is that.

Anne said, "To be frank, Mr. Mayerson, I intend to try to convert as many colonists as possible away from Can-D to the traditional Christian practices; that's the central reason I declined to put together a case that would exempt me from the draft." She smiled at him, a lovely smile which, in spite of himself, warmed him. "Is that wrong? I'll tell you frankly: I think the use of Can-D indicates a genuine hunger on the part of these people to find a return to what we in the Neo-American Church—"

"I think," Barney said, gently, "you should let these people alone." And me, too, he thought. I've got enough troubles as it is; don't add your religious fanaticism and make it worse. But she did not look like his idea of a religious fanatic, nor did she talk like one. He was puzzled. Where had she gotten such strong, steady convictions? He could imagine it existing in the colonies, where the need was so great, but she had acquired it on Earth.

Therefore the existence of Can-D, the experience of group translation, did not fully explain it. Maybe, he thought, it's been the transition by gradual stages of Earth to the hell-like blasted wasteland which all of them could foresee—hell, experience!—that had done it; the hope of another life, on different terms, had been reawakened.

Myself, he thought, the individual I've been, Barney Mayerson of Earth, who worked for P. P. Layouts and lived in the renown conapt building with the unlikely low number 33, is dead. That person is finished, wiped out as if by a sponge.

Whether I like it or not I've been born again.

"Being a colonist on Mars," he said, "isn't going to be like living on Terra. Maybe when I get there—" He ceased; he had intended to say, Maybe I'll be more interested in your dogmatic church. But as yet he could not honestly say that, even as a conjecture; he rebelled from an idea that was still foreign to his makeup. And yet—

"Go ahead," Anne Hawthorne said. "Finish your sentence."

"Talk to me again," Barney said, "when I've lived down in the bottom of a hovel on an alien world for a while. When I've begun my new life, if you can call it a life, as a colonist." His tone was bitter; it surprised him, the ferocity . . . it bordered on being anguish, he realized with shame.

Anne said placidly, "All right. I'll be glad to."

After that the two of them sat in silence; Barney read a homeopape and, beside him, Anne Hawthorne, the fanatic girl missionary to Mars, read a book. He peered at the title, and saw that it was Eric Lederman's great text on colonial living, *Pilgrim without Progress*. God knew where she had gotten a copy; the UN had condemned it, made it incredibly difficult to obtain. And to read a copy of it here on a UN ship—it was a singular act of courage; he was impressed.

Glancing at her he realized that she was really overwhelmingly attractive to him, except that she was just a little too thin, wore no makeup, and had as much of her heavy dark hair as possible covered with a round, white, veil-like cap; she looked, he decided, as if she were dressed for a long

journey which would end in church. Anyhow he liked her
manner of speaking, her compassionate, modulated voice.
Would he run into her again on Mars?

It came to him that he hoped so. In fact—was this improper?—he hoped even to find himself participating with
her in the corporate act of taking Can-D.

Yes, he thought, it's improper because I know what I
intend, what the experience of translation with her would
signify to me.

He hoped it anyhow.

8

Extending his hand, Norm Schein said heartily, "Hi there, Mayerson; I'm the official greeter from our hovel. Welcome—ugh—to Mars."

"I'm Fran Schein," his wife said, also shaking hands with Barney Mayerson. "We have a very orderly, stable hovel here; I don't think you'll find it too dreadful." She added, half to herself, "Just dreadful enough." She smiled, but Mayerson did not smile back; he looked grim, tired, and depressed, as most new colonists did on arrival to a life which they knew was difficult and essentially meaningless. "Don't expect us to sell you on the virtues of this," she said. "That's the UN's job. We're nothing more than victims like yourself. Except that we've been here a while."

"Don't make it sound so bad," Norm said in warning.

"But it is," Fran said. "Mr. Mayerson is facing it; he isn't going to accept any pretty story. Right, Mr. Mayerson?"

"I could do with a little illusion at this point," Barney said as he seated himself on a metal bench within the hovel entrance. The sand-plow which had brought him, meanwhile, unloaded his gear; he watched dully.

"Sorry," Fran said.

"Okay to smoke?" Barney got out a package of Terran cigarettes; the Scheins stared at them fixedly and he then offered them each a chance at the pack, guiltily.

"You arrived at a difficult time," Norm Schein explained. "We're right in the middle of a debate." He glanced around at the others. "Since you're now a member of our hovel I don't see why you shouldn't be brought into it; after all it concerns you, too."

Tod Morris said, "Maybe he'll—you know. Tell."

"We can swear him to secrecy," Sam Regan said, and his wife Mary nodded. "Our discussion, Mr. Geyerson—"

"Mayerson," Barney corrected.

"—Has to do with the drug Can-D, which is the old reliable translating agent we've depended on, versus the newer, untried drug Chew-Z; we're debating whether to drop Can-D once and for all and—"

"Wait until we're below," Norm Schein said, and scowled.

Seating himself on the bench beside Barney Mayerson, Tod Morris said, "Can-D is kaput; it's too hard to get, costs too many skins, and personally I'm tired of Perky Pat—it's too artificial, too superficial, and materialistality in—pardon; that's our word here for—" He groped in difficult explanation. "Well, it's apartment, cars, sunbathing on the beach, ritzy clothes . . . we enjoyed it for a while, but it's not enough in some sort of *un*materialistality way. You see at all, Mayerson?"

Norm Schein said, "Okay, but Mayerson here hasn't had that; he isn't jaded. Maybe he'd appreciate going through all that."

"Like we did," Fran agreed. "Anyhow, we haven't voted; we haven't decided which we're going to buy and use from now on. I think we ought to let Mr. Mayerson try both. Or have you already tried Can-D, Mr. Mayerson?"

"I did," Barney said. "But a long time ago. Too long for me to remember clearly." Leo had given it to him, and offered him more, big amounts, all he wanted. But he had declined; it hadn't appealed to him.

Norm Schein said, "This is rather an unfortunate welcome to our hovel, I'm afraid, getting you embroiled in our controversy like this. But we've run out of Can-D; we either have to restock or switch: this is the critical moment. Of course the Can-D pusher, Impy White, is after us to reorder through her . . . by the end of tonight we'll have decided one way or another. And it will affect all of us . . . for the rest of our lives."

"So be glad you didn't arrive tomorrow," Fran said. "After the vote is taken." She smiled at him encouragingly, trying to make him feel welcome; they had little to offer him except their mutual bond, the fact of their relatedness one to another, and this was extended now to him.

What a place, Barney Mayerson was thinking to himself. *The rest of my life* . . . it seemed impossible, but what they said was true. There was no provision in the UN selective service law for mustering out. And the fact was not an easy one to face; these people were the body-corporate for him now, and yet—how much worse it could be. Two of their women seemed physically attractive and he could tell—or believed he could—that they were, so to speak, interested; he sensed the subtle interaction of the manifold complexities of the interpersonal relationships which built up in the cramped confines of a single hovel. But—

"The way out," Mary Regan said quietly to him, seating herself on the side of the bench opposite Tod Morris, "is through one or the other of the translating drugs, Mr. Mayerson. Otherwise, as you can see—" She put her hand on his shoulder; the physical touch was there already. "It would be impossible. We'd simply wind up killing one another in our pain."

"Yes," he said. "I see." But he had not learned that by coming to Mars; he had, like every other Terran, known that early in life, heard of colony life, the struggle against the lure of internecine termination to it all in one swift surrender.

No wonder induction was fought so rabidly, as had been the case with him originally. It was a fight to hold onto life.

"Tonight," Mary Regan said to him, "we'll procure one drug or the other; Impy will be stopping by about 7 P.M., Fineburg Crescent time; the answer will have to be in by then."

"I think we can vote now," Norm Schein said. "I can see that Mr. Mayerson, even though he's just arrived, is prepared. Am I right, Mayerson?"

"Yes," Barney said. The sand-dredge had completed its autonomic task; his possessions sat in a meager heap, and loose sand billowed across them already—if they were not taken below they would succumb to the dust, and soon. Hell, he thought; maybe it's just as well. Ties to the past . . .

The other hovelists gathered to assist him, passing his suitcases from hand to hand, to the conveyer belt that serviced the hovel below the surface. Even if he was not interested in preserving his former goods they were; they had a knowledge superior to his.

"You learn to get by from day to day," Sam Regan said sympathetically to him. "You never think in longer terms. Just until dinner or until time for bed; very finite intervals and tasks and pleasures. Escapes."

Tossing his cigarette away, Barney reached for the heaviest of his suitcases. "Thanks." It was profound advice.

"Excuse me," Sam Regan said with polite dignity and went to pick up the discarded cigarette for himself.

Seated in the hovel-chamber adequate to receive them all, the collective members, including new Barney Mayerson, prepared to solemnly vote. The time: six o'clock, Fineburg Crescent reckoning. The evening meal, shared as was customary, was over; the dishes now lay lathered and rinsed in the proper machine. No one, it appeared to Barney, had anything to do now; the weight of empty time hung over them all.

Examining the collection of votes, Norm Schein announced, "Four for Chew-Z. Three for Can-D. That's the decision, then. Okay, who wants the job of telling Impy White the bad news?" He peered around at each of them. "She's going to be sore; we better expect that."

Barney said, "I'll tell her."

Astonished, the three couples who comprised the hovel's inhabitants in addition to himself stared at him. "But you don't even know her," Fran Schein protested.

"I'll say it's my fault," Barney said. "That I tipped the balance here to Chew-Z." They would let him, he knew; it was an onerous task.

Half an hour later he lounged in the silent darkness at the lip of the hovel's entrance, smoking and listening to the unfamiliar sounds of the Martian night.

Far off some lunary object streaked the sky, passing between his sight and the stars. A moment later he heard retrojets. Soon, he knew; he waited, arms folded, more or less relaxed, practicing what he intended to say.

Presently a squat female figure dressed in heavy coveralls trudged into view. "Schein? Morris? Well, Regan, then?" She squinted at him, using an infrared lantern. "I don't know you." Warily, she halted. "I have a laser pistol." It manifested itself, pointed at him. "Speak up."

Barney said, "Let's move off out of earshot of the hovel."

With extreme caution Impatience White accompanied him, still pointing the laser pistol menacingly. She accepted his ident-pak, reading it by means of her lantern. "You were with Bulero," she said, glancing up at him appraisingly. "So?"

"So," he said, "we're switching to Chew-Z, we at Chicken Pox Prospects."

"*Why?*"

"Just accept it and don't push any farther here. You can check with Leo at P. P. Or through Conner Freeman on Venus."

"I will," Impatience said. "Chew-Z is garbage; it's habit-forming, toxic, and what's worse leads to lethal, escape-dreams, not of Terra but of—" She gestured with the pistol.

"Grotesque, baroque fantasies of an infantile, totally deranged nature. Explain to me why this decision."

He said nothing; he merely shrugged. It was interesting, however, the ideological devotion on her part; it amused him. In fact, he reflected, its fanaticism was in sharp contrast to the attitude which the girl missionary aboard the Terra-Mars ship had shown. Evidently subject matter had no bearing; he had never realized this before.

"I'll see you tomorrow night at this same time," Impatience White decided. "If you're being truthful, fine. But if you're not—"

"What if I'm not?" he said slowly, deliberately. "Can you force us to consume your product? After all, it is illegal; we could ask for UN protection."

"You're new." Her scorn was enormous. "The UN in this region is perfectly aware of the Can-D traffic; I pay a regular stipend to them, to avoid interference. As far as Chew-Z goes—" She gestured with her gun. "If the UN is going to protect them, and they're the coming thing—"

"Then you'll go over to them," Barney said.

She did not answer; instead she turned and strode off. Almost at once her short shape vanished into the Martian night; he remained where he was and then he made his way back to the hovel, orienting himself by the looming, opaque shape of a huge, apparently discarded tractor-type farm machine parked close by.

"Well?" Norm Schein, to his surprise, said, meeting him at the entrance. "I came up to see how many holes she had lasered in your cranium."

"She took it philosophically."

"Impy White?" Norm laughed sharply. "It's a million-skin business she runs—'philosophically' my ass. What really happened?"

Barney said, "She'll be back after she gets instructions from above." He began to descend into the hovel.

"Yeah, that makes sense; she's small-fry. Leo Bulero, on Terra—"

"I know." He saw no reason to conceal his previous career; in any case it was public record; the hovelists would run across the datum eventually. "I was Leo's Pre-Fash consultant for New York."

"And you voted to switch to Chew-Z?" Norm was incredulous. "You had a falling-out with Bulero, is that right?"

"I'll tell you sometime." He reached the bottom of the ramp and stepped out into the communal chamber where the others waited.

With relief Fran Schein said, "At least she didn't stew you with that little laser pistol she waves around. You must have outstared her."

"Are we rid of her?" Tod Morris asked.

"I'll have that news tomorrow night," Barney said.

Mary Regan said to him, "We think you're very brave. You're going to give this hovel a great deal, Mr. Mayerson. Barney, I mean. To mix a metaphor, a good swift goose to our morale."

"My, my," Helen Morris mocked. "Aren't we getting a little inelegant in our dithering attempt to impress the new citizen?"

Flushing, Mary Regan said, "I wasn't trying to impress him."

"Flatter him, then," Fran Schein said softly.

"You, too," Mary said with anger. "You were the first to fawn over him when he stepped off that ramp—or anyhow you wanted to; you would have, if we hadn't all been here. If your husband especially hadn't been here."

To change the subject, Norm Schein said, "Too bad we can't translate ourselves tonight, get out the good old Perky Pat layout one final time. Barney might enjoy it. He could at least see what he's voted to give up." Meaningfully, he gazed from one of them to the next, pinning each down. "Now come on . . . surely *one* of you has some Can-D you've held back, stuffed in a crack in the wall or under the septic tank for a rainy year. Aw, come on; be generous to the new citizen; show him you're not—"

"Okay," Helen Morris burst in, flushed with sullen resentment. "I have a little, enough for three-quarters of an hour. But that's absolutely all, and suppose that Chew-Z isn't ready for distribution in our area yet?"

"Get your Can-D," Norm said. As she departed he said, "And don't worry; *Chew-Z is here.* Today when I was picking up a sack of salt from that last UN drop I ran into one of their pushers. He gave me his card." He displayed the card. "All we need to do is light a common strontium nitrate flare at 7:30 P.M. and they'll be down from their satellite—"

"Satellite!" Everyone squawked in amazement. "Then," Fran said excitedly, "it must be UN-sanctioned. Or do they have a layout and the disc jockeys on the satellite advertise their new mins?"

"I don't know, yet," Norm admitted. "I mean, at this point there's a lot of confusion. Wait'll the dust settles."

"Here on Mars," Sam Regan said hollowly, "it'll never settle."

They sat in a circle. Before them the Perky Pat layout, complete and elaborate, beckoned; they all felt its pull, and Norm Schein reflected that this was a sentimental occasion because they would never be doing this again . . . unless, of course, they did it—made use of the layout—with Chew-Z. How would that work out? he wondered. Interesting . . .

He had a feeling, unaccountably, that it would not be the same.

And—they might not like the difference.

"You understand," Sam Regan said to the new member Barney Mayerson, "that we're going to spend the translated period listening to and watching Pat's new Great Books animator—you know, the device they've just brought out on Terra . . . you're surely more familiar with it than we are, Barney, so maybe you ought to explain it to us."

Barney, dutifully, said, "You insert one of the Great Books, for instance *Moby Dick,* into the reservoid. Then you set the controls for *long* or *short*. Then for *funny* version, or *same-as-book* or *sad* version. Then you set the style-indicator as to which classic Great Artist you want the book animated like. Dali, Bacon, Picasso . . . the medium-priced Great Books animator is set up to render in cartoon form the styles of a dozen system-famous artists; you specify which ones you want when you originally buy the thing. And there are options you can add later that provide even more."

"Terrific," Norm Schein said, radiating enthusiasm. "So what you get is a whole evening's entertainment, say *sad* version in the style of Jack Wright of like for instance *Vanity Fair*. Wow!"

Sighing, Fran said dreamily, "How it must have resounded in your soul, Barney, to have lived so recently on Terra. You seem to carry the vibrations with you still."

"Heck, we get it all," Norm said, "when we're translated." Impatiently he reached for the undersize supply of Can-D. "Let's start." Taking his own slice he chewed with vigor. "The Great Book I'm going to turn into a full-length *funny* cartoon version in the style of De Chirico will be—" He pondered. "Um, *The Meditations of Marcus Aurelius*."

"Very witty," Helen Morris said cuttingly. "I was going to suggest Augustine's *Confessions* in the style of Lichtenstein—*funny*, of course."

"I mean it! Imagine: the surrealistic perspective, deserted, ruined buildings with Doric columns lying on their sides, hollow heads—"

"Everybody else better get chewing," Fran advised, taking her slice, "so we'll be in synch."

Barney accepted his. The end of the old, he reflected as he chewed; I'm participating in what, for this particular hovel, is the final night, and in its place comes what? If Leo is right it will be intolerably worse, in fact no comparison. Of course, Leo is scarcely disinterested. But he is evolved. And wise.

Minned objects which in the past I judged favorably, he realized. I'll in a moment be immersed in a world composed of them, reduced to their dimension. And, unlike the other hovelists, I can compare my experience of this layout with what I so recently left behind.

And fairly soon, he realized soberly, I will be required to do the same with Chew-Z.

"You're going to discover it's an odd sensation," Norm Schein said to him, "to find yourself inhabiting a body with three other fellas; we all have to agree on what we want the body to do, or anyhow a dominant majority has to form, otherwise we're just plain stuck."

"That happens," Tod Morris said. "Half the time, in fact."

One by one the rest of them began to chew their slices of Can-D; Barney Mayerson was the last and most reluctant. Aw hell, he thought all at once, and strode across the room to a basin; there he spat out the half-chewed Can-D without having swallowed it.

The others, seated at the Perky Pat layout, had already collapsed into a coma and none of them now paid any attention to him. He was, for all intents and purposes, suddenly alone. The hovel for a time was his.

He wandered about, aware of the silence.

I just can't do it, he realized. Can't take the damn stuff like the rest of them do. At least not yet.

A bell sounded.

Someone was at the hovel entrance, requesting permission to enter; it was up to him to admit them. So he made his way in ascent, hoping he was doing the proper thing, hoping that it was not one of the UN's periodic raids; there would not be much he could do to keep them from discovering the other hovelists inert at their layout and, flagrante delicto, Can-D users.

Lantern in hand, at the ground-level entrance, stood a young woman wearing a bulky heat-retention suit and clearly unaccustomed to it; she looked enormously uncomfortable. "Hello, Mr. Mayerson," she said. "Remember me? I tracked you down because I'm just terribly lonely. May I come in?" It was Anne Hawthorne; surprised, he stared at her. "Or are you busy? I could come back another time." She half-turned, starting away.

"I can see," he said, "that Mars has been quite some shock to you."

"It's a sin on my part," Anne said, "but I already hate it; I really do—I know I should adopt a patient attitude of acceptance and all that, but—" She flashed the lantern at the landscape beyond the hovel and in a quavering, despairing voice said, "All I want to do now is find some way to get back to Earth; I don't want to convert anybody or change anything, I just want to get away from here." She added morosely, "But I know I can't. So I thought instead I'd visit you. See?"

Taking her by the hand he led her down the ramp and to the compartment which had been assigned to him as his living quarters.

"Where're your co-hovelists?" She looked about alertly.

"Out."

"Outside?" She opened the door to the communal room, and saw the lot of them slumped at the layout. "Oh, out that way. But not you." She shut the door, frowning, obviously perplexed. "You amaze me. I'd have gladly accepted some Can-D, tonight, the way I feel. Look how well you're standing up under it, compared with me. I'm so—inadequate."

Barney said, "Maybe I have more of a purpose here than you."

"I had plenty of purpose." She removed her bulky suit and seated herself as he began fixing coffee for the two of them. "The people in my hovel—it's half a mile to the north of this one—are out, too, the same way. Did you know I was so close? Would you have looked me up?"

"Sure I would have." He found plastic, insipidly styled cups and saucers, laid them on the foldaway table, and produced the equally foldaway chairs. "Maybe," he said, "God doesn't extend as far as Mars. Maybe when we left Terra—"

"Nonsense," Anne said sharply, rousing herself.

"I thought that would succeed in getting you angry."

"Of course it does. He's everywhere. Even here." She glanced at his partially unpacked possessions, the suitcases and sealed cartons. "You didn't bring very much, did you? Most of mine's still on the way, on an autonomic transport." Strolling over, she stood studying a pile of paperback books. *"De Imitatione Christi,"* she said in amazement. "You're reading Thomas à Kempis? This is a great and wonderful book."

"I bought it," he said, "but never read it."

"Did you try? I bet you didn't." She opened it at random and read to herself, her lips moving. " 'Think the least gift that he giveth is great; and the most despisable things take as special gifts and as great tokens of love.' That would include life here on Mars, wouldn't it? This despisable life, shut up in these—hovels. Well-named, aren't they? Why in the name of God—" She turned to him, appealing to him. "Couldn't it be a *finite* period here, and then we could go home?"

Barney said, "A colony, by definition, has to be permanent. Think of Roanoke Island."

"Yes." Anne nodded. "I have been. I wish Mars was one big Roanoke Island, with everyone going home."

"To be slowly cooked."

"We can evolve, as the rich do; it could be done on a mass basis." She put down the à Kempis book abruptly. "But I don't want that, either; a chitinous shell and the rest. Isn't there any answer, Mr. Mayerson? You know, Neo-Christians are taught to believe they're travelers in a foreign land. Wayfaring strangers. Now we really are; Earth is ceasing to become our natural world, and certainly *this* never will be. We've got no world left!" She stared at him, her nostrils flaring. "No home at all!"

"Well," he said uncomfortably, "there's always Can-D and Chew-Z."

"Do you have any?"

"No."

She nodded. "Back to Thomas à Kempis, then." But she did not pick the book up again; instead she stood head-down, lost in dreary meditation. "I know what's going to happen, Mr. Mayerson. Barney. I'm not going to convert anyone to Neo-American Christianity; instead they'll convert me to Can-D and Chew-Z and whatever other vice is current, here, whatever escape presents itself. Sex. They're terribly promiscuous here on Mars, you know; everyone goes to bed with everyone else. I'll even try that; in fact I'm ready for it right now—I just can't stand the way things are . . . did you get a really *good look* at the surface before nightfall?"

"Yes." It hadn't upset him that much, seeing the half-abandoned gardens and fully abandoned equipment, the great heaps of rotting supplies. He knew from edu-tapes that the frontier was always like that, even on Earth; Alaska had been like that until recent times and so, except for the actual resort towns, was Antarctica right now.

Anne Hawthorne said, "Those hovelists in the other room at their layout. Suppose we lifted Perky Pat entirely from the board and smashed it to bits? What would become of them?"

"They'd go on with their fantasy." It was established, now; the props were no longer necessary as foci. "Why would you want to do that?" It had a decided sadistic quality to it and he was surprised; the girl had not struck him that way at first meeting.

"Iconoclasm," Anne said. "I want to smash their idols and that's what Perky Pat and Walt are. I want to because I—" She was silent, then. "I envy them. It's not religious fervor; it's just a very mean, cruel streak. I know it. If I can't join them—"

"You can. You will. So will I. But not right away." He served her a cup of coffee; she accepted it reflexively, slender now without her heavy outer coat. She was, he saw, almost as tall as he; in heels she would be, if not taller. Her nose was odd. It ended in a near ball, not quite humorously but rather—earthy, he decided. As if it ties her to the soil; it made him think of Anglo-Saxon and Norman peasants tilling their square, small fields.

No wonder she hated it on Mars; historically her people undoubtedly had loved the authentic ground of Terra, the smell and actual texture, and above all the memory it contained, the remnants in transmuted form, of the host of critters who had walked about and then at last dropped dead, in the end perished and turned back—not to dust—but to rich humus. Well, she could start a garden here on Mars; maybe she could make one grow where previous hovelists had pointedly failed. How strange that she was so absolutely depressed. Was this normal for new arrivals? Somehow he himself did not feel it. Perhaps on some deep level he imagined he would find his way back to Terra. In which case it was he who was deranged. Not Anne.

Anne said suddenly, "I have some Can-D, Barney." She reached into the pockets of her UN-issue canvas work-slacks, groped, and brought a small packet out. "I bought it a little while ago, in my own hovel. Flax Back Spit, as they call it. The hovelist who sold it to me believed that Chew-Z would make it worthless so he gave me a good price. I tried to take it—I practically had it in my mouth. But finally like you I couldn't. Isn't a miserable reality better than the most interesting illusion? Or *is* it illusion, Barney? I don't know anything about philosophy; you explain it to me because all I know is religious faith and that doesn't equip me to understand this. These translation drugs." All at once she opened the packet; her fingers squirmed desperately. "I can't go on, Barney."

"Wait," he said, putting his own cup down and starting toward her. But it was too late; she had already taken the Can-D. "None for me?" he asked, a little amused. "You're missing the whole point; you won't have anyone to be with, in translation." Taking her by the arm he led her from the compartment, tugging her hurriedly out into the corridor and across into the large communal room where the others lay; seating her among them, he said, with compassion, "At least this way it'll be a shared experience and I understand that helps."

"Thank you," she said drowsily. Her eyes shut and her body became, by degrees, limp.

Now, he realized, she's Perky Pat. In a world without trouble.

Bending, he kissed her on the mouth.

"I'm still awake," she murmured.

"But you won't remember anyhow," he said.

"Oh yes I will," Anne Hawthorne said faintly. And then she departed; he felt her go. He was alone with seven un-inhabited physical shells and he at once made his way back to his own quarters where the two cups of hot coffee steamed.

I could fall in love with that girl, he said to himself. Not like Roni Fugate or even like Emily but something new. Better? he wondered. Or is this desperation? Exactly what I saw Anne do just now with the Can-D, gulp it down because there is nothing else, only darkness. It is this or the void. And not for a day or a week but—forever. So I've got to fall in love with her.

By himself he sat surrounded by his partly unpacked belongings, drinking coffee and meditating until at last he heard groanings and stirrings in the communal room. His fellow hovelists were returning to consciousness. He put his cup down and walked out to join them.

"Why'd you back out, Mayerson?" Norm Schein said; he rubbed his forehead, scowling. "God, what a headache I've got." He noticed Anne Hawthorne, then; still unconscious, she lay with her back against the wall, her head dropped forward. "Who's she?"

Fran, rising to her feet unsteadily, said, "She joined us at the end; she's a pal of Mayerson's: he met her on the flight. She's quite nice but she's a religious nut; you'll see." Critically, she eyed Anne. "Not too bad looking. I was really curious to see her; I imagined her as more, well, austere."

Coming up to Barney, Sam Regan said, "Get her to join you, Mayerson; we'd be glad to vote to admit her, here. We've got lots of room and you should have a—shall we say—wife." He, too, scrutinized Anne. "Yeah," he said. "Pretty. Nice long black hair; I like that."

"You do, do you," Mary Regan said tartly to him.

"Yeah I do; so what?" Sam Regan glared back at his wife.

Barney said, "She's spoken for."

They all eyed him curiously.

"That's odd," Helen Morris said. "Because when we were together with her just now she didn't tell us that, and as far as we could make out you and she had only—"

Interrupting, Fran Schein said to Barney, "You don't want a Neo-Christian nut to live with you. We've had experience with that; we ejected a couple of them last year. They can cause terrible trouble here on Mars. Remember, *we shared her mind* . . . she's a dedicated member of some high church or other, with all the sacraments and the rituals, all that old outdated junk; she actually believes in it."

Barney said tightly, "I know."

In an easy-going way Tod Morris said, "That's true, Mayerson; honest. We have to live too close together to import any kind of ideological fanaticism from Terra. It's happened at other hovels; we know what we're talking about. It has to be live and let live, with no absolutist creeds and dogma; a hovel is just too small." He lit a cigarette and glanced down at Anne Hawthorne. "Strange that a pretty girl would pick that stuff up. Well, it takes all kinds." He looked puzzled.

"Did she seem to enjoy being translated?" Barney asked Helen Morris.

"Yes, to a certain extent. Of course it upset her . . . the first time you have to expect that; she didn't know how to cooperate in handling the body. But she was quite eager to learn. Now obviously she's got it all to herself so it's easier on her. This is good practice."

Bending down, Barney Mayerson picked up the small doll, Perky Pat in her yellow shorts and red-striped cotton t-shirt and sandals. This now was Anne Hawthorne, he realized. In a sense that no one quite understood. And yet he could destroy the doll, crush it, and Anne, in her synthetic fantasy life, would be unaffected.

"I'd like to marry her," he said aloud, suddenly.

"Who?" Tod asked. "Perky Pat or the new girl?"

"He means Perky Pat," Norm Schein said, and snickered.

"No he doesn't," Helen said severely. "And I think it's fine; now we can be four couples instead of three couples and one man, one odd man."

"Is there any way," Barney said, "to get drunk around here?"

"Sure," Norm said. "We've got liquor—it's dull ersatz gin, but it's eighty proof; it'll do the job."

"Let me have some," Barney said, reaching for his wallet.

"It's free. The UN supply ships drop it in vats." Norm went to a locked cupboard, produced a key, and opened it.

Sam Regan said, "Tell us, Mayerson, why you feel the need to get drunk. Is it us? The hovel? Mars itself?"

"No." It was none of those; it had to do with Anne and the disintegration of her identity. Her use of Can-D all at once, a symptom of her inability to believe or to cope, her giving up. It was an omen, in which he, too, was involved; he saw himself in what had happened.

If he could help her perhaps he could help himself. And if not—

He had an intuition that otherwise they were both finished. Mars, for both himself and Anne, would mean death. And probably soon.

9

After she emerged from the experience of translation Anne Hawthorne was taciturn and moody. It was not a good sign; he guessed that she, too, now had a premonition similar to his. However, she said nothing about it; she merely went at once to get her bulky outer suit from his compartment.

"I have to get back to Flax Back Spit," she explained. "Thank you for letting me use your layout," she said to the hovelists who stood here and there, watching her as she dressed. "I'm sorry, Barney." She hung her head. "It was unkind to leave you the way I did."

He accompanied her, on foot, across the flat, nocturnal sands to her own hovel; neither of them spoke as they plodded along, keeping their eyes open, as they had been told to, for a local predator, a jackal-like telepathic Martian life form. However, they saw nothing.

"How was it?" he asked her at last.

"You mean being that little brassy blonde-haired doll with all her damn clothes and her boyfriend and her car and her—" Anne, beside him, shuddered. "Awful. Well, that's not it. Just—pointless. I found nothing there. It was like going back to my teens."

"Yeah," he agreed. There was that about Perky Pat.

"Barney," she said quietly, "I have to find something else and soon. Can you help me? You seem smart and grown-up and experienced. Being translated is not going to help me . . . Chew-Z won't be any better because something in me rebels, won't take it—see? Yes, you see; I can tell. Hell, you wouldn't even try it *once,* so you must understand." She squeezed his arm, and clung tightly to him in the darkness. "I know something else, Barney. *They're tired of it, too;* all they did was bicker while they—we—were inside those dolls. They didn't enjoy it for a second, even."

"Gosh," he said.

Flashing her lantern ahead, Anne said, "It's a shame; I wish they did. I feel sorrier for them than I do for—" She ceased, walked on for a time in silence, and then abruptly said, "I've changed, Barney. I feel it in myself. I want to sit down here—wherever we are. You and I alone in the dark. And then you know what . . . I don't have to say, do I?"

"No," he admitted. "But the thing is, you'd regret it afterward. I would, too, because of your reaction."

"Maybe I'll pray," Anne said. "Praying is hard to do; you have to know how. You don't pray for yourself; you pray what we call an intercessive prayer: for others. And what you pray to isn't the God Who's in the heavens out there somewhere . . . it's to the Holy Spirit within; that's different, that's the Paraclete. Did you ever real Paul?"

"Paul who?"

"In the New Testament. His letters to for instance the Corinthians or the Romans . . . you know. Paul says our enemy is death; it's the final enemy we overcome, so I guess it's the greatest. We're all blighted, according to Paul, not just our bodies but our souls, too; both have to die and then we can be born again, with new bodies not of flesh but incorruptible. See? You know, when I was Perky Pat, just now . . . I had the oddest feeling that I was—it's wrong to say this or believe it, but—"

"But," Barney finished for her, "it seemed like a taste of

that. But you expected it, though; you knew the resemblance—you mentioned it yourself, on the ship." A lot of people, he reflected, had noticed it, too.

"Yes," Anne admitted. "But what I didn't realize is—" In the darkness she turned toward him; he could just barely make her out. *"Being translated is the only hint we can have of it this side of death.* So it's a temptation. If it wasn't for that dreadful doll, that Perky Pat—"

"Chew-Z," Barney said.

"That's what I was thinking. If it was like that, like what Paul says about the corruptible man putting on incorruption—I couldn't stop myself, Barney; I'd have to chew Chew-Z. I wouldn't be able to wait until the end of my life . . . it might be fifty years living here on Mars—half a century!" She shuddered. "Why wait when I could have it *now?*"

"The last person I talked to," Barney said, "who had taken Chew-Z, said it was the worst experience of his life."

That startled her. "In what way?"

"He fell into the domain of someone or something he considered absolutely evil, someone he was terrified of. And he was lucky—and he knew it—to get away again."

"Barney," she said, "why are you on Mars? Don't say it's because of the draft; a person as smart as you could have gone to a psychiatrist—"

"I'm on Mars," he said, "because I made a mistake." In your terminology, he reflected, it would be called a sin. And in my terminology, too, he decided.

Anne said, "You hurt someone, didn't you?"

He shrugged.

"So now for the rest of your life you're here," Anne said. "Barney, can you get me a supply of Chew-Z?"

"Pretty soon." It would not be long before he ran into one of Palmer Eldritch's pushers; he was certain of that. Putting his hand on her shoulder he said, "But you can get it for yourself just as easily."

She leaned against him as they walked, and he hugged her; she did not resist—in fact she sighed with relief. "Barney, I have something to show you. A leaflet that one of the people in my hovel gave me; she said a whole bundle had been dropped the other day. It's from the Chew-Z people." Reaching into her bulky coat she rummaged about, then; in the glare of the lantern he saw the folded paper. "Read it. You'll understand why I feel as I do about Chew-Z . . . why it's such a spiritual problem for me."

Holding the paper to the light he read the top line; it blazed out in huge black letters.

GOD PROMISES ETERNAL LIFE. WE CAN DELIVER IT.

"See?" Anne said.

"I see." He did not even bother to read the rest; folding the paper back up he returned it to her, feeling heavy-hearted. "Quite a slogan."

"A true one."

"Not the big lie," Barney said, "but instead the big truth." Which, he wondered, is worse? Hard to tell. Ideally, Palmer Eldritch would drop dead for the *blasphemia* shouted by the pamphlet, but evidently that was not going to occur. An evil visitor oozing over us from the Prox system, he said to himself, offering us what we've prayed for over a period of two thousand years. And why is this so palpably bad? Hard to say, but nevertheless it is. Because maybe it'll mean bondage to Eldritch, such as Leo experienced; Eldritch will be with us constantly from now on, infiltrating our lives. And He who has protected us in the past simply sits passive.

Each time we're translated, he thought, we'll see—not God—but Palmer Eldritch.

Aloud he said, "If Chew-Z fails you—"

"Don't say that."

"If Palmer Eldritch fails you, then maybe—" He stopped. Because ahead of them lay the hovel Flax Back Spit; its entrance light glowed dimly in the Martian gloom. "You're home." He did not like to let her go; his hand on her shoulder, he clung to her, thinking back to what he had said to his fellow hovelists about her. "Come back with me," he said. "To Chicken Pox Prospects. We'll get formally, legally married."

She stared at him and then—incredibly—she began to laugh.

"Does that mean no?" he asked, woodenly.

"What," Anne said, "is 'Chicken Pox Prospects'? Oh, I see; that's the code name of your hovel. I'm sorry, Barney; I didn't mean to laugh. But the answer of course is no." She moved away from him, and opened the outer door of the hovel's entrance-chamber. And then she set down her lantern and stepped toward him, arms held out. "Make love to me," she said.

"Not here. Too close to the entrance." He was afraid.

"Wherever you want. Take me there." She put her arms around his neck. "Now," she said. "Don't wait."

He didn't.

Picking her up in his arms, he carried her away from the entrance.

"Golly," she said, when he laid her down in the darkness; she gasped, presently, perhaps from the sudden cold that spilled over them, penetrating their heavy suits which no longer served, which in fact were a hindrance to true warmth.

One of the laws of thermal dynamics, he thought. The exchange of heat; molecules passing between us, hers and mine mingling in—entropy? Not yet, he thought.

"Oh my," she said, in the darkness.

"I hurt you?"

"No. I'm sorry. Please."

The cold numbed his back, his ears; it radiated down from the sky. He ignored it as best he could, but he thought of a blanket, a thick wool layer—strange, to be preoccupied with that at such a time. He dreamed of its softness, the scratch of its fibers against his skin, its heaviness. Instead of the brittle, frigid, thin air which made him pant in huge gulps, as if finished.

"Are—you dying?" she asked.

"Just can't breathe. This air."

"Poor, poor—good lord. I've forgotten your name."

"Hell of a thing."

"Barney!"

He clutched her.

"No! Don't stop!" She arched her back. Her teeth chattered.

"I wasn't going to," he said.

"Oooaugh!"

He laughed.

"Don't please laugh at me."

"Not meant unkindly."

A long silence, then. Then, "Oof." She leaped, galvanized as if lost to the shock of a formal experiment. His pale, dignified, unclothed possession: become a tall and very thin greenless nervous system of a frog; probed to life by outside means. Victim of a current not her own but not protested, in any way. Lucid and real, accepting. Ready this long time.

"You all right?"

"Yes," she said. "Yes Barney. I certainly very much am. Yes!"

Later as he tramped back alone, leadenly, in the direction of his own hovel he said to himself, Maybe I'm doing Palmer Eldritch's work. Breaking her down, demoralizing her . . . as if she weren't already. As if we all weren't.

Something blocked his way.

Halting, he located in his coat the side arm which had been provided him; there were, especially at night, in addition to the fearsome telepathic jackal, vicious domestic organisms that stung and ate—he flashed his light warily, expecting some bizarre multi-armed contraption composed perhaps of slime. Instead he saw a parked ship, the small, swift type with slight mass; its tubes still smoked, so evidently it had just now landed. Must have coasted down, he realized, since he hadn't heard any retro noise.

From the ship a man crept, shook himself, snapped on his own lantern, made out Barney Mayerson, and grunted. "I'm Allen Faine. I've been looking all over for you; Leo wants to keep in touch with you through me. I'll be telecasting in code to you at your hovel; here's your code book." Faine held out a slender volume. "You know who I am, don't you?"

"The disc jockey." Weird, this meeting here on the open Martian desert at night between himself and this man from the P. P. Layouts satellite; it seemed unreal. "Thanks," he said, accepting the code book. "What do I do, write it down as you say it and then sneak off to decode it?"

"There'll be a private TV receiver in your compartment in the hovel; we've arranged for it on the grounds that being new to Mars you crave—"

"Okay," Barney said, nodding.

"So you have a girl already," Faine said. "Pardon my use of the infrared searchlight, but—"

"I don't pardon it."

"You'll find that there's little privacy on Mars in matters of that nature. It's like a small town and all the hovelists are starved for news, especially any kind of scandal. I ought to know; it's my job to keep in touch and pass on what I can— naturally there's a lot I can't. Who's the girl?"

"I don't know," Barney said sardonically. "It was dark; I couldn't see." He started on, then, going around the parked ship.

"Wait. You're supposed to know this: a Chew-Z pusher is already operating in the area and we calculate that he'll be approaching your particular hovel as early as tomorrow morning. So be ready. Make sure you buy the bindle in front of witnesses; they should see the entire transaction and then when you chew it make sure they can clearly identify what you're consuming. Got it?" Faine added, "And try to draw the pusher out, get him to give as complete a warranty, verbally of course, as you possibly can. Make him sell you on the product; don't *ask* for it. See?"

Barney said, "And what do I get for doing this?"

"Pardon?"

"Leo never at any time bothered to—"

"I'll tell you what," Faine said quietly. "We'll get you off Mars. That's your payment."

After a time Barney said, "You mean it?"

"It'll be illegal, of course. Only the UN can legally route you back to Terra and that's not going to happen. What we'll do is pick you up some night and transfer you to Winnie-ther-Pooh Acres."

"And there I'll stay."

"Until Leo's surgeons can give you a new face, finger- and footprints, cephalic wave pattern, a new identity throughout; then you'll emerge, probably at your old job for P. P. Layouts. I understand you were their New York man. Two, two and a half years from now, you'll be at that again. So don't give up hope."

Barney said, "Maybe I don't want that."

"What? Sure you do. Every colonist wants—"

"I'll think it over," Barney said, "and let you know. But maybe I'll want something else." He was thinking about Anne. To go back to Terra and pick up once again, perhaps even with Roni Fugate—at some deep, instinctive stratum it did not have the appeal to him that he would have expected. Mars—or the experience of love with Anne Hawthorne—had even further altered him, now; he wondered which it was. Both. And anyhow, he thought, I asked to come here—I wasn't really drafted. And I must never let myself forget that.

Allen Faine said, "I know some of the circumstances, Mayerson. What you're doing is atoning. Correct?"

Surprised, Barney said, "You, too?" Religious inclinations seemed to permeate the entire milieu, here.

"You may object to the word," Faine said, "but it's the proper one. Listen, Mayerson; by the time we get you to

Winnie-ther-Pooh Acres you'll have atoned sufficiently. There's something you don't know yet. Look at this." He held out, reluctantly, a small plastic tube. A container.

Chilled, Barney said. "What's this?"

"Your illness. Leo believes, on professional advice, that it's not enough for you merely to state in court that you've been damaged; they'll insist on thoroughly examining you."

"Tell me specifically what it is in this thing."

"It's epilepsy, Mayerson. The Q form, the strain whose causes no one is sure of, whether it's due to organic injury that can't be detected with the EEG or whether it's psychogenic."

"And the symptoms?"

Faine said, "Grand mal." After a pause he said, "Sorry."

"I see," Barney said. "And how long will I have them?"

"We can administer the antidote after the litigation but not before. A year at the most. So now you can see what I meant when I said that you're going to be in a position to more than atone for not bailing out Leo when he needed it. You can see how this illness, claimed as a side-effect of Chew-Z, will—"

"Sure," Barney said. "Epilepsy is one of the great scarewords. Like cancer, once. People are irrationally afraid of it because they know it can happen to them, any time, with no warning."

"Especially the more recent Q form. Hell, they don't even have a theory about it. What's important is that with the Q form no organic alteration of the brain is involved, and that means we can restore you. The tube, there. It's a metabolic toxin similar in action to metrazol; similar, but unlike metrazol it continues to produce the attacks—with the characteristically deranged EEG pattern during those intervals—until it's neutralized—which as I say we're prepared to do."

"Won't a blood-fraction test show the presence of this toxin?"

"It will show the presence of *a* toxin, and that's exactly what we want. Because we will sequester the documents pertaining to the physical and mental induction exams which you recently took . . . and we'll be able to prove that when you arrived on Mars there was no Q-type epilepsy and no toxicity. And it'll be Leo's—or rather your—contention that the toxicity in the blood is a derivative of Chew-Z."

Barney said, "Even if I lose the suit—"

"It will still greatly damage Chew-Z sales. Most colonists have a nagging feeling anyhow that the translation drugs are in the long run biochemically harmful." Faine added, "The toxin in that tube is relatively rare. Leo obtained it through highly specialized channels. It originates on Io, I believe. One certain doctor—"

"Willy Denkmal," Barney said.

Faine shrugged. "Possibly. In any case there it is in your hand; as soon as you've been exposed to Chew-Z you're to take it. Try to have your first grand mal attack where your fellow hovelists will see you; don't be off somewhere on the desert farming or bossing autonomic dredges. As soon as you've recovered from the attack, get on the vidphone and ask the UN for medical assistance. Have their disinterested doctors examine you; don't apply for private medication."

"It would probably be a good idea," Barney said, "if the UN doctors could run an EEG on me during an attack."

"Absolutely. So try if possible to get yourself into a UN hospital; in all there're three on Mars. You'll be able to put forward a good argument for this because—" Faine hesitated. "Frankly, with this toxin your attacks will involve severe destructiveness, toward yourself and to others. Technically they'll be of the hysterical, aggressive variety concluding in a more or less complete loss of consciousness. It'll be obvious what it is right from the start, because—or so I'm told—you'll reveal the typical tonic stage, with great muscular contractions, and then the clonic stage of rhythmic contraction alternating with relaxation. After which of course the coma supervenes."

"In other words," Barney said, "the classic convulsive form."

"Does it frighten you?"

"I don't see where that matters. I owe Leo something; you and I and Leo know that. I still resent the word 'atonement,' but I suppose this is that." He wondered how this artificially induced illness would affect his relationship with Anne. Probably this would terminate the thing. So he was giving up a good deal for Leo Bulero. But then Leo was doing something for him, too; getting him off Mars was no minor consideration.

"We're taking it for granted," Faine said, "that they'll make an attempt to kill you the moment you retain an attorney. In fact they'll—"

"I'd like to go back to my hovel, now." He moved off. "Okay?"

"Fine. Go pick up the routine there. But let me give you a word of advice as regards that girl. Doberman's Law—remember, he was the first person to marry and then get divorced on Mars?—states that in proportion to your emotional attachment to someone on this damn place the relationship deteriorates. I'd give you two weeks at the most, and not because you'll be ill but because that's standard. Martian musical chairs. And the UN encourages it because it means, frankly, if I may say so, more children to populate the colony. Catch?"

"The UN," Barney said, "might not sanction my relationship with her because it's on a somewhat different basis than you're describing."

"No it's not," Faine said calmly. "It may seem so to you, but I watch the whole planet, day in, night out. I'm just stating a fact; I'm not being critical. In fact I'm personally sympathetic."

"Thanks," Barney said, and walked away, flashing his light ahead of him in the direction of his hovel; tied about his throat the small bleeper signal which told him when he was nearing—and more important when he was *not* nearing—his hovel began to sound louder: a one-frog pond of comfort close to his ear.

I'll take the toxin, he said to himself. And I'll go into court and sue the bastards for Leo's sake. Because I owe that to him. But I'm not returning to Earth; either I make it here or not at all. With Anne Hawthorne, I hope, but if not, then alone or with someone else; I'll live out Doberman's Law, as Faine predicts. Anyhow it'll be here on this miserable planet, this "promised land."

Tomorrow morning, he decided, I'll begin clearing away the sand of fifty thousand centuries for my first vegetable garden. That's the initial step.

10

Next day both Norm Schein and Tod Morris spent the early hours with him, teaching him the knack of operating the bulldozers and dredges and scoops which had fallen into various stages of ruin; most of the equipment, like old tomcats, could be coaxed into one more effort. But the results did not amount to much; they had been discarded for too long.

By noon he was exhausted. So he treated himself to a break, resting in the shade of a mammoth, rusty tractor, eating a cold-rations lunch and drinking tepid tea from a thermos which Fran Schein had been kind enough to bring up to him.

Below, in the hovel, the others did whatever it was they customarily did; he didn't care.

On all sides of him their abandoned, decaying gardens could be seen and he wondered if soon he would forget his, too. Maybe each new colonist had started out this way, in an agony of effort. And then the torpor, the hopelessness, claimed them. And yet, was it so hopeless? Not really.

It's an attitude, he decided. And we—all of us who comprised P. P. Layouts—contributed willingly to it. We gave them an out, something painless and easy. And now Palmer Eldritch has arrived to put the finish on the process. We laid the path for him, myself included, and so what now? Is there any way that I can, as Faine put it, atone?

Approaching him, Helen Morris called cheerfully, "How's the farming coming?" She dropped down beside him and opened a fat seed catalog with the UN stamp plainly marked throughout. "Observe what they'll provide *free;* every seed known to thrive here, including turnips." Resting against him, she turned the pages. "However, there's a little mouse-like burrowing mammal that shows up on the surface late at night; be prepared for that. It eats everything. You'll have to set out a few self-propelling traps."

"Okay," Barney said.

"It's quite some sight, one of those homeostatic traps taking off across the sand in pursuit of a marsle-mouse. God, they go fast. Both the mouse and the trap. You can make it more interesting by placing a bet. I usually bet on the trap. I admire them."

"I think I'd probably bet on the trap, too." I've got a great respect for traps, he reflected. In other words a situation in which none of the doors lead out. No matter how they happen to be marked.

Helen said, "Also the UN will supply two robots free of charge for your use. For a period not to exceed six months. So better plan ahead wisely as to how you want to employ them. The best is to set them to work constructing irrigation ditches. Ours is mostly no good now. Sometimes the ditches have to run two hundred miles, even more. Or you can hatch out a deal—"

"No deals," Barney said.

"But these are *good* deals; find someone nearby in one of the other hovels who's started his own irrigation system and then abandoned it: buy it from him and tap it. Is your girl at Flax Back Spit going to come over here and join you?" She eyed him.

He did not answer; he watched, in the black Martian sky with its noontime stars, a circling ship. The Chew-Z man? The time, then, had come for him to poison himself so that an economic monopoly could be kept alive, a sprawling, interplan empire from which he now derived nothing.

Amazing, he thought, how strong the self-destructive drive can be.

Helen Morris, straining to see, said, "Visitors! It's not a UN ship, either." She started toward the hovel at once. "I'll go tell them."

With his left hand he reached into his coat and touched the tube deep in the interior pocket, thinking to himself, Can I actually do this? It didn't seem possible; there was nothing in his makeup historically which would explain it. Maybe, he thought, it's from despair at having lost everything. But he didn't think so; it was something else.

As the ship landed on the flat desert not far off he thought, Maybe it's to reveal something to Anne about Chew-Z. Even if the demonstration is faked. Because, he thought, if I accept the toxin into my system *she won't try Chew-Z*. He had a strong intuition of that. And it was enough.

From the ship stepped Palmer Eldritch.

No one could fail to identify him; since his crash on Pluto the homeopapes had printed one pic after another. Of course the pics were ten years out of date, but this was still the man. Gray and bony, well over six feet tall, with swinging arms and a peculiarly rapid gait. And his face. It had a ravaged quality, eaten away; as if, Barney conjectured, the fat-layer had been consumed, as if Eldritch at some time or other had fed off himself, devoured perhaps with gusto the superfluous portions of his own body. He had enormous steel teeth, these having been installed prior to his trip to Prox by Czech dental surgeons; they were welded to his jaws, were permanent: he would die with them. And—his right arm was artificial. Twenty years ago in a hunting accident on Callisto he had lost the original; this one of course was superior in that it provided a specialized variety of interchangeable hands. At the moment Eldritch made use of the five-finger humanoid manual extremity; except for its metallic shine it might have been organic.

And he was blind. At least from the standpoint of the natural-born body. But replacements had been made—at the prices which Eldritch could and would pay; that had been done just prior to his Prox voyage by Brazilian oculists. They had done a superb job. The replacements, fitted into the bone sockets, had no pupils, nor did any ball move by muscular action. Instead a panoramic vision was supplied by a wide-angle lens, a permanent horizontal slot running from edge to edge. The accident to his original eyes had been no accident; it had occurred in Chicago, a deliberate acid-throwing attack by persons unknown, for equally unknown reasons . . . at least as far as the public was concerned. Eldritch probably knew. He had, however, said nothing, filed no complaint; instead he had gone straight to his team of Brazilian oculists. His horizontally slotted artificial eyes seemed to please him; almost at once he had appeared at the dedication ceremonies of the new St. George opera house in Utah, and had mixed with his near-peers without embarrassment. Even now, a decade later, the operation was rare and it was the first time Barney had ever seen the Jensen wide-angle, luxvid eyes; this, and the artificial arm with its enormously variable manual repertory, impressed him more than he would have expected . . . or was there something else about Eldritch?

"Mr. Mayerson," Palmer Eldritch said, and smiled; the steel teeth glinted in the weak, cold Martian sunlight. He extended his hand and automatically Barney did the same.

Your voice, Barney thought. It originates somewhere other than—he blinked. The entire figure was insubstantial; dimly, through it, the landscape showed. It was a figment of some sort, artifically produced, and the irony came to him: so much of the man was artificial already, and now even the flesh and blood portions were, too. Is this what arrived home from Prox? Barney wondered. If so, Hepburn-Gilbert has been deceived; this is no human being. In no sense whatsoever.

"I'm still in the ship," Palmer Eldritch said; his voice boomed from a loudspeaker mounted on the ship's hull. "A precaution, in as much as you're an employee of Leo Bulero." The figment-hand touched Barney's; he experienced a pervasive coldness slop over to him, obviously a purely psychological aversion-reaction since nothing was there to produce the sensation.

"An ex-employee," Barney said.

Behind him, now, the others of the hovel emerged, the Scheins and Morrises and Regans; they approached like wary children as one by one they identified the nebulous man confronting Barney.

"What's going on?" Norm Schein said uneasily. "This is a simulacrum; I don't like it." Standing beside Barney he said, "We're living on the desert, Mayerson; we get mirages all the time, ships and visitors and unnatural life forms. That's what this is; this guy isn't really here and neither is that ship parked there."

Tod Morris added, "They're probably six hundred miles away; it's an optical phenomenon. You get used to it."

"But you can hear me," Palmer Eldritch pointed out; the speaker boomed and echoed. "I'm here, all right, to do business with you. Who's your hovel team-captain?"

"I am," Norm Schein said.

"My card." Eldritch held out a small white card and reflexively Norm Schein reached for it. The card fluttered through his fingers and came to rest on the sand. At that Eldritch smiled. It was a cold, hollow smile, an implosion, as if it had drawn back into the man everything nearby, even the thin air itself. "Look down at it," Eldritch suggested. Norm Schein bent, and studied the card. "That's right," Eldritch said. "I'm here to sign a contract with your group. To deliver to you—"

"Spare us the speech about your delivering what God only promises," Norm Schein said. "Just tell us the price."

"About one-tenth that of the competitor's product. And much more effective; you don't even require a layout." Eldritch seemed to be talking directly to Barney; his gaze, however, could not be plotted because of the structure of the lens apertures. "Are you enjoying it here on Mars, Mr. Mayerson?"

"It's great fun," Barney said.

Eldritch said, "Last night when Allen Faine descended from his dull little satellite to meet with you . . . what did you discuss?"

Rigidly, Barney said, "Business." He thought quickly, but not quite quickly enough; the next question was already blaring from the speaker.

"So you do still work for Leo. In fact it was deliberately arranged to send you here to Mars in advance of our first distribution of Chew-Z. Why? Have you some idea of blocking it? There was no propaganda in your luggage, no leaflets or other printed matter beyond ordinary books. A rumor, perhaps. Word of mouth. Chew-Z is—what, Mr. Mayerson? Dangerous to the habitual user?"

"I don't know. I'm waiting to try some of it. And see."

"We're all waiting," Fran Schein said; she carried in her arms a load of truffle skins, clearly for immediate payment. "Can you make a delivery right now, or do we have to keep on waiting?"

"I can deliver your first allocation," Eldritch said.

A port of the ship snapped open. From it popped a small jet-tractor; it sped toward them. A yard away it halted and ejected a carton wrapped in familiar plain brown paper; the carton lay at their feet and then at last Norm Schein bent and picked it up. *It* was not a phantasm. Cautiously Norm tore the wrappings off.

"Chew-Z," Mary Regan said breathlessly. "Oh, what a lot! How much, Mr. Eldritch?"

"In toto," Eldritch said, "five skins." The tractor extended a small drawer, then, precisely the size to receive the skins.

After an interval of haggling the hovelists came to an arrangement; the five skins were deposited in the drawer—at once it was withdrawn and the tractor swiveled and zipped back to the mother ship. Palmer Eldritch, insubstantial and gray and large, remained. He appeared to be enjoying himself, Barney decided. It did not bother him to know that Leo Bulero had something up his sleeve; Eldritch thrived on this.

The realization depressed him and he walked, alone, to the meager cleared place which was eventually to be his garden. His back to the hovelists and Eldritch, he activated an autonomic unit; it began to wheeze and hum; sand disappeared into it as it sucked noisily, having difficulty. He wondered how long it would continue functioning. And what one did here on Mars to obtain repairs. Perhaps one gave up; maybe there were no repairs.

From behind Barney, Palmer Eldritch's voice came. "Now, Mr. Mayerson, you can begin to chew away for the rest of your life."

He turned, involuntarily, because this was not a phantasm; the man had finally come forth. "That's right," he said. "And nothing could delight me more." He continued, then, tinkering with the autonomic scoop. "Where do you go to get equipment fixed on Mars?" he asked Eldritch. "Does the UN take care of that?"

Eldritch said, "How would I know?"

A portion of the autonomic scoop broke loose in Barney's hands; he held it, weighed it. The piece, shaped like a tire iron, was heavy and he thought, I could kill him with this. Right here, in this spot. Wouldn't that solve it? No toxin to produce grand mal seizures, no litigation . . . but there'd be retaliation from them. I'd outlive Eldritch by only a few hours.

But—isn't it still worth it?

He turned. And then it happened so swiftly that he had no valid concept of it, not even an accurate perception. From the parked ship a laser beam reached forth and he felt the intense impact as it touched the metal section in his hands. At the same time Palmer Eldritch danced back, lithely, bounding upward in the slight Martian gravity; like a balloon—Barney stared but did not believe—he floated off, grinning with his huge steel teeth, waggling his artificial arm, his lank body slowly rotating. Then, as if reeled in by a transparent line, he progressed in a jerky sine-wave motion toward the ship. All at once he was gone. The nose of the ship clamped shut after him; Eldritch was inside. Safe.

"Why'd he do that?" Norm Schein said, eaten with curiosity, where he and the other hovelists stood. "What in God's name went on, there?"

Barney said nothing; shakily he set the remains of the metal piece down. They were ashlike remnants only, brittle and dry; they crumbled away as they touched the ground.

"They got into a hassle," Tod Morris said. "Mayerson and Eldritch; they didn't hit it off, not one bit."

"Anyhow," Norm said, "we got the Chew-Z. Mayerson, you better stay away from Eldritch in the future; let me handle the transaction. If I had known that because you were an employee of Leo Bulero—"

"Former," Barney said reflexively, and resumed his tinkering with the defective autonomic scoop. He had failed in his first try at killing Palmer Eldritch. Would he ever have a chance again?

Had he really had a chance just now?

The answer to both, he decided was no.

Late that afternoon the hovelists of Chicken Pox Prospects gathered to chew. The mood was one of tension and solemnity; scarcely anything was said as the bindles of Chew-Z, one by one, were unwrapped and passed around.

"Ugh," Fran Schein said, making a face. "It tastes *awful.*"

"Taste, schmaste," Norm said impatiently. He chewed, then. "Like a decayed mushroom; you sure are right." Stoically, he swallowed, and continued chewing. "Gak," he said, and retched.

"To be doing this without a layout—" Helen Morris said. "Where will we go, just anywhere? I'm scared," she said all at once. "Will we be together? Are you positive of that, Norm?"

"Who cares," Sam Regan said, chewing.

"Watch me," Barney Mayerson said.

They glanced at him with curiosity; something in his tone made them do as he said.

"I put the Chew-Z in my mouth," Barney said, and did so. "You see me doing it. Right?" He chewed. "Now I'm chewing it." His heart labored. God, he thought. Can I go through with this?"

"Yeah, we see you," Tod Morris agreed, nodding. "So what? I mean, are you going to blow up or float off like Eldritch or something?" He, too, began on his bindle, then. They were all chewing, all seven of them, Barney realized. He shut his eyes.

The next he knew, his wife was bending over him.

"I said," she said, "do you want a second Manhattan or not? Because if you do I have to request the refrig for more cracked ice."

"Emily," he said.

"Yes, dear," she said tartly. "Whenever you say my name like that I know you're about to launch in on one of your lectures. What is it this time?" She seated herself on the arm of the couch opposite him, smoothing her skirt; it was the striking blue-and-white hand-printed Mexican wraparound that he had gotten her at Christmas. "I'm ready," she said.

"No—lecture," he said. Am I really that way? he asked himself. Always delivering tirades? Groggily, he rose to his feet; he felt dizzy and he steadied himself by holding onto the nearby pole lamp.

Eying him, Emily said, "You're blammed."

Blammed. He hadn't heard that term since college; it was long out of style, and naturally Emily still used it. "The word," he said as distinctly as possible, "is now fnugled. Can you remember that? Fnugled." He walked unsteadily to the sideboard in the kitchen where the liquor was.

"Fnugled," Emily said and sighed. She looked sad; he noticed that and wondered why. "Barney," she said, then, "don't drink so much, okay? Call it blammed or fnugled or anything you want, it's still the same. I guess it's my fault; you drink so much because I'm so inadequate." She wiped briefly with her knuckle at her right eye, an annoying, familiar, ticlike motion.

"It's not that you're so inadequate," he said. "It's just that I have high standards." I was taught to expect a lot from others, he said to himself. To expect they'd be as reputable and stable as I am, and not sloppily emotional all the time, not in control of themselves.

But an artist, he realized. Or rather so-called artist. Bohemian. That's closer to it. The artistic life without the talent. He began fixing himself a fresh drink, this one bourbon and water, without ice; he poured directly from the bottle of Old Crow, ignoring the shot glass.

"When you pour that way," Emily said, "I know you're angry and we're in for it. And I just hate it."

"So then leave," he said.

"Goddam you," Emily said. "I don't *want* to leave! Couldn't you just—" She gestured with hopeless futility. "Be a little nicer, more charitable or something? Learn to overlook . . ." Her voice sank, almost inaudibly she said, "My shortcomings."

"But," he said, "they can't be overlooked. I'd like to. You think I want to live with someone who can't finish anything they start or accomplish anything socially? For instance when—aw, the hell with it." What was the use? Emily couldn't be reformed; she was purely and simply a slob. Her idea of a well-spent day was to wallow and putter and fool with a mess of greasy, excretionlike paints or bury her arms for hours on end in a great crock of wet gray clay. And meanwhile—

Time was escaping from them. And all the world, including all of Mr. Bulero's employees, especially his Pre-Fash consultants, grew and augmented themselves, bloomed into maturity. I'll never be the New York Pre-Fash consultant, he said to himself. I'll always be stuck here in Detroit where *nothing,* absolutely nothing new originates.

If he could snare the position of New York Pre-Fash consultant—my life would mean something, he realized. I'd be happy because I'd be doing a job that made full use of my ability. What the hell else would I need? Nothing else; *that's all I ask.*

"I'm going out," he said to Emily and set down his glass; going to the closet, he got his coat.

"Will you be back before I go to bed?" Mournfully, she followed him to the door of the conapt, here in building 11139584—counting outward from downtown New York—where they had lived two years, now.

"We'll see," he said, and opened the door.

In the hallway stood a figure, a tall gray man with bulging steel teeth, dead pupilless eyes, and a gleaming artificial hand extended from his right sleeve. The man said, "Hello, Mayerson." He smiled; the steel teeth shone.

"Palmer Eldritch," Barney said. He turned to Emily. "You've seen his pics in the homeopapes; he's that incredibly famous big industrialist." Naturally he had recognized Eldritch, and at once. "Did you want to see me?" he asked hesitantly; it all had a mysterious quality to it, as if it had all somehow happened before but in another way.

"Let me talk to your husband a moment," Eldritch said to Emily in a peculiarly gentle voice; he motioned and Barney stepped out into the hall. The door shut behind him; Emily had closed it obediently. Now Eldritch seemed grim; no longer gentle or smiling he said, "Mayerson, you're using your time badly. You're doing nothing but repeating the past. What's the use of my selling you Chew-Z? You're perverse; I've never seen anything like it. I'll give you ten more minutes and then I'm bringing you back to Chicken Pox Prospects where you belong. So you better figure out very damn fast what you want and if you understand anything finally."

"What the hell," Barney said, "is Chew-Z?"

The artificial hand lifted; with enormous force Palmer Eldritch shoved him and he toppled.

"Hey," Barney said weakly, trying to fight back, to nullify the pressure of the man's immense strength. "What—"

And then he was flat on his back. His head rang, ached; with difficulty he managed to open his eyes and focus on the room around him. He was waking up; he had on, he discovered, his pajamas, but they were unfamiliar: he had never seen them before. Was he in someone else's conapt, wearing their clothes? Some other man . . .

In panic he examined the bed, the covers. Beside him—

He saw an unfamiliar girl who slept on, breathing lightly through her mouth, her hair a tumble of cottonlike white, shoulders bare and smooth.

"I'm late," he said, and his voice came out distorted and husky, almost unrecognizable.

"No, you're not," the girl murmured, eyes still shut. "Relax. We can get in to work from here in—" She yawned and opened her eyes. "Fifteen minutes." She smiled at him; his discomfort amused her. "You always say that, every morning. Go see about coffee. I've *got* to have coffee."

"Sure," he said, and scrambled out of bed.

"Mr. Rabbit," the girl said mockingly. "You're so scared. Scared about me, about your job—and always running."

"My God," he said. "I've turned my back on everything."

"What everything?"

"Emily." He stared at the girl, Roni Something-or-other, at her bedroom. "Now I've got nothing," he said.

"Oh fine," Roni said with embittered sarcasm. "Now maybe I can say some nice things to you, to make *you* feel good."

He said, "And I did it just now. Not years ago. Just before Palmer Eldritch came in."

"How could Palmer Eldritch 'come in'? He's in a hospital bed out in the Jupiter or Saturn area; the UN took him there after they pried him from the wreck of his ship." Her tone was scornful, and yet there was a note of curiosity in it.

"Palmer Eldritch appeared to me just now," he said, doggedly. He thought, *I have to get back to Emily.* Sliding, stooping, he grabbed up his clothes, stumbled with them to the bathroom, and slammed the door behind him. Rapidly he shaved, changed, emerged, and said to the girl, who still lay in bed. "I have to go. Don't be sore at me; I have to do it."

A moment later, without having had breakfast, he was descending to the ground-level floor and after that he stood under the antithermal shield, searching up and down for a cab.

The cab, a fine, shiny new model, whipped him in almost no time to Emily's conapt building; in a blur he paid it, hurried inside, and in a matter of seconds was ascending. It seemed as if *no* time had passed, as if time had ceased and everything waited, frozen, for him; he was in a world of fixed objects, the sole moving thing.

At her door he rang the buzzer.

The door opened and a man stood there. "Yes?" The man was dark, reasonably good-looking, with heavy eyebrows and carefully combed, somewhat curly hair; he held the morning 'pape in one hand—behind him Barney saw a table of breakfast dishes.

Barney said, "You're—Richard Hnatt."

"Yes." Puzzled, he regarded Barney intently. "Do I know you?"

Emily appeared, wearing a gray turtle-neck sweater and stained jeans. "Good heavens. It's Barney," she said to Hnatt. "My former. Come in." She held the door wide open for him and he entered the apt. She seemed pleased to see him.

"Glad to meet you," Hnatt said in a neutral tone, starting to extend his hand and then changing his mind. "Coffee?"

"Thanks." Barney seated himself at the breakfast table at an unset place. "Listen," he said to Emily; he couldn't wait: it had to be said now even with Hnatt present. "I made a mistake in divorcing you. I'd like to remarry you. Go back on the old basis."

Emily, in a way which he remembered, laughed with delight; she was overcome and she went off to get him a cup and saucer, unable to answer. He wondered if she would ever answer; it was easier for her—it appealed to the lazy slob in her—just to laugh. Christ, he thought and stared straight ahead, fixedly.

Across from him Hnatt seated himself and said, "We're married. Did you suppose we were just living together?" His face was dark but he seemed in control of himself.

Barney said, speaking to Emily and not to Hnatt, "Marriages can be broken. Will you remarry me?" He rose and took a few hesitant steps in her direction; at that moment she turned and, calmly, handed him his cup and saucer.

"Oh no," she said, still smiling; her eyes poured over with light, that of compassion. She understood how he felt, that this was not an impulse only. But the answer was still no, and, he knew, it would always be; her mind was not even made up—there was, to her, simply no reality to which he was referring. He thought, I cut her down, once, cut her off, lopped her, with thorough knowledge of what I was doing, and this is the result; I am seeing the bread as they say which was cast on the water drifting back to choke me, water-soaked bread that will lodge in my throat, never to be swallowed or disgorged, either one. It's precisely what I deserve, he said to himself; I *made* this situation.

Returning to the kitchen table he numbly seated himself, sat as she filled his cup; he stared at her hands. Once these were my wife's, he said to himself. And I gave it up. Self-destruction; I wanted to see myself die. That's the only possible satisfactory explanation. Or was I that stupid? No; stupidity wouldn't encompass such an enormity, so complete a willful—

Emily said, "How are things, Barney?"

"Oh hell, just plain great." His voice shook.

"I hear you're living with a very pretty little redhead," Emily said. She seated herself at her own place, and resumed her meal.

"That's over," Barney said. "Forgotten."

"Who, then?" Her tone was conversational. Passing the time of day with me as if I were an old pal or perhaps a neighbor from another apt in this building, he thought. Madness! How can she—*can* she—feel like this? Impossible. It's an act, burying something deeper.

Aloud he said, "You're afraid that if you get mixed up with me again I'll—toss you out again. Once burned, twice warned. But I won't; I'll never do anything like that again."

In her placid, conversational voice Emily said, "I'm sorry you feel so bad, Barney. Aren't you seeing an analyst? Somebody said they saw you carrying a psychiatric suitcase around with you."

"Dr. Smile," he said, remembering. Probably he had left him at Roni Fugate's apt. "I need help," he said to Emily. "Isn't there any way—" He broke off. Can't the past be altered? he asked himself. Evidently not. Cause and effect work in only one direction, and change is real. So what's gone is gone and I might as well get out of here. He rose to his feet. "I must be out of my mind," he said to both her and Richard Hnatt. "I'm sorry; I'm only half awake—this morning I'm disoriented. It started when I woke up."

"Drink your coffee, why don't you?" Hnatt suggested. "How about some bear's claw to go with it?" The darkness had left his face; he, like Emily, was now tranquil, uninvolved.

Barney said, "I don't understand it. Palmer Eldritch said to come here." Or had he? Something like that; he was certain of it. "This was supposed to work out, I thought," he said, helplessly.

Hnatt and Emily glanced at each other.

"Eldritch is in a hospital somewhere—" Emily began.

"Something's gone wrong," Barney said. "Eldritch must have lost control. I better find him; he can explain it to me." And he felt panic, mercury-swift, fluid, pervasive panic; it filled him to his fingertips. "Goodbye," he managed to say, and started toward the door, groping for escape.

From behind him Richard Hnatt said, "Wait."

Barney turned. At the breakfast table Emily sat with a fixed, faint smile on her face, sipping her coffee, and across from her Hnatt sat facing Barney. Hnatt had one artificial hand, with which he held his fork, and when he lifted a bite of egg to his mouth Barney saw huge, jutting stainless steel teeth. And Hnatt was gray, hollowed out, with dead eyes, and much larger than before; he seemed to fill the room with his presence. But it was still Hnatt. I don't get it, Barney said, and stood at the door, not leaving the apt and not returning; he did as Hnatt suggested: he waited. Isn't this something like Palmer Eldritch? he asked himself. In pics . . . he has an artificial limb and steel teeth and Jensen eyes, but this was not Eldritch.

"It's only fair to tell you," Hnatt said matter-of-factly, "that Emily is a lot fonder of you than what she says suggests. I know because she's told me. Many times." He glanced at Emily, then. "You're a duty type. You feel it's the moral thing to do at this point, to suppress your emotions toward Barney; it's what you've been doing all along anyhow. But forget your duty. You can't build a marriage on it; there has to be spontaneity there. Even if you feel it's wrong to—" He made a gesture. "Well, let's say *deny* me . . . still, you should face your feelings honestly and not cover them with a self-sacrificing façade. That's what you did with Barney here; you let him kick you out because you thought it was your duty not to interfere with his career." He added, "You're still behaving that way and it's still a mistake. Be true to yourself." And, all at once, he grinned at Barney, grinned—and one dead eye flicked off, as if in a mechanical wink.

It was Palmer Eldritch now. Completely.

Emily, however, did not appear to notice; her smile had faded and she looked confused, upset, and increasingly furious. "You make me so damn angry," she said to her husband. "I *said* how I feel and I'm not a hypocrite. And I don't like to be accused of being one."

Across from her the seated man said, "You have only one life. If you want to live it with Barney instead of me—"

"I don't." She glared at him.

"I'm going," Barney said; he opened the hall door. It was hopeless.

"Wait." Palmer Eldritch rose, and sauntered after him. "I'll walk downstairs with you."

Together the two of them trudged down the hall toward the steps.

"Don't give up," Eldritch said. "Remember: this is only the initial time you've made use of Chew-Z; you'll have other times later. You can keep chipping away until eventually you get it."

Barney said, "What the hell is Chew-Z?"

From close beside him a girl's voice was repeating, "Barney Mayerson. Come on." He was being shaken; he blinked, squinted. Kneeling, her hand on his shoulder, was Anne Hawthorne. "What was it like? I stopped by and I couldn't find anyone around; then I ran across all of you here in a circle, completely passed out. What if I had been a UN official?"

"You woke me," he said to Anne, realizing what she had done; he felt massive, resentful disappointment. However, the translation for the time being was over and that was that. But he experienced the craving within him, the yearning. To do it again, and as soon as possible. Everything else was unimportant, even the girl beside him and his inert very quiet fellow-hovelists slumped here and there.

"It was that good?" Anne said perceptively. She touched her coat. "He visited our hovel, too; I bought. The man with the strange teeth and eyes, that gray, big man."

"Eldritch. Or a simulacrum of him." His joints ached, as if he had been sitting doubled up for hours, and yet, examining his watch, he saw that only a few seconds, a minute at the most, had passed. "Eldritch is everywhere," he said to Anne. "Give me your Chew-Z," he said to her.

"No."

He shrugged, concealing his disappointment, the acute, physical impact of deprivation. Well, Palmer Eldritch would be returning; he surely knew the effects of his product. Possibly even later today.

"Tell me about it," Anne said.

Barney said, "It's an illusory world in which Eldritch holds the key positions as god; he gives you a chance to do what you can't really ever do—reconstruct the past as it ought to have been. But even for him it's hard. Takes time." He was silent, then; he sat rubbing his aching forehead.

"You mean he can't—and you can't—just wave your arms and get what you want? As you can in a dream?"

"It's absolutely not like a dream." It was worse, he realized. More like being in hell, he thought. Yes, that's the way hell must be: recurrent and unyielding. But Eldritch thought in time, with sufficient patience and effort, *it could be changed*.

"If you go back—" Anne began.

" 'If.' " He stared at her. "I've got to go back. I wasn't able to accomplish anything this time." Hundreds of times, he thought. It might take that. "Listen. For God's sake give me that Chew-Z bindle you've got there. I know I can convince her. I've got Eldritch himself on my side, plugging away. Right now she's mad, and I took her by surprise—" He became silent; he stared at Anne Hawthorne. There's something wrong, he thought. Because—

Anne had one artificial arm and hand; the plastic and metal fingers were only inches from him and he could discern them clearly. And when he looked up into her face he saw the hollowness, the emptiness as vast as the intersystem space out of which Eldritch had emerged. The dead eyes, filled with space beyond the known, visited worlds.

"You can have more later," Anne said calmly. "One session a day is enough." She smiled. "Otherwise you'd run out of skins; you wouldn't be able to afford any more, and then what the hell would you do?"

Her smile glinted, the shiny opulence of stainless steel.

The other hovelists, on all sides of him, groaned into wakefulness, recovering by slow, anguished stages; they sat up, mumbled, and tried to orient themselves. Anne had gone somewhere. By himself he managed to get to his feet. Coffee, he thought. I'll bet she's fixing coffee.

"Wow," Norm Schein said.

"Where'd you go?" Tod Morris demanded, thick-tongued; blearily he too stood, then assisted his wife Helen. "I was back in my teens, in high school, when I was on my first complete date—first, you get me, successful one, you follow?" He glanced nervously at Helen, then.

Mary Regan said, "It's *much* better than Can-D. Infinitely. Oh, if I could tell you what I was doing—" She giggled self-consciously. "I just can't, though." Her face shone hot and red.

Going off to his own compartment Barney Mayerson locked the door, and got out the tube of toxin that Allen Faine had given him; he held it in his hand, thinking, *Now is the time.* But—are we back? Did I see nothing more than a residual view of Eldritch, superimposed on Anne? Or perhaps it had been genuine insight, perception of the actual, of their unqualified situation; not just his but all of theirs together.

If so it was not the time to receive the toxin. Instinct offered him that point of observation.

Nevertheless he unscrewed the lid of the tube.

A tiny, frail voice, emanating from the opened tube, piped, "You're being watched, Mayerson. And if you're up to some kind of tactic we'll be required to step in. You will be severely restricted. Sorry."

He put the lid back on the tube, and screwed it tight with shaking fingers. And the tube had been—empty!

"What is it?" Anne said, appearing; she had been in the kitchen of his compartment; she wore an apron which she had discovered somewhere. "What's that?" she asked, seeing the tube in his hand.

"Escape," he grated. "From this."

"From exactly what?" Her normal appearance had reasserted itself; nothing now was amiss. "You look positively sick, Barney; you really do. Is it an after-effect of the Chew-Z?"

"A hangover." Is Palmer Eldritch actually inside this? he wondered, examining the closed tube; he revolved it in the palm of his hand. "Is there any way to contact the Faines' satellite?"

"Oh, I imagine so. You probably just put in a vidcall or whatever their means of—"

"Go ask Norm Schein to make the contact for me," he said.

Obligingly, Anne departed; the compartment door shut after her.

At once he dug the code book which Faine had presented him from its hiding place beneath the kitchen stove. This would have to be encoded.

The pages of the code book were blank.

Then it won't go in code, he said to himself, and that's that. I'll have to do the best I can and let it go, however unsatisfactory.

The door swung open; Anne appeared and said, "Mr. Schein is placing the call for you. They request particular tunes all the time, he says."

He followed her down the corridor and into a cramped

little room where Norm sat at a transmitter; as Barney entered he turned his head and said, "I've got Charlotte—will that do?"

"Allen," Barney said.

"Okay." Presently Norm said, "Now I've got Ol' Eggplant Al. Here." He handed the microphone to Barney. On the tiny screen Allen Faine's face, jovial and professional, appeared. "A new citizen to talk to you," Norm explained, reclutching the microphone briefly. "Barney Mayerson, meet half of the team that keeps us alive and sane here on Mars." To himself he muttered, "God, have I got a headache. Excuse me." He vacated the chair at the transmitter and disappeared totteringly down the hall.

"Mr. Faine," Barney said carefully, "I was speaking with Mr. Palmer Eldritch earlier today. He mentioned the conversation that you and I had. He was aware of it so as far as I can see there's no—"

Coldly, Allen Faine said, "What conversation?"

For an interval Barney was silent. "Evidently they had an infrared camera going," he continued at last. "Probably in a satellite that was making its pass. However, the contents of our conversation, it would appear, is still not—"

"You're a nut," Faine said. "I don't know you; I never had any conversation with you. Well, man, have you a request or not?" His face was impassive, oblique with detachment, and it did not seem simulated.

"You don't know who I am?" Barney said, unbelievingly.

Faine cut the connection at his end and the tiny vidscreen fused over, now showing only emptiness, the void. Barney shut off the transmitter. He felt nothing. Apathy. He walked past Anne and out into the corridor; there he halted, got out his package—was it the last?—of Terran cigarettes, and lit up, thinking, What Eldritch did to Leo on Luna or Sigma 14-B or wherever he's done to me, too. And eventually he'll snare us all. Just like this. Isolated. The communal world is gone. At least for me; he began with me.

And, he thought, I'm supposed to fight back with an empty tube that once may or may not have contained a rare, expensive, brain-disorganizing toxin—but which now contains only Palmer Eldritch, and not even all of him. Just his voice.

The match burned his fingers. He ignored it.

11

Referring to his bundle of notes Felix Blau stated, "Fifteen hours ago a UN-approved Chew-Z-owned ship landed on Mars and distributed its initial bindles to the hovels in the Fineburg Crescent."

Leo Bulero leaned toward the screen, folded his hands, and said, "Including Chicken Pox Prospects?"

Briefly, Felix nodded.

"By now," Leo said, "he should have consumed the dose of that brain-rotting filth and we should have heard from him via the satellite system."

"I fully realize that."

"William C. Clarke is still standing by?" Clarke was P. P. Layouts' top legal man on Mars.

"Yes," Felix said, "but Mayerson hasn't contacted him either; he hasn't contacted *anybody*." He shoved his documents aside. "That is all, absolutely all, I have at this point."

"Maybe he died," Leo said. He felt morose; the whole thing depressed him. "Maybe he had such a severe convulsion that—"

"But then we'd have heard, because one of the three UN hospitals on Mars would have been notified."

"Where is Palmer Eldritch?"

"No one in my organization knows," Felix said. "He left Luna and disappeared. We simply lost him."

"I'd give my right arm," Leo said, "to know what's going on down in that hovel, that Chicken Pox Prospects where Barney is."

"Go to Mars yourself."

"Oh no," Leo said at once. "I'm not leaving P. P. Layouts, not after what happened to me on Luna. Can't you get a man in there from your organization who can report directly to us?"

"We have that girl, that Anne Hawthorne. But she hasn't checked in either. Maybe I'll go to Mars. If you're not."

"I'm not," Leo repeated.

Felix Blau said, "It'll cost you."

"Sure," Leo said. "And I'll pay. But at least we'll have some sort of chance; I mean, as it stands we've got nothing." And we're finished, he said to himself. "Just bill me," he said.

"But do you have any idea what it would cost you if I died, if they got me there on Mars? My organization would—"

"Please," Leo said. "I don't want to talk about that; what is Mars, a graveyard that Eldritch is digging? Eldritch probably ate Barney Mayerson. Okay, you go; you show up at Chicken Pox Prospects." He rang off.

Behind him Roni Fugate, his acting New York Pre-Fash consultant, sat intently listening. Taking it all in, Leo said to himself.

"Did you get a good earful?" he demanded roughly.

Roni said, "You're doing the same thing to him that he did to you."

"Who? What?"

"Barney was afraid to follow you when you disappeared on Luna. Now you're afraid—"

"It's just not wise. All right," he said. "I'm too goddam scared of Palmer to set foot outside this building; of course

I'm not going to Mars and what you say is absolutely true."

"But no one," Roni said softly, "is going to fire you. The way you did Barney."

"I'm firing myself. Inside. It hurts."

"But not enough to make you go to Mars."

"All right!" Savagely he snapped the vidset back on again and dialed Felix Blau. "Blau, I take it all back. I'm going myself. Although it's insane."

"Frankly," Felix Blau said, "in my opinion you're doing exactly what Palmer Eldritch wants. All questions of bravery versus—"

"Eldritch's power works through that drug," Leo said. "As long as he can't administer any to me I'm fine. I'll take a few company guards along to watch that I'm not slipped an injection like last time. Hey, Blau. You still come along; okay?" He swung to face Roni. "Is that all right?"

"Yes." She nodded.

"See? She says it's okay. So will you come along with me to Mars and you know, hold my hand?"

"Sure, Leo," Felix Blau said. "And if you faint I'll fan you back to consciousness. I'll meet you at your office in—" He examined his wristwatch. "Two hours. We'll map out details. Have a fast ship ready. And I'll bring a couple of men along I have confidence in, too."

"That's it," Leo said to Roni as he broke the connection. "Look what you got me to do. You seized Barney's job and if I don't get back from Mars maybe you can nail down my job, too." He glared at her. Women can get a man to do anything, he realized. Mother, wife, even employee; they twist us like hot little bits of thermoplastic.

Roni said, "Is that really why I said it, Mr. Bulero? Do you really believe that?"

He took a good, long, hard look at her. "Yes. Because you're insatiably ambitious. I really believe that."

"You're wrong."

"If *I* don't come back from Mars will you come after me?"

He waited but she did not answer; he saw hesitation on her face, and at that he loudly laughed. "Of course not," he said.

Stonily, Roni Fugate said, "I must get back to my office; I have new flatware to judge. Modern patterns from Cape-town." Rising, she departed; he watched her go, thinking, She's the real one. Not Palmer Eldritch. If I do get back I've got to find some method of quietly dumping her. I don't like to be manipulated.

Palmer Eldritch, he thought suddenly, appeared in the form of a small girl, a little child—not to mention later on when he was that dog. Maybe there is no Roni Fugate; maybe it's Eldritch.

The thought chilled him.

What we have here, he realized, is not an invasion of Earth by Proxmen, beings from another system. Not an invasion by the legions of a pseudo human race. No. It's Palmer Eldritch who's everywhere, growing and growing like a mad weed. Is there a point where he'll burst, grow too much? All the manifestations of Eldritch, all over Terra and Luna and Mars, Palmer puffing up and bursting—pop, pop, POP! Like Shakespeare says, some damn thing about sticking a mere pin in through the armor, and goodbye king.

But, he thought, what in this case is the pin? And is there an open spot into which we can thrust it? I don't know and Felix doesn't know and Barney; I'll make book that he doesn't have the foggiest idea of how to cope with Eldritch. Kidnap Zoe, the man's elderly, ugly daughter? Palmer wouldn't care. Unless Palmer is also Zoe; maybe there is no Zoe, independent of him. And that's the way we'll all wind up unless we figure out how to destroy him, he realized. Replicas, extensions of the man, inhabiting three planets and six moons. The man's a protoplasm, spreading and re-producing and dividing, and all through that damn lichen-derived non-Terran drug, that horrible, miserable Chew-Z.

Once more at the vidset he dialed Allen Faine's satellite. Presently, a trifle insubstantial and weak but nevertheless there, the face of his prime disc jockey appeared. "Yes, Mr. Bulero."

"You're positive Mayerson hasn't contacted you? He's got the code book, hasn't he?"

"Got the book, but still nothing from him. We've been monitoring every transmission from Chicken Pox Prospects. We saw Eldritch's ship land near the hovel—that was hours ago—and we saw Eldritch get out and go up to the hovelists, and although our cameras didn't pick this up I'm sure the transaction was consummated at that instant." Faine added, "And Barney Mayerson was one of the hovelists who met Eldritch at the surface."

"I believe I know what happened," Leo said. "Okay, thanks, Al." He rang off. *Barney went below with the Chew-Z,* he realized. *And right away they all sat down and chewed; that was the end, just as it was for me on Luna. Our tactics required that Barney chew away,* Leo realized, *and so we played right into Palmer's dirty, semimechanical hands; once he had the drug in Barney's system we were through. Because Eldritch somehow controls each of the hallucinatory worlds induced by the drug; I know it—know it!—that the skunk is in all of them.*

The fantasy worlds that Chew-Z induces, he thought, *are in Palmer Eldritch's head. As I found out personally.*

And the trouble is, he thought, *that once you get into one of them you can't quite scramble back out; it stays with you, even when you think you're free. It's a one-way gate, and for all I know I'm still in it* now.

However that did not seem likely. And yet, he thought, *it shows how afraid I am—as Roni Fugate pointed out. Afraid enough to (I'll admit it) abandon Barney there like he abandoned me. And Barney was using his precog ability, so he had foresight, almost to the point where it was like what I have now, like hindsight. He knew in advance what I had to learn by experience. No wonder he balked.*

Who gets sacrificed? Leo asked himself. *Me, Barney, Felix*

Blau—which of us gets melted down for Palmer to guzzle? Because that's what we are potentially for him: food to be consumed. It's an oral thing that arrived back from the Prox system, a great mouth, open to receive us.

But Palmer's not a cannibal. Because I know he's not human; that's not a man there in that Palmer Eldritch skin.

But what it was he had no concept at all. So much could happen in the vast expanses between Sol and Proxima, either going or coming. Maybe it happened, he thought, when Palmer was going; maybe he ate the Proxmen during those ten years, cleaned the plate there, and so then came back to us. Ugh. He shivered.

Well, he thought, two more hours of independent life, plus the time it takes to travel to Mars. Maybe ten hours of private existence, and then—swallowed. And all over Mars that hideous drug is being distributed; think, picture, the numbers confined to Palmer's illusory worlds, his nets that he casts. What do those Buddhists in the UN like Hepburn-Gilbert call it? Maya. The veil of illusion. Sheoot, he thought dismally, and reached to snap on his intercom in order to requisition a fast ship for the flight. And I want a good pilot, he remembered; too many autonomic landings of late have been failures: I don't intend to be splattered all over the countryside—especially *that* countryside.

To Miss Gleason he said, "Who's the best interplan pilot we have?"

"Don Davis," Miss Gleason said promptly. "He has a perfect record in—you know. His flights from Venus." She did not refer explicitly to their Can-D enterprise; even the intercom might be tapped.

Ten minutes later the travel arrangements had all been made.

Leo Bulero leaned back in his chair, lit a large green Havana-leaf claro cigar which had been housed in a helium-filled humidor, probably for years . . . the cigar, as he bit the end off, seemed dry and brittle; it cracked under the pressure of his teeth and he felt disappointment. It had appeared so good, so perfectly preserved in its coffin. Well, you never know, he informed himself. Until you get right to it.

His office door opened. Miss Gleason, the ship-requisition papers in her hands, entered.

The hand which held the papers was artificial; he made out the glint of undisguised metal and at once he raised his head to scrutinize her face, the rest of her. Neanderthal teeth, he thought; that's what those giant stainless steel molars look like. Reversion, two hundred thousand years back; revolting. And the luxvid or vidlux or whatever they were eyes, without pupils, only slits. Jensen Labs of Chicago's product, anyhow.

"Goddam you, Eldritch," he said.

"I'm your pilot, too," Palmer Eldritch, from within the shape of Miss Gleason, said. "And I was thinking of greeting you when you land. But that's too much, too soon."

"Give me the papers to sign," Leo said, reaching out.

Surprised, Palmer Eldritch said, "You still intend to make the trip to Mars?" He looked decidedly taken aback.

"Yes," Leo said, and waited patiently for the requisition papers.

Once you've taken Chew-Z you're delivered over. At least that's how dogmatic, devout, fanatical Anne Hawthorne would phrase it. Like sin, Barney Mayerson thought; it's the condition of slavery. Like the Fall. And the temptation is similar.

But what's missing here is a way by which we can be freed. Would we have to go to Prox to find it? Even there it may not exist. Not in the universe anywhere.

Anne Hawthorne appeared at the door of the hovel's transmitter room. "Are you all right?"

"Sure," Barney said. "You know, we got ourselves into this. No one *made* us chew Chew-Z." He dropped his cigarette to the floor and erased its life with the toe of his boot. "And you won't give me your bindle," he said. But it was not Anne denying it to him. It was Palmer Eldritch, operating through her, holding back.

Even so, I can take it from her, he realized.

"Stop," she said. Or rather it said.

"Hey," Norm Schein yelled from the transmitter room, jumping to his feet, amazed. "What are you doing, Mayerson? Let her—"

The strong artificial arm struck him; the metal fingers clawed and it was almost enough; they pried at his neck, knowingly, alert to the spot where death could most effectively be administered. But he had the bindle and that was it; he let the creature go.

"Don't take it, Barney," she said quietly. "It's just too soon after the first dose. Please."

Without answering he started off, toward his own compartment.

"Will you do one thing for me?" she called after him. "Divide it in half, let me take it with you. So I can be along."

"Why?" he said.

"Maybe I can help you by being there."

Barney said, "I can make it on my own." If I can reach Emily before the divorce, before Richard Hnatt shows up— as I first did, he thought. That's the only place I have any real chance. Again and again, he thought. Try! Until I'm successful.

He locked the door.

As he devoured the Chew-Z he thought about Leo Bulero. You got away. Probably because Palmer Eldritch was weaker than you. Is that it? Or was Eldritch simply paying out the line, letting you dangle? You could come here and stop me; now, though, there's no stopping. Even Eldritch warned me; speaking through Anne Hawthorne; it was too much even for him, and now what? Have I gone so far that I've plunged to the bottom out of even *his* sight? Where even Palmer Eldritch can't go, where nothing exists.

And of course, he thought, I can't get back up.

His head ached and he shut his eyes involuntarily. It was

as if his brain, alive and frightened, had physically stirred; he felt it tremble. Altered metabolism, he realized. Shock. I'm sorry, he said to himself, apologizing to his somatic part. Okay?

"Help," he said, aloud.

"Aw, help—my ass," a man's voice grated. "What do you want me to do, hold your hand? Open your eyes or get out of here. That period you spent on Mars, it ruined you and I'm fed up. Come on!"

"Shut up," Barney said. "I'm sick; I went too far. You mean all you can do is bawl me out?" He opened his eyes, and faced Leo Bulero, who was at his big, littered oak desk. "Listen," Barney said. "I'm on Chew-Z; I can't stop it. If you can't help me then I'm finished." His legs bent as if melting as he made his way to a nearby chair and seated himself.

Regarding him thoughtfully, smoking a cigar, Leo said, "You're on Chew-Z *now?*" He scowled. "As of two years ago—"

"It's banned?"

"Yeah. Banned. My God. I don't know if it's worth my talking you; what are you, some kind of phantasm from the past?"

"You heard what I said; *I said I'm on it.*" He clenched his fists.

"Okay, okay." Leo puffed masses of heavy gray smoke, agitatedly. "Don't get excited. Hell, I went ahead and saw the future, too, and it didn't kill me. And anyhow, for chrissakes, you're a precog—you ought to be used to it. Anyhow—" he leaned back in his chair, swiveled about, then crossed his legs. "I saw this monument, see? Guess to who. To me." He eyed Barney, then shrugged.

Barney said, "I have nothing to gain, nothing at all, from this time period. I want my wife back. I want Emily." He felt enraged, upsurging bitterness. The bile of disappointment.

"Emily." Leo Bulero nodded. Then, into his intercom, he

said, "Miss Gleason, please don't let anything bother us for a while." He again turned his attention to Barney, surveying him acutely. "That fellow Hnatt—is that his name?—got hauled in by the UN police along with the rest of the Eldritch organization; see, Hnatt had this contract that he signed with Eldritch's business agent. Well, they gave him the choice of a prison sentence—okay, I admit it's unfair, but don't blame me—or emigrating. He emigrated."

"What about her?"

"With that pot business of hers? How the hell could she conduct it from a hovel underneath the Martian desert? Naturally she dumped the dumb jerk. Well so see if you had waited—"

Barney said, "Are you really Leo Bulero? Or are you Palmer Eldritch? And this is to make me feel even worse—is that it?"

Raising an eyebrow, Leo said, "Palmer Eldritch is dead."

"But this isn't real; this is a drug-induced fantasy. Translation."

"The hell it isn't real." Leo glared at him. "What does that make me, then? Listen." He pointed his finger angrily at Barney. "There's nothing unreal about *me;* you're the one who's a goddam phantasm, like you said, out of the past. I mean, you've got the situation completely backward. You hear this?" He banged on the surface of his desk with all the strength in his hands. "The sound reality makes. And I say that your ex-wife and Hnatt are divorced; I know because she sells her pots to us for minning. In fact, she was in Roni Fugate's office last Thursday." Grumpily, he smoked his cigar, still glaring at Barney.

"Then all I have to do," Barney said, "is look her up." It was as simple as that.

"Oh yeah," Leo agreed, nodding. "But just one thing. What are you going to do with Roni Fugate? You're living with her in this world that you seem to like to imagine as unreal."

Astounded, Barney said, "After *two years?*"

"And Emily knows it because since she's been selling her pots to us through Roni the two of them have become buddies; they tell each other their secrets. Look at it from Emily's viewpoint. If she lets you come back to her Roni'll probably stop accepting her pots for minning. It's a risk, and I bet Em won't want to take it. I mean, we give Roni absolute say-so, like you had in your time."

Barney said, "Emily would never put her career ahead of her own life."

"*You* did. Maybe Em learned from you, got the message. And anyhow, even without that Hnatt guy, why would Emily want to go back to you? She's leading a very successful life, with her career; she's planet-famous and she's got skin after skin salted away . . . you want the truth? She's got all the men she wants. Any darn time. Em doesn't need you; face it, Barney. Anyhow, what's lacking about Roni? Frankly I wouldn't mind—"

"I think you're Palmer Eldritch," Barney said.

"Me?" Leo tapped his chest. "Barney, I killed Eldritch; that's why they put up that monument to me." His voice was low and quiet but he had flushed deep red. "Do I have stainless steel teeth? I have an artificial arm?" Leo lifted up both his hands. "Well? And my eyes—"

Barney moved toward the door of the office.

"Where are you going?" Leo demanded.

"I know," Barney said as he opened the door, "that if I can see Emily even for just a few minutes—"

"No you can't, fella," Leo said. He shook his head, firmly.

Waiting in the corridor for the elevator Barney thought, Maybe it really was Leo. And maybe it's true.

So I cannot succeed without Palmer Eldritch.

Anne was right; I should have given half the bindle back to her and then we could have tried this together. Anne, Palmer . . . it's all the same, it's all him, the creator. That's who and what he is, he realized. The owner of these worlds.

The rest of us just inhabit them and when he wants to he can inhabit them, too. Can kick over the scenery, manifest himself, push things in any direction he chooses. Even be any of us he cares to. All of us, in fact, if he desires. Eternal, outside of time and spliced-together segments of all other dimensions . . . *he can even enter a world in which he's dead.*

Palmer Eldritch had gone to Prox a man and returned a god.

Aloud, as he stood waiting for the elevator, Barney said, "Palmer Eldritch, help me. Get my wife back for me." He looked around; no one was present to overhear him.

The elevator arrived. The doors slid aside. Inside the elevator waited four men and two women, silently.

All of them were Palmer Eldritch. Men and women alike: artificial arm, stainless steel teeth . . . the gaunt, hollowed-out gray face with Jensen eyes.

Virtually in unison, but not quite, as if competing with each other for first chance to utter it, the six people said, "You're not going to be able to get back to your own world from here, Mayerson; you've gone too far, this time, taken a massive overdose. As I warned you when you snatched it away from me at Chicken Pox Prospects."

"Can't you help me?" Barney said. "I've got to get her back."

"You don't understand," the Palmer Eldritches all said, collectively shaking their heads; it was the same motion that Leo had just now made, and the same firm no. "As we pointed out to you: since this is your future you're already established here. So there's no place for you; that's a matter of simple logic. Who'm I supposed to snare Emily for? You? Or the legitimate Barney Mayerson who lived naturally up to this time? And don't think he hasn't tried to get Emily back. Don't you suppose—and obviously you haven't—that as the Hnatts split up *he made his move?* I did what I could for him, then; it was quite a few months ago, just after Richard Hnatt was shipped to Mars, kicking and protesting the whole way. Personally I don't blame Hnatt; it was a dirty deal, all engineered by Leo, of course. And look at yourself." The six Palmer Eldritches gestured contemptuously. "You're a phantasm, as Leo said; I can see through you, literally. I'll tell you in more accurate terminology what you are." From the six the calm, dispassionate statement came, then. "You're a ghost."

Barney stared at them and they stared back placidly, unmoved.

"Try building your life on that premise," the Eldritches continued. "Well, you got what St. Paul promises, as Anne Hawthorne was blabbing about; you're no longer clothed in a perishable, fleshly body—you've put on an ethereal body in its place. How do you like it, Mayerson?" Their tone was mocking, but compassion showed on the six faces; it showed in the weird, slitted mechanical eyes of each of them. "You can't die; you don't eat or drink or breathe air . . . you can, if you wish, pass directly through walls, in fact through any material object you care to. You'll learn that, in time. Evidently on the road to Damascus Paul experienced a vision relating to this phenomenon. That and a lot more besides." The Eldritches added, "I'm inclined, as you can see, to be somewhat sympathetic to the Early- and Neo-Christian point of view, such as Anne holds. It assists in explaining a great deal."

Barney said, "What about you, Eldritch? You're dead, killed two years ago by Leo." And I know, he thought, that you're suffering what I am; the same process must have overtaken you, somewhere along the route. You gave yourself an overdose of Chew-Z and now for you there's no return to your own time and world, either.

"That monument," the six Eldritches said, murmuring together like a rattling, far-off wind, "is highly inaccurate. A ship of mine had a running gun-battle with one of Leo's, just off Venus; I was aboard, or supposed to be aboard, ours. Leo was aboard his. He and I had just held a conference together with Hepburn-Gilbert on Venus and on the way back to Terra Leo took the opportunity to jump our ship. It's on that premise that the monument was erected—due to Leo's astute economic pressure, applied in all the proper political bodies. He got himself into the history books once and for all."

Two persons, a well-dressed executive-type young man and a girl who was possibly a secretary, strolled down the hall; they glanced curiously at Barney and then at the six creatures within the elevator.

The creatures ceased to be Palmer Eldritch; the change took place before him. All at once they were six individual, ordinary men and women. Utterly heterogeneous.

Barney walked away from the elevator. For a measureless interval he roamed the corridors and then, by ramp, descended to ground level where the P. P. Layouts directory was situated. There, reading it, he located his own name and office number. Ironically—and this bordered on being just too much—he held the title he had tried to pry by force out of Leo not so long ago; he was listed as Pre-Fash Supervisor, clearly outranking every individual consultant. So again, if he had only waited—

Beyond doubt Leo had managed to bring him back from Mars. Rescued him from the world of the hovel. And this implied a great deal.

The planned litigation—or some substitute tactic—had succeeded. Would, rather. And perhaps soon.

The mist of hallucination cast up by Palmer Eldritch, the fisherman of human souls, was enormously effective, but not perfect. Not in the long run. So had he stopped consuming Chew-Z after the initial dose—

Perhaps Anne Hawthorne's possession of a bindle had been deliberate. A means of maneuvering him into taking it once again and very quickly. If so, her protests had been spurious; she had intended that he seize it, and, like a beast in a superior maze, he had scrambled for the glimpsed way out. Manipulated by Palmer Eldritch through every inch of the way.

And there was no path back.

If he was to believe Eldritch, speaking through Leo. Through his congregation everywhere. But that was the key word, if.

By elevator he ascended to the floor of his own office.

When he opened the office door the man seated at the desk raised his head and said, "Close that thing. We don't have a lot of time." The man, and it was himself, rose; Barney scrutinized him and then, reflexively, shut the door as instructed. "Thanks," his future self said, icily. "And stop worrying about getting back to your own time; you will. Most of what Eldritch did—or does, if you prefer to regard it that way—consists of manufacturing surface changes: he makes things *appear* the way he wants, but that doesn't mean they are. Follow me?"

"I'll—take your word for it."

His future self said, "I realize that's easy for me to say, now; Eldritch still shows up from time to time, sometimes even publicly, but I know and everyone else right down to the most ignorant readers of the lowest level of 'papes know that it's nothing but a phantasm; the actual man is in a grave on Sigma 14-B and that's verified. You're in a different spot. For you the actual Palmer Eldritch could enter at any minute; what would be actual for you would be a phantasm for me, and the same is going to be true when you get back to Mars. You'll be encountering a genuine living Palmer Eldritch and I don't frankly envy you."

Barney said, "Just tell me how to get back."

"You don't care about Emily any more?"

"I'm scared." And he felt his own gaze, the perception and comprehension of the future, sear him. "Okay," he blurted, "what am I supposed to do, pretend otherwise to impress you? Anyhow you'd know."

"Where Eldritch had the advantage over everyone and

anyone who's consumed Chew-Z is that recovery from the drug is excessively retarded and gradual; it's a series of levels, each progressively less an induced illusion and more compounded of authentic reality. Sometimes the process takes years. *This* is why the UN belatedly banned it and turned against Eldritch; Hepburn-Gilbert initially approved it because he honestly believed that it aided the user to penetrate to concrete reality, and then it became obvious to everyone who used it or witnessed it being used that it did exactly the—"

"Then I never recovered from my first dose."

"Right; you never got back to clear-cut reality. As you would have if you had abstained another twenty-four hours. Those phantasms of Eldritch, imposed on normal matter, would have faded away entirely; you would have been free. But Eldritch got you to accept that second, stronger dose; he knew you had been sent to Mars to operate against him, although he didn't have any idea in what way. He was afraid of you."

It sounded strange to hear that; it did not ring right. Eldritch, with all he had done and could do—but Eldritch had seen the monument of the future; he knew that somehow, in some manner, they were going to kill him after all.

The door of the office abruptly opened.

Roni Fugate looked in and saw the two of them; she said nothing—she simply stared, open-mouthed. And then at last murmured, "A phantasm. I think it's the one standing, the one nearest me." Shakily, she entered the office, shutting the door after her.

"That's right," his future self said, scrutinizing her sharply. "You can test it out by putting your hand into it."

She did so; Barney Mayerson saw her hand pass into his body and disappear. "I've seen phantasms before," she said, withdrawing her hand; now she was more composed. "But never of you, dear. Everyone who consumed that abomination became a phantasm at one time or another, but recently they've become less frequent to us. At one time, about

a year ago, you saw them everytime you turned around."
She added, "Hepburn-Gilbert finally saw one of himself; just
what he deserved."

"You realize," his future self said to Roni, "that he's under
the domination of Eldritch, even though to us the man is
dead. So we have to work cautiously. Eldritch can begin to
affect his perception at any time, and when that happens
he'll have no choice but to react accordingly."

Speaking to Barney, Roni said, "What *can* we do for you?"

"He wants to get back to Mars," his future self said.
"They've got an enormously complicated scheme screwed
together to destroy Eldritch via the interplan courts; it in-
volves him taking an Ionian epilepsygenic, KV-7. Or can't
you remember back to that?"

"But it never got into the courts," Roni said. "Eldritch
settled. They dropped litigation."

"We can transport you to Mars," his future self said to
Barney, "in a P. P. Layouts ship. But that won't accomplish
anything because Eldritch will not only follow you and be
with you on the trip; he'll be there to greet you—a favorite
outdoor sport of his. Never forget that a phantasm can go
anywhere; it's not bounded by time or space. That's what
makes it a phantasm, that and the fact that it has no metabolism, at least not as we understand the word. Oddly, however, it is affected by gravity. There have been a number of
studies lately on the subject; anyhow not much is yet known."
Meaningfully he finished, "Especially on the subtopic, How
does one return a phantasm to its own space and time—
exorcise it."

Barney said, "You're anxious to get rid of me?" He felt
cold.

"That's right," his future self said calmly. "Just as anxious
as you are to get back; you know now you made a mistake,
you know that—" He glanced at Roni and immediately
ceased. He did not intend to refer to the topic of Emily in
front of her.

"They've made some attempts with high-voltage, low-amperage electroshock," Roni said. "And with magnetic fields. Columbia University has—"

"The best work so far," his future self said, "is in the physics department of Cal, out on the West Coast. The phantasm is bombarded by Beta particles which disintegrate the essential protein basis for—"

"Okay," Barney said. "I'll leave you alone. I'll go to the physics department at Cal and see what they can do." He felt utterly defeated; he had been abandoned even by himself, the ultimate, he thought with impotent, wild fury. Christ!

"That's strange," Roni said.

"What's strange," his future self said, tipping his chair back, folding his arms and regarding her.

"Your saying that about Cal," Roni said. "As far as I know they've never done any work with phantasms out there." To Barney she said quietly, "Ask to see both his hands."

Barney said, "Your hands." But already the creeping alteration in the seated man had begun, in the jaw especially, the idiosyncratic bulge which he recognized so easily. "Forget it," he said thickly; he felt dizzy.

His future self said mockingly, "God helps those who help themselves, Mayerson. Do you really think it's going to do any good to go knocking all around trying to dream up someone to take pity on you? Hell, *I* pity you; I told you not to consume that second bindle. I'd release you from this if I knew how, and I know more about the drug than anyone else alive."

"What's going to happen to him?" Roni asked his future self, which was no longer his future self; the metamorphosis was complete and Palmer Eldritch sat tilted back at the desk, tall and gray, rocking slightly in the wheeled chair, a great mass of timeless cobwebs shaped, almost as a cavalier gesture, in quasi-human form. "My good God, is he just going to wander around here *forever*?"

"Good question," Palmer Eldritch said gravely. "I wish I knew; for myself as well as him. I'm in it a lot deeper than he, remember." Addressing Barney he said, "You grasp the point, don't you, that it isn't necessary for you to assume your normal Gestalt; you can be a stone or a tree or a jet-hopper or a section of antithermal roofing. I've been all those things and a lot more. If you become inanimate, an old log for instance, you're no longer conscious of the passage of time. It's an interesting possible solution for someone who wants to escape his phantasmic existence. I don't." His voice was low. "Because for me, returning to my own space and time means death, at Leo Bulero's instigation. On the contrary; I can live on only in this state. But with you—" He gestured, smiling faintly. "Be a rock, Mayerson. Last it out, however long it is before the drug wears off. Ten years, a century. A million years. Or be an old fossil bone in a museum." His gaze was gentle.

After a time Roni said, "Maybe he's right, Barney."

Barney walked to the desk, picked up a glass paperweight, and then set it down.

"We can't touch him," Roni said, "but he can—"

"The ability of phantasms to manipulate material objects," Palmer Eldritch said, "makes it clear that they *are* present and not merely projections. Remember the poltergeist phenomenon . . . they were capable of hurling objects all around the house, but they were incorporeal, too."

Mounted on the wall of the office gleamed a plaque; it was an award which Emily had received, three years before his own time, for ceramics she had entered in a show. Here it was; he still kept it.

"I want to be that plaque," Barney decided. It was made of hardwood, probably mahogany, and brass; it would endure a long time and in addition he knew that his future self would never abandon it. He walked toward the plaque, wondering how he ceased being a man and became an object of brass and wood mounted on an office wall.

Palmer Eldritch said, "You want my help, Mayerson?"

"Yes," he said.

Something swept him up; he put out his arms to steady himself and then he was diving, descending an endless tunnel that narrowed—he felt it squeeze around him, and he knew that he had misjudged. Palmer Eldritch had once more thought rings around him, demonstrated his power over everyone who used Chew-Z; Eldritch had done something and he could not even tell what, but anyhow it was not what he had said. Not what had been promised.

"Goddam you, Eldritch," Barney said, not hearing his voice, hearing nothing; he descended on and on, weightless, not even a phantasm any longer; gravity had ceased to affect him, so even that was gone, too.

Leave me something, Palmer, he thought to himself. Please. A prayer, he realized, which had already been turned down; Palmer Eldritch had long ago acted—it was too late and it always had been. Then I'll go ahead with litigation, Barney said to himself; I'll find my way back to Mars somehow, take the toxin, spend the rest of my life in the interplan courts fighting you—and winning. Not for Leo and P. P. Layouts but for me.

He heard, then, a laugh. It was Palmer Eldritch's laugh but it was emerging from—

Himself.

Looking down at his hands, he distinguished the left one, pink, pale, made of flesh, covered with skin and tiny, almost invisible hair, and then the right one, bright, glowing, spotless in its mechanical perfection, a hand infinitely superior to the original one, long since gone.

Now he knew what had been done to him. A great translation—from his standpoint, anyhow—had been accomplished, and possibly everything up to now had worked with this end in mind.

It will be me, he realized, that Leo Bulero will kill. Me the monument will present a narration of.

Now I am Palmer Eldritch.

In that case, he thought after a while as the environment surrounding him seemed to solidify and clear, I wonder how he is making out with Emily.

I hope pretty badly.

12

With vast trailing arms he extended from the Proxima Centaurus system to Terra itself, and he was not human; this was not a man who had returned. And he had great power. He could overcome death.

But he was not happy. For the simple reason that he was alone. So he at once tried to make up for this; he went to a lot of trouble to draw others along the route he had followed.

One of them was Barney Mayerson.

"Mayerson," he said, conversationally, "what the hell have you got to lose? Figure it out for yourself; you're washed up as it stands—no woman you love, a past you regret. You realize you took a decisively wrong course in your life and nobody *made* you do it. And it can't be repaired. Even if the future lasts for a million years it can't restore what you lost by, so to speak, your own hand. You grasp my reasoning?"

No answer.

"And you forget one thing," he continued, after waiting. "She's devolved, from that miserable evolution therapy that ex-Nazi-type German doctor runs in those clinics. Sure, she—actually her husband—was smart enough to discontinue the treatments right away, and she can still turn out pots that sell; she didn't devolve that much. But—you wouldn't like her. You'd know; she'd be just a little more shallow, a shade sillier. It would not be like the past, even if you got her back; *it'd be changed.*"

Again he waited. This time there was an answer. "All right!"

"Where would you like to go?" he continued, then. "Mars? I'll bet. Okay, then back to Terra."

Barney Mayerson, not himself, said, "No. I left voluntarily; I was through; the end had come."

"Okay. Not Terra. Let's see. Hmmm." He pondered. "Prox," he said. "You've never seen the Prox system and the Proxers. I'm a bridge, you know. Between the two systems. They can come here to the Sol system through me any time they want—and I allow them. But I haven't allowed them. But how they are eager." He chuckled. "They're practically lined up. Like the kiddies' Saturday afternoon movie matinee."

"Make me into a stone."

"Why?"

Barney Mayerson said, "So I can't feel. There's nothing for me anywhere."

"You don't even like being translated into one homogeneous organism with me?"

No answer.

"You can share my ambitions. I've got plenty of them, big ones—they make Leo's look like dirt." Of course, he thought, Leo will kill me not long from now. At least as time is reckoned outside of translation. "I'll acquaint you with one. A minor one. Maybe it'll fire you up."

"I doubt it," Barney said.

"I'm going to become a planet."

Barney laughed.

"You think that's funny?" He felt furious.

"I think you're nuts. Whether you're a man or a thing from intersystem space; you're still out of your mind."

"I haven't explained," he said with dignity, "precisely what I meant when I said that. What I mean is, I'm going to be everyone on the planet. You know what planet I'm talking about."

"Terra."

"Hell no. Mars."

"Why Mars?"

"It's—" He groped for the words. "New. Undeveloped. Full of potential. I'm going to be all the colonists as they arrive and begin to live there. I'll guide their civilization; I'll *be* their civilization!"

No answer.

"Come on. Say something."

Barney said, "How come, if you can be so much, including a whole planet, I can't be even that plaque on the wall of my office at P. P. Layouts?"

"Um," he said disconcerted. "Okay, okay. You can be that plaque; what the hell do I care? Be anything you want— you took the drug; you're entitled to be translated into whatever pleases you. It's not real, of course. That's the truth. I'm letting you in on the innermost secret; it's an hallucination. What makes it seem real is that certain prophetic aspects get into the experience, exactly as with dreams. I've walked into and out of a million of them, these so-called 'translation' worlds; I've seen them all. And you know what they are? They're nothing. Like a captive white rat feeding electric impulses again and again to specific areas of his brain—its disgusting."

"I see," Barney Mayerson said.

"You want to wind up in one of them, knowing this?"

After a time Barney said, "Sure."

"Okay! I'll make you a stone, put you by a seashore; you can lie there and listen to the waves for a couple of million years. That ought to satisfy you." You dumb jerk, he thought savagely. A stone! Christ!

"Am I softened or something?" Barney asked, then; in his voice were for the first time strong overtones of doubt.

"Is this what the Proxers wanted? Is this why you were sent?"

"I wasn't sent. I showed up here on my own. It beats living out in dead space between hot stars." He chuckled. "Certainly you're soft—and you want to be a stone. Listen, Mayerson; being a stone isn't what you really want. What you want is death."

"Death?"

"You mean you didn't know?" He was incredulous. "Aw, come on!"

"No. I didn't know."

"It's very simple, Mayerson; I'll give you a translation world in which you're a rotting corpse of a run-over dog in some ditch—think of it: what a goddam relief it'll be. You're going to be me; you are me, and Leo Bulero is going to kill you. That's the dead dog, Mayerson; that's the corpse in the ditch." And I'll live on, he said to himself. That's my gift to you, and remember: in German *Gift* means poison. I'll let you die in my place a few months from now and that monument on Sigma 14-B will be erected but I'll go on, in your living body. When you come back from Mars to work at P. P. Layouts again you'll be me. And so I avoid my fate.

It was so simple.

"Okay, Mayerson," he concluded, weary of the colloquy. "Up and at 'em, as they say. Consider yourself dumped off; we're not a single organism any more. We've got distinct, separate destinies again, and that's the way you wanted it. You're in a ship of Conner Freeman's leaving Venus and I'm down in Chicken Pox Prospects; I've got a thriving vegetable garden up top, and I get to shack up with Anne Hawthorne any time I want—it's a good life, as far as I'm concerned. I hope you like yours equally well." And, at that instant, he emerged.

He stood in the kitchen of his compartment at Chicken Pox Prospects; he was frying himself a panful of local mushrooms . . . the air smelled of butter and spices and, in the living room, his portable tape recorder played a Haydn symphony. Peaceful, he thought with pleasure. Exactly what I want; a little peace and quiet. After all, I was used to that, out in intersystem space. He yawned, stretched with luxury, and said, "I did it."

Seated in the living room, reading a homeopape taken from the news-service emanating from one of the UN satellites, Anne Hawthorne glanced up and said, "You did what, Barney?"

"Got just the right amount of seasoning in this," he said, still exulting. I am Palmer Eldritch and I'm here, not there. I'll survive Leo's attack and I know how to enjoy, use, this life, here, as Barney didn't or wouldn't.

Let's see how he prefers it when Leo's fighter guns his merchant ship into particles. And he sees the last of a life bitterly regretted.

In the glare of the overhead light Barney Mayerson blinked. He realized after a second that he was on a ship; the room appeared ordinary, a combination bedroom and parlor, but he recognized it by the bolted-down condition of the furniture. And the gravity was all wrong; artificially produced, it failed to duplicate Earth's.

And there was a view out. Limited, no larger in fact than a comb of bees' wax. But still the thick plastic revealed the emptiness beyond, and he went over to fixedly peer. Sol, blinding, filled a portion of the panorama and he reflexively reached up to click the black filter into use. And, as he did so, he perceived his hand. His artificial, metallic, superbly efficient mechanical hand.

At once he stalked from the cabin and down the corridor until he reached the locked control booth; he rapped on it with his steel knuckles and after an interval the heavy reinforced bulkhead door opened.

"Yes, Mr. Eldritch." The young blond-haired pilot, nodding with respect.

He said, "Send out a message."

The pilot produced a pen and poised it over his notepad

mounted at the rim of the instrument board. "Who to, sir?"

"To Mr. Leo Bulero."

"To Leo . . . Bulero." The pilot wrote rapidly. "Is this to be relayed to Terra, sir? If so—"

"No. Leo is near us in his own ship. Tell him—" He pondered rapidly.

"You want to talk with him, sir?"

"I don't want him to kill me," he answered. "That's what I'm trying to say. And you with me. And whoever else is on this slow transport, this idiotically huge target." But it's hopeless, he realized. Somebody in Felix Blau's organization, carefully planted on Venus, saw me board this ship; Leo knows I'm here and that's it.

"You mean business competition is that tough?" the pilot said, taken by surprise; he blanched.

Zoe Eldritch, his daughter in dirndl and fur slippers, appeared. "What is it?"

He said, "Leo's nearby. He's got an armed ship, by UN permission; we were lured into a trap. We never should have gone to Venus. Hepburn-Gilbert was in on it." To the pilot he said, "Just keep trying to reach him. I'm going back to my cabin." There's nothing I can do here, he said to himself, and started out.

"Hell," the pilot said, "you talk to him; it's you he's after." He slid from his seat, leaving it pointedly vacant.

Sighing, Barney Mayerson seated himself and clicked on the ship's transmitter; he set it to the emergency frequency, lifted the microphone, and said into it, "You bastard, Leo. You've got me; you coaxed me out where you could get at me. You and that damn fleet of yours, already set up and operating before I got back from Prox—you had the head start." He felt more angry than frightened, now. "We've got nothing on this ship. Absolutely nothing to protect ourselves with—you're shooting down an unarmed target. This is a cargo carrier." He paused, trying to think what else to say. Tell him, he thought, that I'm Barney Mayerson and that Eldritch will never be caught and killed because he'll translate himself from life to life forever? And that in actuality you're killing someone you know and love?

Zoe said, "*Say* something."

"Leo," he said into the microphone, "let me go back to Prox. Please." He waited, listening to the static from the receiver's speaker. "Okay," he said, then. "I take it back. I'll never leave the Sol system and you can never kill me, even with Hepburn-Gilbert's help, or whoever it is in the UN you're operating in conjunction with." To Zoe he said, "How's that? You like that?" He dropped the microphone with a clatter. "I'm through."

The first bolt of laser energy nearly cut the ship in half.

Barney Mayerson lay on the floor of the control booth, listening to the racket of the emergency air pumps wheezing into shrill, clacking life. I got what I wanted, he realized. Or at least what Palmer said I wanted. I'm getting death.

Beyond his ship Leo Bulero's UN-model trim fighter maneuvered for the placing of a second, final bolt. He could see, on the pilot's view-screen, the flash of its exhausts. It was very close indeed.

Lying there he waited to die.

And then Leo Bulero walked across the central room of his compartment toward him.

Interested, Anne Hawthorne rose from her chair, said, "So you're Leo Bulero. There're a number of questions, all pertaining to your product Can-D—"

"I don't produce Can-D," Leo said. "I emphatically deny that rumor. None of my commercial enterprises are in any way illegal. Listen, Barney; did you or did you not consume that—" He lowered his voice; bending over Barney Mayerson, he whispered hoarsely. "You know."

"I'll step outside," Anne said, perceptively.

"No," Leo grunted. He turned to Felix Blau, who nodded. "We realize you're one of Blau's people," Leo said to her. Again he prodded Barney Mayerson, irritably. "I don't think he took it," he said, half to himself. "I'll search him." He began to rummage in Barney's coat pockets and then in his inside shirt. "Here it is." He fished out the tube containing the brain-metabolism toxin. Unscrewing the cap he peered in. "Unconsumed," he said to Blau, with massive disgust. "So naturally Faine heard nothing from him. He backed out."

Barney said, "I didn't back out." I've been a long way, he said to himself. Can't you tell? "Chew-Z," he said. "Very far."

"Yeah, you've been out about two minutes," Leo said with contempt. "We got here just as you locked yourself in; some fella—Norm something—let us in with his master key; he's in charge of this hovel, I guess."

"But remember," Anne said, "the subjective experience with Chew-Z is disconnected to our time-rate; to him it may have been hours or even days." She looked sympathetically in Barney's direction. "True?"

"I died," Barney said. He sat up, nauseated. "You killed me."

There was a remarkable, nonplused silence.

"You mean me?" Felix Blau asked at last.

"No," Barney said. It didn't matter. At least not until the next time he took the drug. Once that happened the finish would arrive; Palmer Eldritch would be successful, would achieve survival. And that was the unbearable part; not his own death—which eventually would arrive anyhow—but Palmer Eldritch's putting on immortality. Grave, he thought; where's your victory over this—thing?

"I feel insulted," Felix Blau complained. "I mean, what's this about someone killing you, Mayerson? Hell, we roused you out of your coma. And it was a long, difficult trip here and for Mr. Bulero—my client—in my opinion a risky one; this is the region where Eldritch operates." He glanced about apprehensively. "Get him to take that toxic substance," he said to Leo, "and then let's get back to Terra before something terrible happens. I can feel it." He started toward the door of the compartment.

Leo said, "Will you take it, Barney?"

"No," he said.

"Why not?" Weariness. Even patience.

"My life means too much to me." I've decided to halt in my atoning, he thought. At last.

"What happened to you while you were translated?"

He rose to his feet; he barely made it.

"He's not going to say," Felix Blau said, at the doorway.

Leo said, "Barney, it's all we've come up with. I'll get you off Mars; you know that. And Q-type epilepsy isn't the end of—"

"You're wasting your time," Felix said, and disappeared out into the hall. He gave Barney one final envenomed glance. "What a mistake you made, pinning your hopes on this guy."

Barney said, "He's right, Leo."

"You'll never get off Mars," Leo said. "I'll never wangle a passage back to Terra for you. No matter what happens from here on out."

"I know it."

"But you don't care. You're going to spend the rest of your life taking that drug." Leo glared at him, baffled.

"Never again," Barney said.

"Then what?"

Barney said, "I'll live here. As a colonist. I'll work on my garden up top and whatever else they do. Build irrigation systems and like that." He felt tired and the nausea had not left him. "Sorry," he said.

"So am I," Leo said. "And I don't understand it." He glanced at Anne Hawthorne, saw no answer there either, shrugged, then walked to the door. There he started to say something more but gave up; with Felix Blau he departed. Barney listened to the sound of them clanking up the steps to the mouth of the hovel and then finally the sound died away and there was silence. He went to the sink and got himself a glass of water.

After a time Anne said, "I understand it."

"Do you?" The water tasted good; it washed away the last traces of Chew-Z.

"Part of you has become Palmer Eldritch," she said. "And part of him became you. Neither of you can ever become completely separated again; you'll always be—"

"You're out of your mind," he said, leaning with exhaustion against the sink, steadying himself; his legs were too weak, still.

"Eldritch got what he wanted out of you," Anne said.

"No," he said. "Because I came back too soon. I would have had to be there another five or ten minutes. When Leo fires his second shot it'll be Palmer Eldritch there in that ship, not me." And that's why there is no need for me to derange my brain metabolism in a hasty, crackpot scheme concocted out of desperation, he said to himself. The man will be dead soon enough . . . or rather *it* will be.

"I see," Anne said. "And you're sure this glimpse of the future you had during translation—"

"It's valid." Because he was not dependent on what had been available to him during his experience with the drug.

In addition he had his own precog ability.

"And Palmer Eldritch knows it's valid, too," he said. "He'll do, is doing, everything possible to get out of it. But he won't. Can't." Or at least, he realized, it's *probable* that he can't. But here was the essence of the future: interlaced possibilities. And long ago he had accepted this, learned how to deal with it; he intuitively knew which time-line to choose. By *that* he had held his job with Leo.

"But because of this Leo won't pull strings for you," Anne said. "He really won't get you back to Earth; he meant it. Don't you comprehend the seriousness of that? I could tell by the expression on his face; as long as he lives he'll never—"

"Earth," Barney said, "I've had." He too had meant what he had said, his anticipations for his own life which lay ahead here on Mars.

If it was good enough for Palmer Eldritch it was good
enough for him. Because Eldritch had lived many lives; there
had been a vast, reliable wisdom contained within the substance of the man or creature, whatever it was. The fusion
of himself with Eldritch during translation had left a mark
on him, a brand for perpetuity: it was a form of absolute
awareness. He wondered, then, if Eldritch had gotten anything back from him in exchange. Did I have something worth
his knowing? he asked himself. Insights? Moods or memories
or values?

Good question. The answer, he decided, was no. Our op-
ponent, something admittedly ugly and foreign that entered
one of our race like an ailment during the long voyage between Terra and Prox . . . and yet it knew much more than
I did about the meaning of our finite lives, here; it saw in
perspective. From its centuries of vacant drifting as it waited
for some kind of life form to pass by which it could grab and
become . . . maybe that's the source of its knowledge: not
experience but unending solitary brooding. And in comparison I knew—had done—nothing.

At the door of the compartment Norm and Fran Schein
appeared. "Hey, Mayerson; how was it? What'd you think
of Chew-Z the second time around?" They entered, expec-
tantly awaiting his answer.

Barney said, "It'll never sell."

Disappointed, Norm said, "That wasn't my reaction; I
liked it, and a lot better than Can-D. Except—" He hesitated, frowned, and glanced at his wife with a worried expression. "There was a creepy presence though, where I was; it
sort of marred things." He explained, "Naturally I was
back—"

Fran interrupted, "Mr. Mayerson looks tired. You can give
him the rest of the details later."

Eying Barney, Norm Schein said, "You're a strange bird,
Barney. You came out of it the first time and snatched this
girl's bindle, here, this Miss Hawthorne, and ran off and
locked yourself in your compartment so you could take it,

and now you say—" He shrugged philosophically. "Well, maybe you just got too much in your craw all at once. You weren't moderate, man. Me, I intend to try it again. Carefully, of course. Not like you." Reassuring himself he said loudly, "I mean it; I liked the stuff."

"Except," Barney said, "for the presence that was there with you."

"I felt it, too," Fran said quietly. "I'm not going to try it again. I'm—afraid of it. Whatever it was." She shivered and moved closer to her husband; automatically, from long habit, he put his arm around her waist.

Barney said, "Don't be afraid of it. It's just trying to live, like the rest of us are."

"But it was so—" Fran began.

"Anything that old," Barney said, "would have to seem unpleasant to us. We have no conception of age to that dimension. That enormity."

"You talk like you know what it was," Norm said.

I know, Barney thought. Because as Anne said, part of it's here inside me. And it will, until it dies a few months from now, retain its portion of me incorporated within its own structure. So when Leo kills it, he realized, it will be a bad instant for me. I wonder how it will feel . . .

"That thing," he said, speaking to them all, especially to Norm Schein and his wife, "has a name which you'd recognize if I told it to you. Although it would never call itself that. We're the ones who've titled it. From experience, at a distance, over thousands of years. But sooner or later we were bound to be confronted by it. Without the distance. Or the years."

Anne Hawthorne said, "You mean God."

It did not seem to him necessary to answer, beyond a slight nod.

"But—*evil?*" Fran Schein whispered.

"An aspect," Barney said. "Our experience of it. Nothing more." Or didn't I make you see that already? he asked himself. Should I tell you how it tried to help me, in its own way? And yet—how fettered it was, too, by the forces of fate, which seem to transcend all that live, including it as much as ourselves.

"Gee whiz," Norm said, the corners of his mouth turning down in almost tearful disappointment; he looked, for a moment, like a cheated small boy.

13

Later, when his legs had ceased collapsing under him, he took Anne Hawthorne to the surface and showed her the beginnings of his garden.

"You know," Anne said, "it takes courage to let people down."

"You mean Leo?" He knew what she meant; there was no dispute about what he had just now done to Leo and to Felix Blau and the whole P. P. Layouts and Can-D organization. "Leo's a grown man," he pointed out. "He'll get over it. He'll recognize that he has to handle Eldritch himself and he will." And, he thought, the litigation against Eldritch would not have accomplished that much; my precog ability tells me that, too.

"Beets," Anne said. She had seated herself on the fender of an autonomic tractor and was examining packages of seeds. "I hate beets. So please don't plant any, even mutant ones that are green, tall, and skinny and taste like last year's plastic doorknob."

"Were you thinking," he said, "of coming here to live?"

"No." Furtively, she inspected the homeostatic control-box of the tractor, and picked at the frayed, partially incinerated insulation of one of its power cables. "But I expect to have dinner with your group every once in a while; you're the closest neighbor we have. Such as you are."

"Listen," he said, "that decayed ruin that you inhabit—" He broke off. Identity, he thought; I'm already acquiring it in terms of this substandard communal dwelling that could use fifty years of constant, detailed repair work by experts. "My hovel," he said to her, "can lick your hovel. Any day of the week."

"What about Sunday? Can you do it twice, then?"

"Sunday," he said, "we're not allowed to. We read the Scriptures."

"Don't joke about it," Anne said quietly.

"I wasn't." And he hadn't been, not at all.

"What you said earlier about Palmer Eldritch—"

Barney said, "I only wanted to tell you one thing. Maybe two at the most. First, that he—you know what I refer to— really exists, really is there. Although not like we've thought and not like we've experienced him up to now—not like we'll perhaps ever be able to. And second—" He hesitated.

"Say it."

"He can't help us very much," Barney said. "Some, maybe. But he stands with empty, open hands; he understands, he wants to help. He tries, but . . . it's just not that simple. Don't ask me why. Maybe even he doesn't know. Maybe it puzzles him, too. Even after all the time he's had to mull over it." And all the time he'll have later on, Barney thought, if he gets away from Leo Bulero. Human, one-of-us Leo. Does Leo know what he's up against? And if he did . . . would he try anyhow, keep on with his schemes?

Leo would. A precog can see something that's foreordained.

Anne said, "What met Eldritch and entered him, what we're confronting, is a being superior to ourselves and as you say we can't judge it or make sense out of what it does or wants; it's mysterious and beyond us. But I know you're wrong, Barney. Something which stands with empty, open hands is not God. It's a creature fashioned by something higher than itself, as we were; God wasn't fashioned and He isn't puzzled."

"I felt," Barney said, "about him a presence of the deity. It was there." Especially in that one moment, he thought, when Eldritch shoved me, tried to make *me* try.

"Of couse," Anne agreed. "I thought you understood about that; He's here inside each of us and in a higher life form such as we're talking about He would certainly be even more manifest. But—let me tell you my cat joke. It's very short and simple. A hostess is giving a dinner party and she's got a lovely five-pound T-bone steak sitting on the sideboard in the kitchen waiting to be cooked while she chats with the guests in the living room—has a few drinks and whatnot. But then she excuses herself to go into the kitchen to cook the steak—and it's gone. And there's the family cat, in the corner, sedately washing its face."

"The cat got the steak," Barney said.

"Did it? The guests are called in; they argue about it. The steak is gone, all five pounds of it; there sits the cat, looking well-fed and cheerful. 'Weigh the cat,' someone says. They've had a few drinks; it looks like a good idea. So they go into the bathroom and weigh the cat on the scales. It reads exactly five pounds. They all perceive this reading and one guest says, 'Okay, that's it. There's the steak.' They're satisfied that they know what happened, now; they've got empirical proof. Then a qualm comes to one of them and he says, puzzled, 'But where's the cat?' "

"I heard that joke before," Barney said. "And anyhow I don't see its application."

Anne said, "That joke poses the finest distillation of the problem of ontology ever invented. If you ponder it long enough—"

"Hell," he said angrily, "it's five pounds of cat; it's nonsense—there's no steak if the scale shows five pounds."

"Remember the wine and the wafer," Anne said quietly.

He stared at her. The idea, for a moment, seemed to come through.

"Yes," she said. "The cat was not the steak. But the cat might be a manifestation which the steak was taking at that moment. The key word happens to be *is*. Don't tell us, Barney, that whatever entered Palmer Eldritch *is* God, because you don't know that much about Him; no one can. But that living entity from intersystem space may, like us, be shaped in His image. A way He selected of showing Himself to us. If the map is not the territory, *the pot is not the potter*. So don't talk ontology, Barney; don't say *is*." She smiled at him hopefully, to see if he understood.

"Someday," Barney said, "we may worship at that monument." Not the deed by Leo Bulero, he thought; as admirable as it was—will be, more accurately—that won't be our object. No, we'll all of us, as a culture, do as I already am tending toward: we'll invest it wanly, pitifully, with our conception of infinite powers. And we'll be right in a sense because those powers are there. But as Anne says, as to its acutal nature—

"I can see you want to be alone with your garden," Anne said. "I think I'll start back to my hovel. Good luck. And, Barney—" She reached out, took him by the hand, and held onto him earnestly. "Never grovel. God, or whatever superior being it is we've encountered—it wouldn't want that and even if it did you shouldn't do it." She leaned forward, kissed him, and then started off.

"You think I'm right?" Barney called after her. "Is there any point in trying to start a garden here?" Or will we go the familiar way, too . . .

"Don't ask me. I'm no authority."

"You just care about your spiritual salvation," he said savagely.

"I don't even care about that any more," Anne said. "I'm terribly, terribly confused and everything upsets me, here. Listen." She walked back to him, her eyes dark and shaded, without light. "When you grabbed me, to take that bindle of Chew-Z; you know what I saw? I mean actually *saw,* not just believed."

"An artificial hand. And a distortion of my jaw. And my eyes—"

"Yes," she said tightly. "The mechanical, slitted eyes. What did it mean?"

Barney said, "It meant that you were seeing into absolute reality. The essence beyond the mere appearance." In your terminology, he thought, what you saw is called—stigmata.

For an interval she regarded him. "That's the way you really are?" she said, then, and drew away from him, with aversion manifest on her face. "Why aren't you what you seem? You're not like that now. I don't understand." She added, tremulously, "I wish I hadn't told that cat joke."

He said, "I saw the same thing in you, dear. At that instant. You fought me off with fingers decidedly not those you were born with." And it could so easily slip into place again. The Presence abides with us, potentially if not actually.

"Is it a curse?" Anne asked. "I mean, we have the account of an original curse of God; is it like that all over again?"

"You ought to be the one who knows; you remember what you saw. All three stigmata—the dead, artificial hand, the Jensen eyes, and the radically deranged jaw." Symbols of its inhabitation, he thought. In our midst. But not asked for. Not intentionally summoned. And—we have no mediating sacraments through which to protect ourselves; we can't compel it, by our careful, time-honored, clever, painstaking rituals, to confine itself to specific elements such as bread and water or bread and wine. It is out in the open, ranging in every direction. It looks into our eyes; and it looks *out* of our eyes.

"It's a price," Anne decided. "That we must pay. For our desire to undergo that drug experience with that Chew-Z. Like the apple originally." Her tone was shockingly bitter.

"Yes," he agreed, "but I think I already paid it." Or came within a hair of paying it, he decided. That thing, which we know only in its Terran body, wanted to substitute me at the instant of its destruction; instead of God dying for man, as we once had, we faced—for a moment—a superior—*the* superior power asking us to perish for *it*.

Does that make it evil? he wondered. Do I believe the argument I gave Norm Schein? Well, it certainly makes it inferior to what came two thousand years before. It seems to be nothing more or less than the desire of, as Anne puts it, an out-of-dust created organism to perpetuate itself; we all have it, we all would like to see a goat or a lamb cut to pieces and incinerated instead of ourselves. Oblations have to be made. And we don't care to be them. In fact our entire lives are dedicated to that one principle. And so is its.

"Goodbye," Anne said. "I'll leave you alone; you can sit in the cab of that dredge and dig away to your heart's content. Maybe when I next see you, there'll be a completed water-system installed here." She smiled once more at him, briefly, and then hiked off in the direction of her own hovel.

After a time he climbed the steps to the cab of the dredge which he had been using and started the creaky, sand-impregnated mechanism. It howled mournfully in protest. Happier, he decided, to remain asleep; this, for the machine, was the ear-splitting summons of the last trumpet, and the dredge was not yet ready.

He had scooped perhaps a half mile of irregular ditch, as yet void of water, when he discovered that an indigenous life form, a Martian something, was stalking him. At once he halted the dredge and peered into the glare of the cold Martian sun to make it out.

It looked a little like a lean, famished old grandmother on all fours and he realized that this was probably the jackal-creature which he had been warned repeatedly about. In any case, whatever it was, it obviously hadn't fed in days; it eyed him ravenously, while keeping its distance—and then, projected telepathically, its thoughts reached him. So he was right. This was it.

"May I eat you?" it asked. And panted, avidly slack-jawed.

"Christ no," Barney said. He fumbled about in the cab of the dredge for something to use as a weapon; his hands closed over a heavy wrench and he displayed it to the Martian predator, letting it speak for him; there lay a great message in the wrench and the way he gripped it.

"Get down off that contraption," the Martian predator thought, in a mixture of hope and need. "I can't reach you up there." The last was intended, certainly, to be a private thought, retained in camera, but somehow it had gotten projected, too. The creature had no finesse. "I'll wait," it decided. "He has to get down eventually."

Barney swung the dredge around and started it back in the direction of Chicken Pox Prospects. Groaning, it clanked at a maddeningly slow rate; it appeared to be failing with each yard. He had the intuition that it was not going to make it. Maybe the creature's right, he said to himself; it is possible I'll have to step down and face it.

Spared, he thought bitterly, by the enormously higher life form that entered Palmer Eldritch that showed up in our system from out there—and then eaten by this stunted beast. The termination of a long flight, he thought. A final arrival that even five minutes ago, despite my precog talent, I didn't anticipate. Maybe I didn't want to . . . as Dr. Smile, if he were here, would triumphantly bleat.

The dredge wheezed, bucked violently, and then, painfully contracting itself, curled up; its life flickered a moment and then it died to a stop.

For a time Barney sat in silence. Placed directly ahead of him the old-grandmother jackal Martian flesh-eater watched, never taking its eyes from him.

"All right," Barney said. "Here I come." He hopped from the cab of the dredge, flailing with the wrench.

The creature dashed at him.

Almost to him, five feet away, it suddenly squealed, veered, and ran past, not touching him. He spun, and watched it go. "*Unclean*," it thought to itself; it halted at a safe distance and fearfully regarded him, tongue lolling. "You're an unclean thing," it informed him dismally.

Unclean, Barney thought. How? Why?

"You just are," the predator answered. "Look at yourself. I can't eat you; I'd be sick." It remained where it was, drooping with disappointment and—aversion. He had horrified it.

"Maybe we're all unclean to you," he said. "All of us from Earth, alien to this world. Unfamiliar."

"Just you," it told him flatly. "Look at—ugh!—your right arm, your hand. There's something intolerably wrong with you. How can you live with yourself? Can't you cleanse yourself some way?"

He did not bother to look at his arm and hand; it was unnecessary.

Calmly, with all the dignity that he could manage, he walked on, over the loosely packed sand, toward his hovel.

That night, as he prepared to go to bed in the cramped bunk provided by his compartment at Chicken Pox Prospects, someone rapped on his closed door. "Hey, Mayerson. Open up."

Putting on his robe he opened the door.

"That trading ship is back," Norm Schein, excited, grabbing him by the lapel of his robe, declared. "You know, from the Chew-Z people. You got any skins left? If so—"

"If they want to see me," Barney said, disengaging Norm Schein's grip from his robe, "they'll have to come down here. You tell them that." He shut the door, then.

Norm loudly departed.

He seated himself at the table on which he ate his meals, got a pack—his last—of Terran cigarettes from the drawer, and lit up; he sat smoking and meditating, hearing above and around his compartment the scampering noises of his fellow hovelists. Large-scale mice, he thought. Who have scented the bait.

The door to his compartment opened. He did not look up; he continued to stare down at the table surface, at the ashtray and matches and pack of Camels.

"Mr. Mayerson."

Barney said, "I know what you're going to say."

Entering the compartment, Palmer Eldritch shut the door, seated himself across from Barney, and said, "Correct, my friend. I let you go just before it happened, before Leo fired the second time. It was my carefully considered decision. And I've had a long time to dwell on the matter; a little over three centuries. I won't tell you why."

"I don't care why," Barney said. He continued to stare down.

"Can't you look at me?" Palmer Eldritch said.

"I'm unclean," Barney informed him.

"WHO TOLD YOU THAT?"

"An animal out in the desert. And it had never seen me before; it knew it just by coming close to me." While still five feet away, he thought to himself. Which is fairly far.

"Hmm. Maybe its motive—"

"It had no goddam motive. In fact just the opposite—it was half-dead from hunger and yearning to eat me. So it must be true."

"To the primitive mind," Eldritch said, "the unclean and the holy are confused. Merged merely as taboo. The ritual for them, the—"

"Aw hell," he said bitterly. "It's true and you know it. I'm alive, I won't die on that ship, but I'm defiled."

"By me?"

Barney said, "Make your own guess."

After a pause Eldritch shrugged and said, "All right. I was cast out from a star system—I won't identify it because to you it wouldn't matter—and I took up residence where that wild, get-rich-quick operator from your system encountered me. And some of that has been passed on to you. But not much. You'll gradually, over the years, recover; it'll diminish until it's gone. Your fellow colonists won't notice because it's touched them, too; it began as soon as they participated in the chewing of what we sold them."

"I'd like to know," Barney said, "what you were trying to do when you introduced Chew-Z to our people."

"Perpetuate myself," the creature opposite him said quietly.

He glanced up, then. "A form of reproduction?"

"Yes, the only way I can."

With overwhelming aversion Barney said, "My God. We would all have become your children."

"Don't fret about that now, Mr. Mayerson," it said, and laughed in a humanlike, jovial way. "Just tend your little garden up top, get your water system going. Frankly I long for death; I'll be glad when Leo Bulero does what he's already contemplating . . . he's begun to hatch it, now that you've refused to take the brain-metabolism toxin. Anyhow, I wish you luck here on Mars; I would have enjoyed it, myself, but things didn't work out and that's that." Eldritch rose to his feet, then.

"You could revert," Barney said. "Resume the form you were in when Palmer encountered you. You don't have to be there, inhabiting that body, when Leo opens fire on your ship."

"Could I?" Its tone was mocking. "Maybe something worse is waiting for me if I fail to show up there. But you wouldn't know about that; you're an entity whose lifespan is relatively short, and in a short span there's a lot less—" It paused, thinking.

"Don't tell me," Barney said. "I don't want to know."

The next time he looked up, Palmer Eldritch was gone.

He lit another cigarette. What a mess, he thought. This is how we act when finally we do contact at long last another sentient race within the galaxy. And how *it* behaves, badly as us and in some respects much worse. And there's nothing to redeem the situation. Not now.

And Leo thought that by going out to confront Eldritch with that tube of toxin we had a chance. Ironic.

And here I am, without having even consummated the miserable act for the courts' benefit, physically, basically, unclean.

Maybe Anne can do something for me, he thought suddenly. Maybe there are methods to restore one to the original condition—dimly remembered, such as it was—before the late and more acute contamination set in. He tried to remember but he knew so little about Neo-Christianity. Anyhow it was worth a try; it suggested there might be hope, and he was going to need that in the years ahead.

After all, the creature residing in deep space which had taken the form of Palmer Eldritch bore some relationship to God; if it was not God, as he himself had decided, then at least it was a portion of God's Creation. So some of the responsibility lay on Him. And, it seemed to Barney, He was probably mature enough to recognize this.

Getting Him to admit it, though. That might be something else again.

However, it was still worth talking to Anne Hawthorne; she might know of techniques for accomplishing even that.

But he somehow doubted it. Because he held a terrifying insight, simple, easy to think and utter, which perhaps applied to himself and those around him, to this situation.

There was such a thing as salvation. But—

Not for everyone.

On the trip back to Terra from their unsuccessful mission to Mars, Leo Bulero endlessly nitpicked and conferred with his colleague, Felix Blau. It was now obvious to both of them what they would have to do.

"He's all the time traveling between a master-satellite

around Venus and the other planets, plus his demesne on Luna," Felix pointed out in summation. "And we all recognize how vulnerable a ship in space is; even a small puncture can—" He gestured graphically.

"We'd need the UN's cooperation," Leo said gloomily. Because all he and his organization were allowed to possess were side arms. Nothing that could be used by one ship against another.

"I've got what may be some interesting data on that," Felix said, rummaging in his briefcase. "Our people in the UN reach into Hepburn-Gilbert's office, as you may or may not know. We can't *compel* him to do anything, but we can at least discuss it." He produced a document. "Our Secretary-General is worried about the consistent appearance of Palmer Eldritch in every one of the so-called 'reincarnations' that users of Chew-Z experience. He's smart enough to correctly interpret what that implies. So if it keeps happening undoubtedly we can get more cooperation from him, at least on a sub rosa basis; for instance—"

Leo broke in, "Felix, let me ask you something. How long have you had an artificial arm?"

Glancing down, Felix grunted in surprise. And then, staring at Leo Bulero, he said, "So do you, too. And there's something the matter with your teeth; open your mouth and let's see."

Without answering, Leo got to his feet and went into the men's room of the ship to survey himself in the floor-length mirror.

There was no doubt of it. Even the eyes, too. Resignedly he returned to his seat beside Felix Blau. Neither of them said anything for a while; Felix rattled his documents mechanically—oh God, Leo thought; *literally* mechanically!— and Leo alternated between watching him and dully staring out the window at the blackness and stars of interplan space.

Finally Felix said, "Sort of throws you at first, doesn't it?"

"It does," Leo agreed hoarsely. "I mean, hey Felix—what do we do?"

"We accept it," Felix said. He was gazing with fixed intensity down the aisle at the people in the other seats. Leo looked and saw, too. The same deformity of the jaw. The same brilliant, unfleshly right hand, one holding a homeopape, another a book, a third its fingers restlessly tapping. On and on and on until the termination of the aisle and the beginning of the pilot's cabin. In there, too, he realized. It's all of us.

"But I just don't quite get what it means," Leo complained helplessly. "Are we in—you know. Translated by that foul drug and this is—" He gestured. "We're both out of our minds, is that it?"

Felix Blau said, "Have you taken Chew-Z?"

"No. Not since that one intravenous injection on Luna."

"Neither have I," Felix said. "Ever. So it's spread. Without the use of the drug. He's everywhere, or rather *it's* everywhere. But this is good; this'll decidedly cause Hepburn-Gilbert to reconsider the UN's stand. He'll have to face exactly what this thing amounts to. I think Palmer Eldritch made a mistake; he went too far."

"Maybe it couldn't help it," Leo said. Maybe the damn organism was like a protoplasm; it had to ingest and grow—instinctively it spread out farther and farther. Until it's destroyed at the source, Leo thought. And we're the ones to do it, because I'm personally Homo sapiens evolvens: I'm the human of the future right here sitting in this seat now. *If* we can get the UN's help.

I'm the Protector, he said to himself, of our race.

He wondered if this blight had reached Terra, yet. A civilization of Palmer Eldritches, gray and hollow and stooped and immensely tall, each with his artificial arm and eccentric teeth and mechanical, slitted eyes. It would not be pleasant. He, the Protector, shrank from the envisioning of it. And suppose it reaches our minds? he asked himself. Not just the anatomy of the thing but the mentality as well . . . what would happen to our plans to kill the thing?

Say, I bet this still isn't real, Leo said to himself. I know

I'm right and Felix isn't; I'm still under the influence of that one dose; I never came back out—that's what's the matter. Thinking this he felt relief, because there was still a real Terra untouched; it was only himself that was affected. No matter how genuine Felix beside him and the ship and the memory of his visit to Mars to see about Barney Mayerson seemed.

"Hey, Felix," he said, nudging him. "You're a figment. Get it? This is a private world of mine. I can't prove it, naturally, but—"

"Sorry," Felix said laconically. "You're wrong."

"Aw, come on! Eventually I'm going to wake up or whatever it is you finally do when that miserable stuff is out of your system. I'm going to keep drinking a lot of liquids, you know, flush it out of my veins." He waved. "Stewardess." He beckoned to her urgently. "Bring us our drinks now. Bourbon and water for me." He glanced inquiringly at Felix.

"The same," Felix murmured. "Except I want a little ice. But not too much because that way when it melts the drink is no good."

The stewardess presently approached, tray extended. "Yours is with ice?" she asked Felix; she was blonde and pretty, with green eyes the texture of good polished stones, and when she bent forward her articulated, spherical breasts were partially exposed. Leo noticed that, liked that; however, the distortion of her jaw ruined the total impression and he felt disappointed, cheated. And now, he saw, the lovely long-lashed eyes had vanished. Been replaced. He looked away, disgruntled and depressed, until she had gone. It was going to be especially hard, he realized, regarding women; he did not for instance anticipate with any pleasure the first sight of Roni Fugate.

"You saw?" Felix said as he drank his drink.

"Yes, and it proves how quickly we've got to act," Leo said. "As soon as we land in New York we look up that wily, no-good nitwit Hepburn-Gilbert."

"What for?" Felix Blau asked.

Leo stared at him, then pointed at Felix's artificial, shiny fingers holding his glass.

"I rather like them now," Felix said meditatively.

That's what I thought, Leo thought. That's exactly what I was expecting. But I still have faith I can get at the thing, if not this week then next. If not this month then sometime. I know it; I know myself now and what I can do. It's all up to me. Which is just fine. I saw enough in the future not to ever give up, even if I'm the only one who doesn't succumb, who's still keeping the old way alive, the pre-Palmer Eldritch way. It's nothing more than faith in powers implanted in me from the start which I can—in the end—draw on and beat him with. So in a sense it isn't me; it's something *in* me that even that thing Palmer Eldritch can't reach and consume because since it's not me it's not mine to lose. I feel it growing. Withstanding the external, nonessential alterations, the arm, the eyes, the teeth—it's not touched by any of these three, the evil, negative trinity of alienation, blurred reality, and despair that Eldritch brought back with him from Proxima. Or rather from the space in between.

He thought, We have lived thousands of years under one old-time plague already that's partly spoiled and destroyed our holiness, and that from a source higher then Eldritch. And if you can't completely obliterate our spirit, how can this? Is it maybe going to finish the job? If it thinks so—if Palmer Eldritch believes that's what he arrived here for— he's wrong. Because that power in me that was implanted without my knowledge—*it wasn't even reached by the original ancient blight.* How about that?

My evolved mind tells me all these things, he thought. Those E Therapy sessions weren't in vain . . . I may not have lived as long as Eldritch in one sense, but in another sense I have; I've lived a hundred thousand years, that of my accelerated evolution, and out of it I've become very wise; I got my money's worth. Nothing could be clearer to me now. And down in the resorts of Antarctica I'll join the others like myself; we'll be a guild of Protectors. Saving the rest.

"Hey Blau," he said, poking with his non-artificial elbow the semi-thing beside him. "I'm your descendant. Eldritch showed up from another space but I came from another time. Got it?"

"Um," Felix Blau murmured.

"Look at my double-dome, my big forehead; I'm a bubble-head, right? And this rind; it's not just on top; it's all over. So in my case the therapy really took. So don't give up yet. Believe in me."

"Okay, Leo."

"Stick around for a while. There'll be action. I may be looking out at you through a couple of Jensen luxvid artificial-type eyes, but it's still me inside here. Okay?"

"Okay," Felix Blau said. "Anything you say, Leo."

" 'Leo'? How come you keep calling me 'Leo'?"

Sitting rigidly upright in his chair, supporting himself with both hands, Felix Blau regarded him imploringly. "Think, Leo. For chrissakes *think*."

"Oh yeah." Sobered, he nodded; he felt chastened. "Sorry. It was just a temporary slip. I know what you're referring to; I know what you're afraid of. But it didn't mean anything." He added, "I'll keep thinking, like you say. I won't forget again." He nodded solemnly, promising.

This ship rushed on, nearer and nearer Earth.

ABOUT THE AUTHOR

PHILIP K. DICK was born in Chicago in 1928 and lived most of his life in California. He briefly attended the University of California, but dropped out before completing any classes. In 1952 he began writing professionally and proceeded to write thirty-six novels and five short story collections. He won the Hugo Award for best novel in 1962 for *The Man in the High Castle* and the John W. Campbell Memorial Award for best novel of the year in 1974 for *Flow My Tears the Policeman Said*. Philip K. Dick died of heart failure following a stroke on March 2, 1982, in Santa Ana, California.